Emily's Hawaii

Emily's Hawaii

By
Ruth M. Tabrah

Illustrations by Pat Hall

Press Pacifica

Library of Congress Cataloging-in-Publication Data

Tabrah, Ruth M., 1921—
   Emily's Hawaii.

   Previously published as: Hawaiian heart.
   Summary: On her trip to the island of Hawaii, young girl visits various places of interest, including some burial caves.
   [1. Hawaii Island (Hawaii)--Fiction] I. Hall, Pat, ill. II. Title.
PZ7.T115Em 1985 [Fic] 85-30071
ISBN 0-916630-45-5

Available from Booklines Hawaii, Ltd.,
94-527 Puahi Street, Waipahu, Hawaii 96797

Printed in Hong Kong

This is a story about the way things once were, and sometimes still are in the remote rural areas of Hawaii nei. Kohala is a real place, and the atmosphere, lore, and history in this story are true but the plantation there no longer exists. The aloha of Kohala people remains warm and vibrant. However, the people in this story, without exception, are all imaginary characters and were so intended to be.

1

Albert Disappears

The Honolulu-bound plane was less than half an hour out of San Francisco when Beener stood in the aisle, beside his sister's seat.

"Em! Do you have him? He's gone!" Beener's voice was wild and woebegone.

"Have who?" Emily got up in alarm.

"He's lost Albert," said their mother coming up behind Beener. "Emily, you haven't seen him? Beener didn't slip him into your flight bag at the airport by mistake?"

"He better not have!" Emily sat down again. If that was why her nine-year-old brother was upset, she did not intend to feel sorry for him. Beener's Albert was cold and squirmy and scratchy. And Albert was supposed to have been left with a friend back home in Sacramento, anyway.

"Emily Ann Fergus!" said her mother.

"Oh, pfui!" Twelve-year-old Emily made a face. Gingerly, she unzipped her flight bag.

The elderly woman who was Emily's seatmate took out a lemon drop and handed it to Beener in a gesture of sympathy. She watched with interest while Emily hesitantly felt all around her camera and her purse and her long, unwieldy, precious treasure box.

"No Albert," Emily said, careful not to sound too relieved.

Her father was in the aisle with Beener now, and so were the stewardess and three curious passengers.

Emily sighed. Here they were, on their way to live for a year on a fourteen-thousand-acre sugar plantation on the Big Island of Hawaii. Emily's father, who was a Sacramento doctor; Emily's mother, who was an artist in her spare time; Emily, who at twelve was sure her nine-year-old brother was the world's worst nuisance; and Beener, who was in trouble already — and Hawaii still stood two thousand miles away!

Because she knew she'd better, Emily hunched down and looked for Albert under her seat. "Not there either," she said.

She might not like turtles herself, but to Beener, Albert was as precious as that long cardboard box sticking out of the flight bag was to her. Emily loved to explore as much as Beener liked to experiment, and, while she explored, Emily loved also to collect. Only, nothing alive! Whereas Beener liked pets, Emily was partial to rock specimens and arrowheads and unusual coins.

By now, the entire tourist section of the plane was involved in the search for Beener's missing pet. The stewardess hunted for Albert in the toilets and in the tiny flight kitchen and on the shelves for hand baggage. The aisle was inspected with flashlights. The passengers all hunted in and under and around their seats. The stewardess had the pilot look in his cabin, just in case.

There was no Albert anywhere.

Beener moped as the jet engine ate up the long blue ocean miles from San Francisco to Honolulu. They would land at two o'clock. An hour later, their interisland flight would leave Honolulu for the Big Island. By suppertime, only a few hours away, they would be on the plantation. The year in which Emily and Beener intended to find out and do all they could in Hawaii would begin.

"Excited?" Emily's seatmate asked.

Emily nodded and smiled.

"Your first trip to Hawaii?"

"First time," Emily confided. "Have you ever been to Hawaii before?" She noticed now that it was not really a dress her seatmate was wearing, but an old-fashioned muumuu, with a dark silk handkerchief knotted in a triangle at the neck.

"I live in Honolulu," the woman smiled. "My name is Kalani McBryde."

"I'm Emily Ann Fergus," Emily introduced herself. "We're going to live in Hawaii, too! Only not in Honolulu. It's in Kohala on the Big Island. Did you ever hear of that place?"

"Kohala? I was born there!" Kalani McBryde smiled. Her dark eyes seemed to look at something far, far away, something very pleasant that she enjoyed remembering from long ago. "Kohala," she sounded envious. "So you will live in Kohala! Lucky you! To me, Emily, *Kohala no ka oi!*"

"Pardon me?" queried Emily.

"*Kohala no ka oi,*" Kalani McBryde repeated. "In Hawaiian that means: Kohala is the best place!"

"You speak Hawaiian?" asked Emily. She had not realized that people still did.

"I speak Hawaiian. I am part Hawaiian. *Hapahaole. Hapa* means half. *Haole* is what Hawaiians call white-skinned foreigners, which is what you will be in the islands, Emily, a *haole* girl."

"How-lee. *Haole.*" The syllables of this word felt queer on Emily's tongue.

"In Hawaii," Kalani McBryde explained, "a *haole* is any Caucasian person, excepting a Portuguese. The Portuguese people came to the islands very early, more than 100 years ago, as contract laborers for the sugar plantations. They are Cauca-

12

sians, but they have always been called by the name of their nationality."

"Many years ago, *haoles* were the owners, the planters, the businessmen, doctors, and missionaries. They were mostly English and Americans, Scotchmen like my grandfather; and a few were Germans and Norwegians. Only a few *haoles* were laborers, and some of the early *haoles* were arrogant people who were much disliked. Some always felt like foreigners in Hawaii. Some became real *kamaainas,* true islanders at heart." Kalani McBryde looked quizzically at Emily. "There are not many *haoles* in Kohala. What are you and your family going to be doing there?"

"You've heard of exchange teachers," said Emily, "well, my father's going to be an exchange doctor. He and his classmate, Dr. Sandy Blythe of Kohala, decided to change practices and houses for one year." Emily looked around to make sure her parents or Beener were not where they might overhear. "Don't tell anybody I said so," she whispered, "but I think we have the best of this deal!

"Only," she stopped whispering, "I hadn't heard about this *haole* business before. I'm not sure I like that! After all, Hawaii's the fiftieth state. We're all Americans."

"Americans with many different kinds of ancestors," Kalani McBryde reminded her. "You will be among few people who have your skin color or

13

your blue eyes where you're going to live this year."

Until now, when she tried to imagine living on the Big Island, Emily had not thought much about the people. Kohala, she had surmised, would be a series of long white beaches where she could sit under a palm tree or go surfing or learn to play a ukulele. Somewhere in the landscape, there would be fourteen thousand acres of sugarcane and mountains that had once been volcanoes, but she had no really clear idea of Kohala in her head.

"Keep your heart open and your eyes open this year, will you, Emily?" Kalani McBryde urged. "If you do, you'll see the Kohala that I love, and my ancestors loved, the Kohala where King Kamehameha was born and grew to manhood, the Kohala where forty thousand of my people once lived."

"There is a beach in Kohala — Keokea is its name." Kalani sighed and looked as if she wished she were in Emily's place. "There was once an ancient *heiau,* a temple, on the cliff above that beach. People say, if you go there on nights of full moon, you can still hear the ghost drums beating in that ancient temple."

"Ghost drums!" Emily looked closely, but Kalani McBryde wasn't teasing her, nor was she just making conversation. She was serious. Emily could tell.

"Once," Kalani reminisced, "when I was a girl your age, twelve maybe, going on thirteen, I went to Keokea one night at the time of the full moon. My grandmother took me, to help her look after certain things in a family cave. The drums sounded all that night we were out. We could hear them clearly above the surf. We thought we could hear them in the cave half a mile away!"

Listening, Emily felt gooseflesh prickle along her skin. Ghost drums. Caves. Being a *haole*. She shivered, as excited by all her traveling companion had said as she was by the stewardess' voice over the loudspeaker.

"Fasten seat belts and observe the no smoking sign, please. We will be landing at Honolulu International Airport soon."

"Come, Emily. Look!" Kalani McBryde beckoned her to the window.

Below, beyond the oily silver wing tip, were the jagged green mountains of the island of Oahu. There, on the near lee coast, Emily could see the long white scallop of Waikiki Beach with hotels like pink, yellow, and white concrete layer cakes, and the dark slim shapes of palm trees everywhere. Long white breakers rolled in on Waikiki Beach bearing specks that were surfboards and outrigger canoes. Offshore, catamarans hovered with pink-and-white striped sails pouting before the wind.

Diamond Head looked just as it looked on calendar pictures — a big, stark, extinct volcano jutting out as a backdrop for Waikiki.

The houses and canals and throughways and skyscraper apartments and office buildings of Honolulu climbed in winding streets up green valleys and steep brown hillsides.

Then, the docks and business buildings of downtown waterfront Honolulu were below. There was the sandspit and blue-green water of Honolulu Harbor. The plane wing dipped lower and lower. There was a swift drop, a light bumping motion — and they were in Hawaii!

"Aloha, aloha nui loa!" Kalani McBryde kissed Emily on the cheek in farewell. "Have a good year, and remember! Keep your eyes and your heart and your mind open — to see my Hawaii, will you, Emily dear?"

"I will!" Emily promised. They had been friends about four hours, but Emily felt as close to her as if she'd known Kalani McBryde all her life.

"Did you enjoy riding with the Princess Kalani?" the stewardess asked, as Emily led the Ferguses toward the warm air of Hawaii waiting outside.

Emily stopped so abruptly that Beener stumbled and gouged his toes painfully into the back of her heels.

"Princess Kalani?" Emily repeated. "Wait, Beener. Don't push!" she said annoyed.

"Princess Kalani McBryde." The stewardess smiled. "She is so very modest, she would never tell you herself, but if Hawaii were still an island kingdom, as it was when she was a girl, she would be Hawaii's queen!"

Emily gasped. "Queen!" If she had only known! All the way across the Pacific she had shared a seat with royalty!

"Beener. I said don't push!" Emily turned to give Beener a small, surreptitious kick she hoped her parents couldn't see.

Something on the cabin floor caught her eye. She looked down — and stopped with her foot just short of Beener's ankle bone.

"Are you ever lucky, Beener!" she pointed.

The small round object on the floor might have been a crumpled old candy wrapper dropped on the threshold of the plane — but it was not!

"Albert!" Beener scooped up his pet and held the shell close to the end of his nose. The turtle's head poked out. It blinked small beady eyes.

"Smart old Albert!" Beener crooned. "He made it to Hawaii, too!"

2

Earthquake

Honolulu airport was like being in some faraway exotic country, with all the different kinds of people and signs in a number of languages, including Japanese and Chinese.

Kohala's Big Island airport of Upolu Point was two hundred and sixteen miles south of Honolulu and another hour's flying time away.

They had to hurry to make their connections with the interisland plane that flew, this one day a week, from Honolulu to Upolu Point.

"Good thing we found you!" Beener told Albert. "There wouldn't have been time between planes to search for you!"

Emily could see, this second time from the air, that Honolulu was a big city straddling the lee coast of its island, Oahu. Freeways poked tunnels through

Oahu's steep, weathered mountains to the crowded island's windward towns.

"This looks interesting, but I'm glad we're going to live in plantation Hawaii," said Mrs. Fergus. "Big cities are too much alike, wherever they are."

Emily flattened her nose against the plane window to see the resort beach and hotels of Waikiki again. She hadn't realized Waikiki Beach was in the city of Honolulu, surrounded by tall skyscraper apartment buildings and hotels, as well as by mountains, palm trees, and Diamond Head.

North of the island of Oahu were Kauai, the garden island, and Niihau, a small island owned by the Robinson family of Kauai. Only Hawaiian people lived on Niihau and still spoke nothing but the Hawaiian language in their homes and church. They spoke English only at school.

Honolulu was the capital of this island state. Oahu was a smaller island than Maui or the Big Island of Hawaii where Emily was going to spend this year, but Oahu had more people living on it than lived on all the rest of the Hawaiian islands.

When they flew over Molokai, an island with steep cliffs rising from the sea, the stewardess showed the Ferguses the lonely peninsula of Kalaupapa, Molokai's leper colony, where there still lived a few people who chose to spend the rest of their lives in what had once been a dreaded place.

Molokai, Maui, and Lanai were three green

islands set close together in the dark blue sea. Lanai was the smallest. The whole island grew nothing but pineapples. The one town, Lanai City, was built in the middle of the island, surrounded by pineapple fields. There were not as many palm trees here as Emily had seen on Oahu. Lanai City, the stewardess told them over the plane's loudspeaker system, was shaded by rows of tall norfolk island pines, the shape of Christmas trees.

Maui's valleys were planted in pineapple and in sugarcane. Sand beaches and coral reefs girdled the shores. In Maui's ten-thousand-foot-high volcanic mountain, Haleakala, was a crater so large that the city of New York could be hidden inside.

"Fasten your seat belts and please observe the no smoking sign!" warned the stewardess. "We shall be landing at Upolu Point in approximately four minutes."

Emily looked down. They were flying away from Maui, and for nearly ten minutes they had been flying over a rough, ugly, whitecapped stretch of ocean. This was the Alenuihaha Channel, which separated Maui and the northwest tip of the Big Island, where Kohala plantation lay.

Emily fastened her seat belt and looked at Beener, who sat with his belt tight and Albert held confidently in his hand.

The plane began to drop swiftly. Emily looked down again. There was no land in sight!

"Beener!" she whispered, scared. The plane was dropping down into that ugly rough ocean. She looked around for the stewardess, then looked out the window again. The ocean was rushing up to meet them, and she caught a first glimpse of a rocky coast below. Emily closed her eyes and grabbed Beener's arm.

"Well, for Pete's sake, what's the matter with you? Airsick?" said Beener.

The plane wheels bounced. Emily opened her eyes and looked out, feeling foolish now. The pilot had landed them exactly where he should have — on the blacktop airport runway, just out of reach of the salt spray of the surf.

Kohala's Upolu Point airport waiting room was an opensided Quonset hut, crowded with women in gay muumuus, girls in dresses, boys in the blue jeans that boys wear anywhere. There were thong slippers, spike-heeled shoes, work boots, bare feet, and Japanese wooden geta.

Hawaiian faces, Oriental faces, Spanish faces, Filipino faces; faces that were a handsome hint of every one of these. Much laughter. Many smiles. A variety of English that was strange to Emily's ear. "Pidgin. Island pidgin," she remembered Princess Kalani had said.

A Filipino woman stood at the edge of the airport lanai, smoking a long thin black cigar.

Two elderly Japanese ladies walked toward the

parking lot under the shade of an oiled paper umbrella with a bamboo pole for a handle. Printed on the umbrella paper was: "Labour Past Is Pleasant" and "Heaven Blesses The Wise," and underneath each saying was a line of characters in Japanese.

The islands, at first glance, were a mixture of East and West, only Emily had not realized until today how much more East than West they would seem.

It made Emily understand, here on this remote island, how her Korean classmate in Sacramento must have felt when she first landed in California from her home in Seoul. Emily felt good inside to remember how she and her classmates and the teacher had tried to help Yum Chun get acquainted. It was a queer feeling to be surrounded by people whose features and color and way of speech were different from anything you had been used to before.

Emily smiled tentatively at a Japanese girl nearby as she walked into the airport to wait for their luggage to be unloaded from the plane. It must be the same in Hawaii as it was in Sacramento, Emily thought. If you were friendly yourself, strangers were likely to be friendly to you. Aloha was the only Hawaiian word Emily had known before she came to the islands, and aloha was the one word that described the atmosphere she had sensed at the Honolulu airport and here. Aloha too was in the welcome from Dr. Wong, Sandy Blythe's partner, who was at the airport gate with flower leis for each of them, as they came across the blacktop strip from the interisland plane.

Dr. Wong was a bachelor, much younger than her father. He was a good-looking man with such a pleasant smile and such a friendly manner that Emily liked him at once.

He introduced the Ferguses to so many of the people in the airport that Emily could not hope to remember to sort out all the right faces with the right names.

Beener helped his father and Dr. Wong load their luggage into Dr. Wong's car. They had brought only the weight limit of forty-four pounds each with them from San Francisco. The rest of what they would need for this year was being shipped airfreight.

The district of Kohala was as large in area as a mainland county might be. In every direction, except seaward, from the airport, were fields of sugarcane.

"You've never seen cane plants before?" Dr. Wong asked as they drove up the paved road flanked by fields of cane. He stopped right there, before they had gone half a mile, so Emily and Beener could get out and take a good, close look.

The stalks of the cane plants were taller and thicker, but similar in appearance to field corn. In the younger fields, the rows of cane were distinctly spaced, but in the mature fields, the cane grew in

23

a dense, high, silvery-green mass, which the wind rippled into waves of motion and varying shades of color.

"The painting I can do here!" exclaimed Mrs. Fergus.

"Boy! The big machinery on this plantation!" Beener looked with interest at a double-trailered cane truck, top-heavy with a load of cut cane stalks, whining in low gear up the hill ahead.

As they drove on, a high, powerful jet of water from the pumps of an overhead irrigating machine, caught and prismed the sunlight in rainbow drops of color.

On a distant slope, across a bare brown newly harvested field, they could see the yellow silhouette of a tractor at work, carving the deep topsoil into contoured ploughed rows.

All Kohala climbed up the gentle slope of the island from the seacoast to the dark green tree line of rounded mountains.

Somewhere on this vast plantation, nearly four thousand people lived. But, from the airport road, not a house or building was in sight.

A dove flew in front of the car, and a covey of mynah birds scolded as they flew up from under the wheels at the last impudent moment.

Emily turned and looked back. Across the Alenuihaha Channel, the island of Maui was a great, blue cloud-hung mountain against the sky.

Kalani McBryde was right, Emily thought. *Kohala no ka oi.*

That night, in a strange bed, in a strange room, in the big old-fashioned plantation house, Kalani's praise of Kohala was farthest from Emily's thoughts.

The windows rattled alarmingly in the wind. The branches of the big monkeypod tree creaked and groaned. Strange animals came snuffling at the ti plants that grew around the house. All the shadows in the high-ceilinged room looked strange and spooky.

Emily lay awake, remembering Kalani McBryde's story about ghost drums and the spirits of old Kohala. This house, Dr. Wong had said, was one of the oldest on the plantation. Such an old house, Emily thought, might have its ghosts too!

Emily pulled the covers up over her ears, wishing she could stop thinking about ghosts.

Suddenly the bedroom windows began rattling violently in their frames — and not from the wind. The bed, the bedroom — the whole house — rocked in a long uneasy shiplike sway. From the depths of the earth came a rumbling, growling sound.

Something hard and swift and heavy hurtled into Emily's bed. "Beener!" she gasped, and she reached out and held her brother as if her two arms could protect him from this old house shaking down.

"Earthquake?" said Beener in a shaky voice.

"Earthquake," said Emily, trying to sound very brave.

The house stopped rocking. There was a second of absolute silence. Then, all the dogs in Kohala began to bark. The roosters began to crow.

From Beener's adjoining room, Dr. and Mrs. Fergus hurried into Emily's bedroom and turned on the light. The plantation house was built in a long series of rooms, each connected with a door between, and each room also opened onto a big screened L-shaped lanai.

"Beener! Here you are!" said Mrs. Fergus, relieved.

"I came in to be with Em in case she got scared," said Beener, sliding out from Emily's covers to sit on the edge of Emily's bed.

"In case *I* got scared! You —" Emily gave Beener a shove.

"Ou-ch," complained Beener, landing on the floor on his rear end.

"Emily!" said Mrs. Fergus.

Beener stuck out his tongue and made a face at his sister from the floor.

"That's enough of that!" said Dr. Fergus sternly. "You two learn to get along better this year, or I'll make life unpleasant for both of you!"

"Get along with him? How could anybody!" protested Emily.

"Get along with her? Impossible!" said Beener,

picking himself up off the floor. He stood glaring at his sister, and then abruptly stopped glaring, and looked thoughtful. "If we had an earthquake, does that mean the volcano's going off?"

Dr. Fergus laughed. "You sound hopeful, Beener. They do call Kilauea the world's only drive-in volcano, and we're at the opposite end of the island — maybe a hundred and thirty miles away. It's supposed to be the world's most active volcano."

"Only not tonight, please! I'm too sleepy for earthquakes or volcanoes or standing here talking about either one," yawned Mrs. Fergus. "It's that three-hour time change from the coast, and we're all tired from the excitement of the trip!"

"Not me!" said Beener. "I feel great! If that volcano goes off, Dad and I'll go. I can think of a neat scientific experiment I want to try!"

"You and your experiments," said Emily, and she yawned too. She watched her mother and father and Beener leave her room. She turned off her light. It was going to be a nuisance, she thought sleepily, having Beener's bedroom connected so handily with hers. Before she fell asleep, she reached under her bed. Her treasure box was safe, both from earthquakes and Beener, under there.

Emily soon was dreaming. Horrible slimy monsters scratched at her feet with horny claws. Cold clammy crawling things came at her. Something scraped over her legs, and up her pajama bottom. Slow feet wriggled across the stretch of open skin at her waist. Something made a queer sound walking on her sheet. Something cool and queer brushed her cheek.

"EEEeeeeee!" Emily screamed.

She shook herself, brushed her cheek with her hands, yanked back the covers, and switched on her light.

Beener, her mother, her father, all with dazed, sleepy faces, hurried in.

"Darn you, Beener!" Emily accused. "You keep that nasty turtle of yours out of my bed!" She was still trembling and still half crying. She was ashamed of herself for being so afraid of Albert, but she was.

"Well, Emily. ·Was that all?" said her mother in disgust.

"Holy kasmoley. Girls!" said Beener. "I just hope you didn't hurt him." He picked Albert tenderly from Emily's pillow and examined him in the light. "He must have dropped out of my pajama pocket when I came in here during the earthquake."

"After this," said Dr. Fergus, "Albert sleeps in his turtle bowl safe on your bureau. Understand, Beener? That turtle leads a charmed life, I swear!" He shook his head, and then he paused on the threshold to look at Emily. She was back in bed, covers pulled to her chin, eyes fixed on the painted board ceiling. She was ashamed of herself. She was furious with Beener. She wished she weren't so terrified by creepy, crawly, wriggly creatures, but she was, and she didn't know how she was ever going to make herself change.

"Emily," said her father, guessing what was going through her mind. "With all the bugs and queer creatures and crawling things in the tropics, I don't know how you're going to manage this year!"

3

Forty-two Friends

In spite of the excitement of the day before, Emily and Beener had been exploring their neighborhood of four big old houses since dawn. "Plantation House #2, Puehú Skilled Camp B," was certainly an unromantic address, Emily thought.

She was more than ready for breakfast when Fumiko, the Blythes' housekeeper, who had stayed on to work for Emily's family, called them in for breakfast. She was a tiny cheerful woman no taller than Beener. While the children ate, she told them about where and how plantation people lived.

There were five small villages, she explained, most of them with a general store or two and a branch post office, scattered across the twelve-mile breadth of the Kohala district.

"Five villages because, many years ago, when I

was small yet, there were five sugar plantations in Kohala," Fumiko said. "Many people those days, with all the planting and harvesting done by hand, and five mills grinding. Now, plenty machines, not so many people. Those five villages, most of them, what you call ghost towns now."

The one paved highway linking the dry and the rainy ends of the district was called the government road, Fumiko told them. Because Kohala was at the island's northern tip, the plantation included two very different climates on its windward and leeward sides.

Built off and away from the five villages, and usually some distance from the government road, as was the Fergus' plantation home, were small neighborhoods of houses, called camps.

Some of these camps were up in the cool high elevations on the mountain slopes. Some were in the hotter, dryer areas near cliffs that dropped off into the sea. Some, like Puehu Skilled Camp B, were halfway between.

"This house is over one hundred years old," Fumiko continued. "All built of redwood lumber brought from California in a sailing ship when people first began growing sugarcane here."

"Wow!" Beener looked at the high, old-fashioned kitchen ceiling and small-paned windows. "No wonder that tree out front is so big! I was going to experiment with a tree house, but holy kasmoley! How do you get up to branches that high?"

"Beener, you stay out of that monkeypod tree!" said Fumiko earnestly. "Maybe you get hurt, climbing way up those big branches. And, anyway, some people say five *obakis* live in that tree."

"Obakis?"

"Obaki. Japanese word for ghosts. Evil spirits. You know?" Fumiko smiled. They could believe her, or not, as they chose, that smile said. Emily, remembering Princess Kalani's stories on the plane yesterday afternoon, chose to think about it and make up her mind to believe or not later.

"Aaaaaah!" scoffed Beener. *"Obakis?* I betcha there are no such things, but I can sure think of an experiment to try and find out!"

"I wouldn't," said Fumiko, with that same smile.

After breakfast, Beener and Emily wandered outside again. They and their stomachs were still on Sacramento time, where it was nine o'clock already. It was only six o'clock here.

Emily sat on the front steps. Beener stretched on the grass to let Albert out of his pocket to exercise for a while.

Across the dusty road from the four widely spaced big houses, was a park the size of half a city block. It was an open grassy park, with a backstop for baseball. A banana grove bordered one edge, between the park and the adjoining cane fields. Three goats, staked out on short tethers, nibbled the park lawn.

Below the park were the red painted roofs of another camp. Beyond them were more cane fields, and beyond these cane fields, Emily could look out at the dark blue edging of the sea.

"Tired, Albert?" said Beener. He put Albert back in his pocket. Emily followed along, when she felt like it, for a second look at the backyard.

"Tangerine. Grapefruit. Orange. I don't know," said Beener, identifying the trees in the back-yard by what was growing on each one.

"Mango, that kind," volunteered Isabelo, the yardman, as Emily and Beener puzzled over the strange purplish-green fruit hanging on long rattail stems.

Beener explored by himself in a strip of wilder-ness, between the backyard fence and the cane fields behind the house. "Dibs on these old rabbit hutches for a clubhouse!" he yelled from a jungle of weeds and castor bean brush.

"If you have Albert along up there in your pocket, you're going to either lose him or smother him," Emily predicted from her lazy full-length stretch on the dewy grass. "And good riddance," she added, remembering the awful feeling of Albert in her bed last night.

Beener came back, covered with sticker burrs and the tiny adhesive pods of pigeon peas. "Albert likes to live close to me," he said fondly, patting his jeans pocket. "He'd like a great big open-air turtle pen, and a pond, too, though, I betcha." Beener stood and looked thoughtful. "By those rabbit hutches — near my clubhouse!" he decided.

He ran over to where Isabelo sat on his haunches, weeding around a bed of orchid plants.

Beener approached Isabelo with a smile that Emily knew could get almost anything out of anybody, even her.

"Can I please use your shovel?" he asked. "I'm going to dig a turtle pond."

Isabelo stared up at Beener from under the rim of his lauhala hat. "Can," he said, as if he'd said "yes."

Emily watched Beener go off with the shovel over his shoulder. She yawned, sleepy from being awake twice in the night, but not wanting to miss one single hour of her first day in Hawaii by staying in bed.

"Missy come by Calipunia?" Isabelo asked Emily.

"Calipunia?" Emily got up and went over to the orchid bed. She wondered if a calipunia was some new kind of island flower, and which one it was. She hadn't come by anything like that this morning, she thought, confused. "No — "

It was not the answer Isabelo expected. His eyes widened. "Doctor yesterday, he say yes!"

Emily jumped at a strange voice behind her.

"Oh, sure," said the strange voice in rapid pidgin English. "They stay stop California. Sacramento. Doctor Blythe, he stay go one year there."

Emily whirled around.

There stood a red-headed girl her own age, dressed in Bermuda shorts and shirt, bare feet, and — best of all, making Emily feel completely at ease — like Emily herself, the red-headed stranger had braces on her front teeth.

"Hi!" said the girl, her braces shining in a big smile. "You must be Emily Fergus. I'm Alix Leith. I live next door!"

Within five minutes, the two girls felt like old friends. They sat crosslegged on the grass, patting Alix's little black dog Aka, while from up in the backyard jungle came the steady whack of Isabelo's machete. Beener needed clearing done before he could start to dig.

Despite the red hair, Alix's dark eyes and golden-bronze skin reminded Emily of Kalani McBryde, the Princess Kalani, and of the Hawaiian stewardess on the interisland airplane.

"Have you always lived in Hawaii?" Emily asked enviously.

"I was born in Kohala. So was my father! He's Scotch-Hawaiian. Mother's a coast *haole*."

"Coast *haole*?" Emily puzzled. "I know what a *haole* is, but — "

Alix giggled. "You're one, Emily. Because you came from California. Mother's one, because she came from Oregon. If you're from the West Coast, you're a coast *haole*. Catch?" Alix paused, and then the friendly smile on her face changed to a frown.

A big cream-colored car with chrome-spiked rear fins screeched up the driveway, leaving a cloud of dust to roll in after it. Brakes slammed. A motor died. Car doors opened.

"The Prices," said Alix.

She gave a quick trapped glance at the hibiscus hedge separating the Fergus and Leith backyards. "Too late," she whispered to Emily. "They've seen me already."

She and Emily stood up.

"Alix!" said the stout blond woman getting out of the car. "I might have known you'd be over here first. Well!" the caller surveyed Emily from her braces down to her pale bare feet.

"You must be the new doctor's daughter. And we could hardly wait for you to get here, could we, Jasmine!" She turned with an impatient gesture to the plump, blond girl following her. "Jasmine. Come meet your new little friend!"

Mrs. Price's eyes quickly took in everything going on in the yard: Isabelo and Beener up in the weeds near the old rabbit hutches, glimpses of Fumiko's head through the kitchen windows in the rear of the house.

"Your mother's up, isn't she?" Mrs. Price asked Emily.

"I think so — " Her father had gone out to the hospital a few minutes ago while she and Alix were getting acquainted, but Emily hadn't seen or heard her mother yet. "Come in, and I'll tell her you're here," said Emily politely.

She led the Prices inside, through the kitchen, and into the living room. Mrs. Price sat down on the sofa and set the basket she carried on a low table.

"Sit down, Jasmine! Don't just stand around like that, ever. I've told you before!" she said sharply.

Jasmine, her head bent in embarrassment, ducked into the nearest chair. She was the most unhappy-looking girl Emily had ever seen.

"Excuse me, I'll tell my mother you're here," said Emily.

As she left the room, Emily heard Mrs. Price say, "I see they still have everything the way the Blythes left it — so far."

Mrs. Fergus looked dazed to be entertaining callers at eight o'clock in the morning, before she had had breakfast.

Fumiko, as if she knew just how Mrs. Fergus must feel, quickly brought in coffee for the two grown-ups, guava juice for the girls, and a plate of fresh, sliced hot banana bread.

"I must say, Fumiko does very well for a Japanese. You're fortunate," said Mrs. Price, stirring three teaspoonfuls of sugar into her cup.

Emily saw her mother sit up, as if something had stung her. Mrs. Fergus opened her mouth to speak, but Mrs. Lulu Price was not easy to interrupt. She poured cream in her coffee, took two slices of banana bread, and went on eating and talking all at the same time without a moment's break.

"We have a Puerto Rican working for us. She's clean enough, but so emotional! You know how Puerto Ricans are. Portuguese, too. Very unstable, but I'll take either one over a Hawaiian. I say to Rowland, that's Mr. Price, it may be one hundred and forty years since the missionaries came to try and teach the Hawaiians how to live, but I haven't found one Hawaiian yet who knows the meaning of hard work. Nobody works like a Japanese, which is one thing I always give them credit for."

Mrs. Price helped herself to more banana bread and kept on talking without giving Mrs. Fergus, or anyone else, a chance to say a word.

"My dear," she said to Mrs. Fergus, "I wonder. How will you stand it living in this neighborhood? I know you've only spent one night here so far, but just wait. Oh, we had a small earthquake, but that's not what I mean!"

Alix looked at Emily. Emily looked at Alix. Mrs. Fergus sat looking more and more dazed, with a peculiar expression on her face.

"What will keep you awake all night every night down here is that racket of fighting chickens," Mrs. Price went on, "from all the Filipinos down camp across the park. They're bachelors, most of those men, and those fighting cocks are their pets. I always think they sound like a bunch of chickens themselves when you hear them around the district talking Filipino. I've never been able to understand one of them, myself. I refuse to cope with pidgin English. I always let Rowland give orders to our yardman. Rowland's English, but he was born in Kohala. We're very particular about the way English is spoken in our home," she said proudly. "That's why we're so happy to have you people in the district. A girl her own age for Jasmine to play with! Why, she's been counting the days. Haven't you, Jasmine?"

Jasmine hung her head. She took the last piece of banana bread and poked at the crumbs on the plate with a moistened forefinger.

"Jasmine is so shy," her mother said in a fond voice. "She takes after her father. Rowland is a very retiring personality, too. Most people would be surprised though to know how he is at home! He knows everything that goes on around this plantation — and I mean everything about everybody — not just us!"

"Us?" Mrs. Fergus said, with a peculiar emphasis in her voice.

"Us," Mrs. Price repeated, looking pleased with

herself. "*Haole* people. You know. I promised myself I'd get you acquainted first thing. You'll just love the district!" she said with enthusiasm. "There are about forty-two of us — forty-six with your family now. We have our little social activities. We won't give you time to get bored! It's hard on the children is my only complaint. Poor Jasmine. She's been the only one in her class since first grade. Except for Alix, of course." Mrs. Price smiled condescendingly at Alix.

Mrs. Fergus put her coffee cup down, still half full. "Mrs. Price, I don't think I understand. Jasmine can't be the only child in her class here! We were told there was a large seventh grade in Kohala."

Mrs. Price looked astonished that the question should have to be asked. "But Jasmine's the only *haole* girl — except for Alix."

Again, Emily winced for Alix at the little note of superiority in Mrs. Price's way of saying that. Alix had sounded so proud of being part-Hawaiian when they were getting acquainted earlier. Emily thought she'd like being part-Hawaiian, herself.

"As I say," Mrs. Price smiled, "there are forty-two of us here. You'll find, Mrs. Fergus, that you will have forty-two nice friends."

She put down her coffee cup. She looked hungrily at the empty bread plate. She picked up her basket, took out a hand of bananas and a jar of jelly and put them on the coffee table.

"We raise the best bananas in the district," she said. "You'll enjoy these. And this is a jar of my special passion fruit jelly. They pleaded with me to give the recipe to the PTA cookbook four years ago, but this jelly's my secret. My specialty." Mrs. Price smiled and stood up.

"Emily, you must come spend the day with Jasmine soon. She has a dozen lovely scrapbooks filled with TV and movie stars. Jasmine," she said in a sharper tone, "remember what I told you to say!"

Jasmine stood up, shoulders hunched, glasses slipped down the bridge of her nose, eyes on the floor. She looked so miserable, Emily felt sorry for her.

"You come over. Any time, yuh?" Jasmine said in an accent that, even to Emily's unaccustomed ear, sounded like the pidgin English Jasmine's mother had condemned a few minutes ago.

"Ask me anything you want to know about the island. Call me up. Come over any time. I want to be your introduction to Kohala," Mrs. Price beamed.

Mrs. Fergus walked with her to the living room door, out across the front lanai, and back up the drive.

Emily and Alix and Jasmine followed, and Emily thought to herself, she had never heard her mother so quiet with company.

Jasmine kept her eyes on her own feet.

"See you around, Jasmine," said Alix.

"Yuh," said Jasmine, and she gave Emily a

quick, shy glance, before following her mother.

"And just call me Lulu!" said Mrs. Price, waving good-bye as she backed the cream-colored car out of the driveway.

Mrs. Fergus just stood there, a queer look on her face, until the Prices were out of sight. "Well!" she said then. "Is that woman any example of island aloha?"

"Mrs. Price?" exclaimed Alix. "Oh, no! She's just Mrs. Price and she's awful. Couldn't you tell? Oh — " Alix clapped her hand to her mouth and looked stricken. "I promised Mother I wouldn't say anything. Please, excuse me, Mrs. Fergus. Emily, forget I said what I did just now, will you?"

But before Emily could answer — before she could properly introduce Alix to her mother as she should have half an hour ago when the Prices first came — Beener came racing down full speed from the weeds and castor beans.

"Look! Buried treasure!" he yelled. "Lookit what I found digging Albert's turtle pen!"

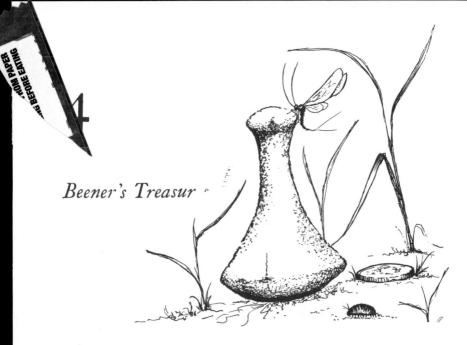

Beener's Treasure

"Look! Come on in the kitchen where I can put 'em down some place safe!" Beener yelled as he ran on ahead.

Emily, Alix, and Mrs. Fergus followed him, up the driveway, across the yard, and through the kitchen door.

"I was digging old Albert's turtle pond and I whacked something funny with the shovel. I took a good look, because you never know what you might dig up on an island this far out in the middle of the Pacific Ocean. And see?" Beener put two small objects carefully down on the kitchen table.

One was a small, strange coin. One was a stone pestle, perfectly shaped and smoothed, three inches high.

"Smart boy, you!" Fumiko admired.

43

"Why, Beener! Benjamin Ebenezer Fergus!" Mrs. Fergus exclaimed.

Emily stood with her mouth open, impressed and already envious. "Wow. Are you ever lucky, Beener!"

"This," Beener fingered the coin, "is real old valuable Hawaiian money."

"Let me see?" Alix asked.

Somewhat reluctantly, Beener handed the coin to her.

"A Kalakaua dime!" Alix turned it from side to side, reading the worn inscription. "That's really rare!"

Watching, Emily sighed. Leave it to Beener. His luck at finding things was uncanny and, to Emily, irritating, since she was the one with a collection and a treasure box.

Beener cared nothing about keeping what he found, but he always drove Emily to a hard bargain in any trade. That old Hawaiian dime was just the kind of souvenir Emily had hoped to be able to add to her treasure box this year, but she could see herself now, emptying the garbage and taking over Beener's chores all this summer — and maybe winter — to get him to give that rare coin to her.

"I have x-ray vision, practically," said Beener. "First I saw the coin in the dirt I dug up. I picked it up. I spit on it and rubbed it shiny. When I read that 'Kalakaua Rex' business on it, boy, I knew! I told Isabelo and Albert so, too!"

"And this little tiny poi pounder," asked Alix, "where'd you find it? This could be really ancient Hawaiian."

"Yeah?" Beener grinned. "That's a really good place to dig up there, I guess. Because after I found the dime, I kept on looking and pretty soon my shovel went whammy on this! Nothing else turned up yet, but boy! Every day, I'm going up there and dig!"

"I might just come dig with you, too," said Mrs. Fergus. "Alix, what did you call this little stone pestle?"

"A poi pounder. Smallest one I ever saw, though." Alix picked up the pounder to demonstrate. "In the old days, Hawaiians lived mostly on fish and on poi, which is mashed, cooked taro root. It's kind of a purple-pink color, and it fills you up like rice and potatoes never can. It's good! We eat poi all the time, only now everybody buys poi at the grocery store. We have a poi factory here in Kohala that makes fresh poi every day. No more poi pounders any more though. They use a machine."

"That little pounder for medicine, maybe?" Fumiko leaned her mop handle against the broom closet door and took the tiny poi pounder from Alix. She rubbed the porous, smooth stone shape with her fingers, then returned it to Beener. "Mr. Fraser, on the other side next door, he knows about old Hawaiian things. You show that one to him!"

45

Alix looked at the kitchen clock. "Almost nine. He'll be home for lunch at eleven-thirty. You can catch him then, Beener."

"Eleven-thirty lunch. That's early. Is he the man we saw drive out at maybe half-past five this morning in a green jeep?"

"That's Uncle Phil. He's head of the harvesting for the whole plantation, and field men have to be on the job early. My dad's office manager, so he goes to work at half-past seven. The plantation day shift starts early, but they're through work, *pau hana,* at half-past three."

"Sandy Blythe wrote us that they harvest and grind cane twenty-four hours a day," said Mrs. Fergus. "It seemed to me, after the earthquake last night, that I could hear trucks rumbling back and forth on the highway."

"That's right," said Alix, "and if we lived closer to the mill, you could hear it running all night, too."

With his left hand, Beener plucked Albert out of his jeans pocket. With his right hand, he picked up the dime and the poi pounder. "Hey, Fumiko. Put Albert in his bowl for me, would you? And guard my treasures while I go up and dig until the man next door comes home?" He gave Fumiko his irresistible smile and his pet and his two discoveries, and ran out to do as he'd said.

"You have a nice boy. Rascal, but nice boy, that Beener," said Fumiko to Mrs. Fergus.

"Rascal, but nice! That's a good description of him, Fumiko!" Mrs. Fergus laughed.

"Rascal, period!" said Emily to Alix in a quick whisper she intended her mother and Fumiko not to hear.

"I need another cup of coffee," said Mrs. Fergus, turning on the flame under the coffee pot.

"May we have some banana bread, Mother? Alix and I didn't get a chance at it when the Prices were here," Emily asked.

At the mention of the Prices, that peculiar expression again crossed Mrs. Fergus' face. She sat down at the table. Fumiko brought another plate of banana bread, and Alix and Emily sat down, too.

"Alix," said Mrs. Fergus, "are there many Mrs. Prices in this district?"

Alix grinned. "Nope. Mostly just the Prices are like that. You know. There are *haoles* and *haoles*. Don't worry. You'll have lots and lots of friends in Kohala, if you want to be friendly, about four thousand of them. I think that's what Daddy said the population is."

Mrs. Fergus looked relieved, but that peculiar expression lingered. "That's what I'd been given to understand before we came — but after this morning — " She shook her head.

"Mrs. Price means all right," said Fumiko charitably.

Mrs. Fergus looked skeptical. "You should have

47

heard all she said, though. And if that's how different kinds of people feel about each other in these islands, Hawaii is not the land of aloha I expected it to be!"

Fumiko tested the coffee pot, poured a cup for Mrs. Fergus, and poured a second cup for herself.

"Mrs. Price, she never got to know much about us, although she's lived here a long time now. But some people, they don't want to know, they don't want to understand. Her way is not how most different kinds of people feel about each other in the islands," Fumiko said. "Most people here are kind. In the camps, if a stranger came, we always tried to make him feel at home. That's how pidgin English started. When my parents first were here from Japan, all different kinds of people lived in the camps and worked together — Chinese, Japanese, Portuguese, Puerto Ricans later on, Koreans, too, Filipinos in my own day. Nobody knew each other's language. Nobody knew English. They wanted to talk to each other so they worked out their own way. A little Hawaiian, some Japanese, some Spanish words, a little bit English. Enough of every language so every person can use it to get along and live and work together and be friends. My daughter explained that to me," said Fumiko proudly. "My youngest daughter. She majored in speech at the University."

What Fumiko said sounded to Emily more the way things ought to be in Hawaii than the way they'd heard this morning from Mrs. Price.

Maybe, Emily thought, it depended on who and what you were yourself, what picture you got of other people.

"Forty-two friends!" said Mrs. Fergus indignantly.

"Not if you want to make more friends than that," said Alix, and Fumiko nodded.

"That Mrs. Price!" said Alix. "Not that I mean to be disrespectful of a grown-up, but — "

Emily wondered about poor, unhappy-looking Jasmine Price. Did she think the way her mother did, too?

The wide verandas of the Frasers' house next door were screened with clematis vines and the tall shiny green leaves of ti.

Across the front of the house, set against a background of torch ginger plants, was a row of carved wooden statues.

"Oh!" Emily stared up at the strange ugly faces. Pearl shell eyes stared back at her, and carved tongues protruded as boldly as Beener's could.

"Those are Hawaiian gods. *Tikis*," said Alix. "Uncle Phil carves them from tree fern logs. That's one of his hobbies, and they're authentic copies of the ancient Hawaiian idols. Some people say there are still plenty of real ones like these hidden away in caves around here."

Beener looked at the *tikis* with more respect than usual. "Wow," he said, taking Albert out of his pocket to look too. "They're fierce!"

Alix led Beener and Emily around to the rear of the house. There were, Emily counted them, seventeen cats and eight kittens curled in the sun, or playing with wads of crumpled paper and string, or frisking with each other around the Frasers' kitchen door.

"Shoo!" said Alix. "Aunt Tuki likes cats," she said, and considered that enough explanation for twenty-five of them.

"Hoo-hoo! Uncle Phil!" Alix called through the screen door.

There was the scraping sound of chair legs from the kitchen. A man with a deeply tanned face and keen blue eyes, his gray hair cut short in a crew cut, came out. "Hi, kids, what can I do for you?"

"Uncle Phil," said Alix, "this is Emily Fergus, and Beener Fergus. Their father's the doctor that Uncle Sandy changed places with this year."

"Glad to meet you." Mr. Fraser held the door open. "Come on in!"

Emily, Alix, and Beener filed into the gayest kitchen Emily had ever seen. From cup hooks screwed to the ceiling, floated gay red and white paper carp. Over the sink was a trio of bright red and blue Japanese paper lanterns. In the center of the kitchen table was a basket heaped with yellow and red and white plumeria blossoms.

"Hi, P'lipo!" said Alix to the fat, sixteen-month-old baby who sat banging his spoon on his high chair tray.

She introduced Emily and Beener to Mrs. Fraser, a dark-eyed woman in a yellow muumuu with a big yellow hibiscus blossom tucked into her long black hair.

"Okay, Beener. Show them!" Alix urged.

Beener set the coin, and then the stone pestle, on the table. From Mr. Fraser's expression, Emily knew that Beener had done it again. The poi pounder and the Hawaiian coin were real finds.

"Hey!" exclaimed Mr. Fraser. "Where'd you find these?"

While Beener told him, Mr. Fraser examined first the Kalakaua dime and then the tiny pounder.

"Not usable as money any more, but a collector's item, that's for sure!" said Mr. Fraser putting the coin down.

Emily looked at the small piece of silver covetously.

"I think I'll just use it for a lucky piece," Beener said, "like I do Albert. Then I betcha I'll find lots more valuable old stuff up there."

"This is a beauty!" Mr. Fraser admired the stone pestle. "And the next question is, how did it get where you found it?" Mr. Fraser looked thoughtful. "There were plenty of Hawaiians living all through this Puehu area in pre-missionary days. There were forty thousand Hawaiians in Kohala when Captain Cook made his voyage along this coast in 1778. In fact, there were still Hawaiians living on their own small *kulianas* here in Kalakaua's time. That might explain the dime being with the poi pounder."

Mr. Fraser read the date on the coin, "1887." That figures. The pounder would be much older. 1787, maybe. Or earlier. Who knows?" He set down both of Beener's treasures, looking at them with an envy Emily well understood.

"Tell you what, kids. I have to hustle this noon. But would you mind bringing these back *pau hana,* after work, about half-past three this afternoon? I have a friend on the staff of Bishop Museum. He's on this island for a bout of fieldwork at Honaunau, sixty miles from here, on the Kona coast. He's driving over for supper with us tonight, and he'll know better than I can tell you whether this little poi pounder is as special as I think!"

Beener picked up the poi pounder with a gesture of reverence. "Holy kasmoley!" he said, impressed. "I'm going home and guard this, me and Albert, until your friend gets here this afternoon!"

"Please, all of you come over, *pau hana,*" Mrs. Fraser invited. "Bring your mother and dad, Emily. And Alix, ask your folks to come, too."

"Thank you! I'll tell them, and I'm sure we can come," said Emily.

"I'll be here, no matter what!" said Beener, holding a treasure in each hand.

"See you this afternoon, Aunt Tuki — and thanks!" said Alix, as the children went out the back door.

Outside, past the twenty-five cats, past a fig tree bearded with Spanish moss and trailing orchid plants, along a stone walk and under the pearly gaze of the carved Hawaiian gods, Emily burst out with her question.

"Alix, are you related to everyone in this neighborhood?"

Alix laughed. "You mean because I call the grown-ups uncle and aunt? That's just being polite, island style. It wouldn't do to call your mother's and father's best friends by their first names, and it sounds funny to say Mr. or Mrs. Fraser all the time, so I call them Aunt Tuki and Uncle Phil. Of course, through Daddy's family, I have lots of calabash relatives on this island, too."

"Calabash?" It was Emily's turn to giggle. "That sounds like what we call shirttail relations at home. Second and third and fifth cousins twice removed?"

"Sure. Only shirttail is a funny way to put it," said Alix.

"Calabash." Emily giggled again. "That's a funny way to put it, too!"

5

An Invitation

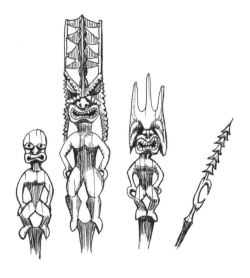

"We've supposed the Hawaiians had these," said Mr. Minetti, the archaeologist from Honolulu's Bishop Museum.

He was intrigued by Beener's tiny poi pounder. "I've never seen one like this before. They were made for children to play with, a toy smaller than a medicine pestle. Probably it was a rare item even with the youngsters who lived in grass houses here in Puehu more than two hundred years ago."

Everyone on the Frasers' lanai was gathered around Beener and his treasures. The grown-ups sat in rattan chairs. P'lipo was in his playpen. Alix and Emily sat perched on the lanai railing. Beener, on the floor, was the center of attention.

Albert had come to the Frasers, too. He was in his plastic bowl on top of the Frasers' fern stand, where Beener could protect him from any cats who came around.

"If you like, Beener might be persuaded to give his find to the museum, Mr. Minetti," Dr. Fergus suggested.

"You mean Beener would be that generous? What a change!" Emily spoke up.

"Emily Ann!" said her mother.

Beener seemed startled by his father's suggestion, but he was challenged now to show his sister she had the wrong opinion of him. "Sure I want my poi pounder to be in the museum. You can just put a card with my name on it in the display case, saying I found it digging a turtle pond in our backyard."

"Thank you, Beener," Mr. Minetti said. "We'll do that!" Then he chuckled. "We might put down Albert's name on the card, since he helped you find it, too!"

A huge wooden tray of what Mrs. Fraser called *pupus* was on a low table which everyone could reach. Emily nibbled *pupus* as she turned over in her mind the chances for wangling Beener into trading the Hawaiian dime.

She had never tasted anything like the thin delicious sun dried strips of beef called *pipi kaula,* or the crisp bites of turtle steak fried in deep fat. Even the strangest food on the big tray — rosy thin slices of raw fish to dip into a hot mustard sauce — tasted good to her.

55

"Ummmmmm! Japanese style *sashimi*," said Alix, helping herself to more raw fish.

Emily admired the way Alix and the Frasers, the Leiths and Mr. Minetti picked up the *pupus* with a neat expert motion of chopsticks.

The only new food there that Emily did not like was pickled Korean style cabbage. It was called *kim chee,* pronounced exactly as it is spelled. It burned like a mouthful of crunchy fire, but the grown-ups, her parents included, ate it with relish.

Beener, who was not adventurous when it came to food, kept scooping handfuls of macadamia nuts for himself, and feeding turtle-sized *pupus* of raw fish to Albert.

"Feed him a piece of turtle steak!" urged Alix.

"You think I want to turn him into a cannibal?" Beener said indignantly.

"If you Ferguses are interested in Hawaiian history, you've certainly come to the right spot," said Mr. Minetti. "Kohala and your neighboring district of Kona — in fact, most of the Big Island — is still untouched, undeveloped, and there is plenty of exploring to be done."

"That's my hobby, and Daddy's," said Emily, "history, Hawaiian or any other kind."

"Exploring's my hobby!" said Beener.

Mr. Minetti looked thoughtful. "You people might be interested in a little Hawaiian archaeology then. I'm over here on a special field assignment.

The National Park Service is developing a Hawaiian historic park over on the Kona coast at Honaunau. There are one hundred and sixty acres of historic sites hidden in brush jungle there. We've found old house platforms, an ancient Hawaiian sled-racing course built down on a lava flow — "

"Sleds!" Beener frowned. "How could they use sleds if it's always summertime over here?"

"They slid on ti leaves, which make a fair toboggan over a smooth grass-slicked lava surface, or a nice steep muddy hill. Island kids still like to go ti-leaf sliding, Beener," said Mr. Minetti, laughing at the expression on Beener's face.

"Mud?"

"That's for you, eh, Beener?" his father smiled.

"You bet!" said Beener. "I'm going to try that ti-leaf sliding myself!"

"Only the chiefs could use the ti-leaf slides in ancient Hawaii," said Mr. Minetti. "The royal slide in Honaunau was *kapu,* which is the Hawaiian word for tabu — forbidden to ordinary people like you and me. There were many *kapus* and sometimes people forgot rules, or wanted to do something forbidden, anyway. If they were caught, the punishment could be death. So, at Honaunau, there was a special walled enclosure called a place of refuge, where people who had broken a rule could go for sanctuary and be safe. There were many other places of refuge in the islands, but the one at Honaunau is the only one left standing today.

"I'll be spending the next few weeks making a final check on the museum's archaeological survey and report there. If you can get over, I'd be happy to take you around and, in fact, if you like, put you to work! The museum can always use good volunteer help."

"Oh, Daddy, can we? Please!" Emily and Beener descended on their father, both at once.

"Hey! Easy, you two! May we, you mean," Dr. Fergus laughed. "That's an attractive invitation, but I don't know whether the museum can use such young volunteers."

"I wouldn't ask every family," said Mr. Minetti. "But if Beener can turn up artifacts on his own and know enough to recognize them for something valuable, and if Emily is as dependable as she looks, the invitation is for the whole family to come!"

"Yipppp-ee!" said Beener, but with restraint. To Emily's relief, for the rest of the afternoon, he did his best to look old enough and dependable enough to be a museum volunteer.

"Looks like you have a real good luck combination with Albert and your Hawaiian dime, eh, Beener?" said Mr. Leith. Alix's father was a tall, heavyset, handsome part-Hawaiian man. "We've had people in Kohala before, who liked to fool around collecting Hawaiian stones and exploring in caves, but some of them were pretty short on luck."

Mr. Leith shook his head. "Phil and Tuki, you remember Dr. Halvorsen, the Norwegian fellow who came to work here for three months the year Sandy Blythe went to Japan? Halvorsen liked to explore caves, because he was interested in Hawaiian history, too."

"Was he the one who took the leg bone out of Red Hill and got cave-sick?" Mr. Minetti asked.

Emily, listening, forgot all about the *pupu* of dried beef halfway to her mouth.

Beener sat listening, his mouth ajar. "Human bone?" he asked.

"Human bone. From a burial and refuge cave here in Kohala," Mr. Minetti nodded. "There are more caves on the Big Island than any place I've ever been. They are lava tubes, really. Kona is honeycombed with them underground. So is Kohala, only Kohala caves are much older because this is the oldest part of the Big Island. I've never been in Red Hill Cave myself, but I've heard a lot about it. That's a cave I want to visit this trip, if I can!"

"I was along the time Halvorsen took that bone," said Phil Fraser. "We all warned him to leave it in the cave and not to touch anything, but he told us he didn't believe in Hawaiian superstitions. He laughed at the rest of us."

"I've heard about these Hawaiian caves!" Dr. Fergus was enthralled. "I'd like to go in one myself!"

"I can take you into a cave when you come to

Kona," Mr. Minetti offered. "This island is a spelunker's paradise. One cave I know, in Kona, is supposed to go for five miles from the mountains to the sea. The Hawaiians have a legend of a cave in Kohala. that connects the Big Island and Maui, twenty-six miles of subterranean lava tube."

"That's for me!" said Beener. "I'm going to be a spelunker someday. I like to explore dangerous places like caves!"

"A cave can be a dangerous place," said Mr. Minetti, "but unless you do something foolish like that fellow Halvorsen, Hawaiian caves are fairly safe. It's only a long chance you'd be caught in one when Madame Pele, the volcano goddess, decides to shake up the Big Island with an earthquake."

"What's cave-sickness?" Mrs. Fergus asked.

"Perhaps," Mr. Minetti's voice was oddly cautious, "it's a disease of the mind." He shrugged. "If you take something out of a cave, and you know you shouldn't, your guilty conscience can make you very ill. Dr. Halvorsen was asked before he went into Red Hill Cave not to take or touch anything inside — but he touched many things, and he took out a leg bone from some old Hawaiian who was buried down there, who knows how many hundreds of years ago."

"Twenty-four hours later he was cave-sick!" Mr. Fraser added. "He had a high fever, a headache, and aching bones!"

"John Kaimana, from the ranch, told him that

60

as soon as he took the leg bone back to the cave, he'd get better. And he did, and he was fine after that — only he had no more interest in Hawaiian history!" Mr. Leith grinned.

"Can anybody get cave-sick?" asked Beener.

"Only if you take or touch something you shouldn't, or if you offend the *akuas*, the guardian spirits of the cave," Mr. Fraser said.

"Phil!" protested his wife. "You sound more Hawaiian than we Hawaiians are!"

Mr. Fraser's eyes were serious. "I'm an Illinois corn belt boy," he said gravely, "but I've sat under these palm trees long enough to have a great deal of respect for what I see and hear. If you offend the *akuas*, the spirits — below or above ground — watch out!"

"By spirits, do you mean ghosts?" asked Emily, feeling pleasantly shivery inside. She looked at Mr. Fraser with eyes wide and, as Princess Kalani had urged, mind open.

"Spirits, ghosts, *akuas* — call them what you like," Mr. Fraser nodded, "Kohala's loaded — or loaded with stories about them, anyway!"

6

Kohala No Ka Oi

By the end of her second week in Kohala, Emily
was as much at home in the big plantation house as
if she had lived there all her life. She was used to,
and liked, Kohala summer weather, which was not
as uncomfortably hot as Sacramento could be.

The trade winds cooled the air, sometimes softly,
sometimes in strong brisk gusts that rattled dry limbs
from the monkeypod tree. There were always clouds
scudding across the sky. Big puffy white clouds.
Occasional low black clouds moved down the mountain slopes to dump a sudden shower and leave a
wet, green Kohala drenched in sunshine again.

"The weather is the same in winter, too," said
Alix. "Only once in a while, when the wind blows
opposite from the trade winds, we have what we call
a Kona storm. Then for a day or so, it's hot and

muggy, and we have heavy rain. Sometimes, too, in winter, when there is snow on top of Mauna Kea, it gets cool enough to wear a sweater to school."

Alix Leith was not Emily's only new friend. Dorothy Fujita lived an easy walking distance away. She, too, was twelve going on thirteen, and all three girls, Emily, Alix, and Dorothy, would be in the same seventh grade — along with Jasmine Price.

These first two weeks, Emily, Alix, and Dorothy became an inseparable threesome. Dorothy's brothers, Ryan and Kazu, were Beener's pals. Ryan and Kazu usually came by every day to help Beener dig his turtle pond and look for more treasures. They worked at least an hour every morning.

"That turtle pond is going to be big enough to hold a dinosaur!" Alix teased Beener one day.

"I never saw a five-and-ten turtle live so long as Albert," said Dorothy. "Most of the kids around here keep turtles a week or two, and then the shell turns soft and the turtles die."

Beener took Albert out of his pocket and carefully felt his shell.

"I should think Albert would die of fright, jouncing around in your pocket all the time," said Alix.

Beener put Albert down in the dirt in the sun. "He's used to me. I feed him on fresh meat and tomatoes and lettuce and give him lots of sunbaths. He likes it here in Hawaii. So do I."

She watched the turtle sun himself and stretch out his funny little head and look all around. He did look as if he liked where he was. Me, too, Emily thought. Already, like Kalani McBryde, she had the feeling that *Kohala no ka oi.*

When they tired of watching the boys dig, the girls played badminton or tether ball in Alix's yard, or played tennis on the school courts, or went for walks along the plantation roads. Sometimes they spent a long lazy afternoon playing *sakura,* a Japanese card game, or listening to records, or watching an old movie on TV.

"Imagine," said Emily, "I thought I'd miss all my favorite programs in Hawaii, and there are four television channels, with all kinds of programs, here!"

The favorite afternoon for the three friends was to go swimming at Mahukona, an abandoned sugar wharf, where the water was warm and deep and clear. Mrs. Leith, Mrs. Fujita, and Emily's mother took turns driving them the six miles.

"Before we came, I thought of all Hawaii as one long continuous beach," said Emily. "I thought, when Uncle Sandy told us we had a view of Maui and the ocean from his house, that I could walk down to the ocean whenever I wanted to and go for a swim!"

"Not off these Puehu cliffs!" said Alix. "Mahukona is the best and safest Kohala swimming place. Some Sunday we'll take you to the white sand beaches at Hapuna and Kawaihae. They're about thirty-five miles from here, and they're what the tourists imagine Hawaiian beaches are like. But you can't see so many fish, and you can't practice diving, like here," said Alix. She strapped her face mask around her head and splashed backwards into the water from the concrete boat launching ramp.

Dorothy was next. Emily followed her. The three girls swam out to the end of the wharf, and then a hundred feet farther out to a can buoy.

Through the glass faceplate of her mask, Emily could see a whole new underwater world. Tiny silver and black fish darted in schools around the seaweed that grew on the buoy's anchor chain. Great blue-green parrot fish swam lazily below. Exotic angel-fish, with long trailing thread-fins, slipped from behind pastel-colored coral heads to join a river of flat yellow fish that looked like sunflowers moving along the bottom of the sea.

"There's a *humu-humu-nuku-nuku-a-puaa!*" Dorothy told Emily. She pointed to a fish with a piglike snout.

There were many people swimming at Mahukona in the afternoons — adults with bamboo-framed goggles, high school boys who slipped off the pier and swam away with spears and aqualungs. Hawaiian *tutus* swam with their grandchildren clinging to their backs.

At Mahukona, there were few bathing suits.

People went swimming in whatever they had on.

Emily was glad she was a good swimmer. With her head underwater, she could hear the clack-clack of crabs and shrimps, the noise of the buoy anchor chain, and the slap of surf against the rocks on the shores of the small bay.

She daydreamed, sitting on the can buoy, resting with Dorothy and Alix. Maybe she'd be an oceanographer instead of an archaeologist someday.

A Hawaiian sugar plantation, Emily discovered these first two weeks, was a busy place.

One morning, Fumiko and Mrs. Fergus shouted to Emily to come and help them take a washing from the clothesline.

The air was thick with smoke. Big, sooty flakes of burned cane trash were drifting down on the damp clothes.

"Beener! Run close all the windows!" Fumiko called. "I should have remembered!" she lamented. "Last night, they were cutting firebreaks around the field up there. This morning, of course, they burn that cane!"

The crackling roaring noise, the flames shooting up, the thick brown smoke billowing down across the yard and toward the house, didn't sound or look like routine procedure to Emily, although she knew by now that it was. Burning a cane field was the first step in harvesting. This, Mr. Fraser explained to her, got rid of the dry leaves and made a quicker job of cutting and hauling the sugar-rich cane stalks to the mill.

Before the burned field behind Beener's treasure-digging jungle was cool, the harvesting began. Cane cutting machines came. Caterpillar tractors, called pushers, piled the cut cane into haystacklike heaps.

Two big yellow cranes with grabs on the ends of their long booms, loaded the cut cane into waiting double-trailered cane trucks fitted with great open-mesh-basket sides that would hold several tons of cane each. A crew of field men worked with machetes to retrieve by hand any stalks the machines missed.

All afternoon and all night the field behind the house rumbled with heavy equipment and trucks, and Puehu Skilled Camp B echoed with the whistle blasts of the crane operator's signaling.

At three o'clock, the work truck picked up the day shift crew and brought the three-to-eleven shift to work. After dark, the floodlights on the machines and big floodlights mounted on the crane's tall booms, lighted the field. At eleven, the night shift came to work.

Beener and Albert spent the night out in the backyard watching the harvesting. "You missed the best part," he said, yawning, to Emily at breakfast. The cranes were still up there, but the field was mostly bare brown stubble. Their house now had an unobstructed view up to the government road.

"They don't need to replant. The cane grows up by itself again. Ratoon they call it," Fumiko said. "You harvest eight crops one field, then you replant. Every sixteen years, because it takes almost two years for one crop of cane to mature in a field."

"When did they replant our field last?" Beener asked her.

Fumiko thought for a few minutes. Time was hard to sort out into years here, where there was little difference of weather changes to remember from season to season. "Two years ago," she remembered finally.

Beener counted on his fingers, ran out of fingers, and used his toes. "Holy kasmoley! If I want to see them use the planting machine in the field, I'll have to come back to Hawaii when I'm twenty-three years old!"

7

Kona Surprise

"Beener!" said Mrs. Fergus. "You are not going to take Albert along for this weekend with Mr. Minetti at Honaunau!"

"Why not?" said Beener.

Mrs. Fergus looked at Dr. Fergus. Dr. Fergus grinned, in Beener's same irresistible way. "Why not?" he asked. "Get in — Albert, too. It's one o'clock and I promised Fred Minetti we'd meet him in Kona by three. It's a long sixty miles from here, so let's go!"

They backed out of the driveway. Dr. Fergus swerved into the hibiscus hedge and jammed on the brakes. "Where'd she come from so fast?" he demanded. "That was close, too close!" He looked angrily at the driver of the big cream-colored car.

"Oh-oh!" said Emily.

"Oh-oh!" said her mother, in the same tone of voice.

It was Mrs. Price, with Jasmine. "Oh, dear!" said Mrs. Price, getting out of her car without a word about the near collision. "You're going somewhere?"

"Kona," Mrs. Fergus managed a polite smile. "For the weekend."

"What a disappointment for Emily!" said Mrs. Price. "I know how much she and Jasmine took to each other that first morning, but I haven't had a chance until now to bring Jasmine over to play. Here. We brought you some more of our wonderful bananas." Mrs. Price thrust a hand of ripe yellow fruit through the station wagon window. "Take them along!"

"How thoughtful. Thank you," said Mrs. Fergus dutifully. "Another day, you and Jasmine must come by."

"Oh, we will! Don't you worry! We'll come on Monday morning. Early!" Mrs. Price beamed. "Hello, Doctor." Mrs. Price turned her head. "Jasmine, say hello to Dr. Fergus!"

"Hallo," said Jasmine. Her glasses were down on her nose. Her hair was twisted into large, limp, sausage-shaped curls. She looked as wistful and unhappy as the first morning when she and her mother had come to call.

"Hey, she handed us bad luck!" said Beener

when they were on the way a second time. "You better get rid of those bananas, and fast! It's the worst kind of bad luck, in Hawaii, to take bananas on any kind of a trip, and especially a fishing trip. Mr. Fraser and Mr. Leith and Ryan and Kazu all told me so!"

"We're not going fishing, so maybe it wouldn't be quite such bad luck, but let's not take chances. Pass them around, Helen," Dr. Fergus said to Mrs. Fergus. "We'll eat up any trouble before we're over Kynnersley Hill."

The mountain road leading out of Kohala was edged with windbreaks of ironwood trees. The first few miles were still plantation; then the cane yielded to ranch country.

Below the road, clumps of prickly pear cactus grew five and ten feet tall. There were dead and dying bleached skeletons of ohia and false sandalwood trees. Deep rocky gulches and semi-arid range ran down far, far below to the bright, surf-stitched edges of the sea.

Above the road, the grass was lush and green. Scattered bunches of Hereford and Black Angus cattle grazed near the darker green tree line on the mountaintops.

"Look behind, quick!" urged Emily. The neighbor island of Maui was a looming blue silhouette framed between the double row of ironwood trees and the dip of the blacktop road.

"Look ahead!" Mrs. Fergus urged. In the distance, on the left and middle horizons, were the great gentle slopes of Mauna Kea and Mauna Loa, thirteen-thousand-foot-high volcanoes. Closer, and to the right, in the leeward district of Kona, was the eighty-five-hundred-foot, cloud-draped peak of volcanic Mt. Hualalai.

"There are your beaches, Em," said Dr. Fergus.

Emily stared at the undulating coastline far, far below where intermittent wide scallops of white sand beaches broke the green and brown and lava-black monotony of the shore.

Between the Kohala Mountains, to whose slopes this road clung, and the three bigger mountains humping against the sky ahead, was a valley forty miles wide. At its upper end were the truck-garden farms and buildings of the ranch town of Kamuela. Most of the lower valley was barren and dry.

"This is the Big Island," Emily realized.

"Wow! Even cowboys!" Beener exclaimed a few miles later when they were stopped by a snorting wild-eyed herd of big humped white Brahman cattle crossing the road.

Beener hung out the car window, grinning at the Hawaiian cowboys with their deeply tanned faces and beaming smiles. The cowboys wore broad-brimmed felt hats, like TV cowboys, but the Hawaiian touch was their flower or feather hatband leis. They twirled braided lassos and shook gourd rattles, yelling at the cattle to keep them on the move. Their horses were big and powerful and fast.

"Someday," wished Beener, "I'd like a horse like that to ride."

"I almost forgot to tell you," said Dr. Fergus as they drove on. "We take care of all these cowboys and their families at our dispensary. The ranch manager was in this morning. He said he'd heard I had a boy who should be interested in roundups, and asked if the whole family would like to come up for their branding next month."

"Did you tell him yes?" demanded Beener.

"I'd like to see a real branding myself," said Emily. "Did he say anything about asking friends? Could we bring Dorothy and Alix?"

"And Ryan and Kazu?"

Dr. Fergus pretended to groan. "I'd better trade in this station wagon for a bus!" He smiled back at Emily and Beener. "Yes. Mr. Williams said bring along whomever we wanted. I've already told him that we'll be there!"

By half-past two, the Ferguses were driving slowly along the main waterfront street of the village of Kailua-Kona. Hotels and restaurants looked out over the clear aquamarine waters of Kailua Bay. The ocean here, Emily noted, was a deeper, darker blue than at Mahukona. She wished she could go for a swim right now. Kona beach air was humid and much hotter than Kohala, and very still.

There were tourists strolling in the road, but just as many Hawaiians too. They were mostly young people in gay colored shirts and surf pants, with little saucy Kona lauhala hats on their heads.

Palms shaded every yard. A giant banyan trailed its branches and aerial roots behind the summer palace where once King Kalakaua had stayed.

Charter fishing boats rode at anchor in the bay, some with blue and white marlin flags suspended from their masts.

"Whew! Laziest air I ever breathed!" said Dr. Fergus. "It'll feel good to cool off underground in a few minutes."

"Underground?" repeated Emily.

"Underground!" Beener let out a whoop.

"Underground," confirmed their father. "Fred Minetti is introducing us to Hawaiian archaeology by taking us into an old Hawaiian refuge cave."

8

Ohia Cave

Emily tried to feel as enthusiastic as Beener and her father looked as they drove on beyond the resort village, along a beach road, and then, after several miles, turned up toward the mountains.

The black scars of rough, clinkered lava were everywhere, overgrown here and there with small jungles of haole koa trees or the umbrella shapes of monkeypod trees like the big one in Kohala in the Puehu plantation house frontyard.

Mr. Minetti sat parked in his jeep, a mile up this winding mountainside road, waiting for them.

"I can tell you're new to Hawaii!" he smiled. "You're on time!" He was dressed in khaki pants and shirt, field boots, and a red cotton bandanna knotted pirate style over his bald head.

"All set for some spelunking?" he asked, winking at Beener and Emily.

"You bet!" Beener said eagerly.

Emily just nodded and gave Mr. Minetti a polite smile.

Mr. Minetti pointed to a cavity half hidden by an overgrowth of brush, alongside a sharp curve in the road. "There are several caves close by that I could show you, but I chose this special cave with Emily and Beener in mind. This is the lava tube the Kona Explorer Scouts visit every year."

Beener looked disappointed. "Pretty safe, then, huh?"

The main entrance to Ohia Cave was shaded by a haole koa tree. Emily took one quick glance down, and all she could think of were the creepy, crawly, scarey creatures that must live down there in the dark.

"I'll go first," said Mr. Minetti, as if this was an ordinary enterprise for him. "I have the rope secured to swing down on. My knapsack and lantern are below. I'll be at the bottom to help you land."

Emily watched Mr. Minetti grip the rope that was tied to the trunk of the tree that grew at the edge of the drop-through. The entrance hole was five feet in diameter and perhaps fifteen feet deep.

Mr. Minetti swung down the rope, hand over hand. The rope swayed and quivered as he leaped out of sight. There was a muffled thunk when he landed below. The rope hung slack.

"Next!" he called up.

"Me, please, Dad?" Beener begged.

Emily watched her brother swing down like a monkey and disappear. "Hey. Neat!" she heard him exclaim.

"You want to go next, Em?" asked Mrs. Fergus.

"No. After you — " Emily said, wondering if she looked as reluctant as she felt. She watched her mother go down.

"Emily," said Dr. Fergus. "Maybe this is something you'd rather not do. You can wait for us here, if you like."

Emily hesitated. It was too hot up here to just sit around. If she didn't go into the cave, she was sure she might miss something she ought to see. Worst of all, if she stayed behind, Beener would never stop teasing her for being scared.

"I'm coming down. Only, I want to be last," Emily decided.

"Okay!" Her father grabbed the rope and slid down into the yawning darkness.

Emily was left all alone in the hot sunshine. Cautiously, she clutched the slack rope. She kicked herself out over the abyss. She swung — eyes closed and feet groping for a toehold — in sickening arcs in space.

"Reach out with your feet toward the ledge!" called Mr. Minetti.

Emily opened her eyes and saw what he meant.

"Now, jump!" commanded Dr. Fergus.

Emily took a deep apprehensive breath and did. She plummeted through the air. Thunk! Here she was, on her two feet — upright — on the floor of the entrance to Ohia Cave.

"Hey!" she exclaimed, surprised at how much easier it had been than it looked. "It's nice and cool down here!"

They stood on a jumble of rocks and earth that had once been part of the ceiling of the large lava bubble chamber. Sunlight filtered down from above. Ahead, a lava tube led off into the darkness.

Mr. Minetti clambered over the rubble and adjusted a gas pressure lantern. It hissed and glowed with a brilliant white light. "Did you all bring flashlights?" he asked.

"And extra batteries." Dr. Fergus opened the pack sack he'd brought along. He handed flashlights to each one.

Emily watched Mr. Minetti tie one end of a cone of butcher string to a boulder. "What's that for?"

"Trailmarker," he answered as he tested to see if the end was secure. "We'll be like spiders, spinning our own web through the cave so no matter how far we go up and down side tubes, we can always retrace our route by the string and find our way out. One direction looks like another underground. I've been here many times, but I could still get lost."

"Does everyone have a hat or scarf for head protection from low ceiling bumps?" Mr. Minetti continued to check, "Emergency water in your canteens, matches, candles? Although, with this type lantern, we never have to worry about adequate light."

Emily put on one of her father's old hunting caps, and looked at the gas pressure lantern. It was certainly bright, but it gave off a faint, ominous hissing sound as it burned.

"These sound alarming, but I've used this lantern on cave trips for ten years, with no trouble," said Mr. Minetti. He picked up the lantern by its bail handle. He handed the cone of string to Mrs. Fergus to pay out. Dr. Fergus shouldered the pack of emergency supplies.

"I left a map locating the cave, with a diagram of our route underground and our names on a note with Mrs. Dacuycuy, my neighbor at Honaunau. If we're not back at the cottage by nine o'clock, she will call Henry Jacoby to come in after us. His hobby is spelunking, and he knows this cave better than anyone else."

"Then this is a dangerous expedition, sort of?" said Beener, pleased.

"Not really, or I wouldn't bring you kids along," laughed Mr. Minetti. "Sorry to disappoint you, Beener, but, here in Hawaii, with Pele giving us an occasional shake-up, it is always possible that an earthquake could cause a slide or tube collapse down here. When I'm spelunking or mountain climbing or traveling in rough country, I like to observe three rules for safety — never go alone, always let someone know when and where you are going and when to expect you back, and always go prepared for every emergency."

"Those are good rules for you to learn," Dr. Fergus told Beener.

"Don't worry!" said Beener, peering at something in his pocket. "I'll never go down in a cave by myself!" To demonstrate, he pulled out Albert. "I've got my good luck with me, and company. Double protection!" From his other jeans pocket, Beener pulled out a handkerchief which was carefully knotted around his Kalakaua dime.

"This is one time you'd better keep both hands in your pockets and carry that flashlight in your teeth," advised his father. "If you lose Albert or that dime in this cave, Beener — aloha *oe!* Farewell!"

"There are two kinds of lava," Mr. Minetti explained as they started off up the tube. "Aa flows are big rough clinkers. They move quite slowly. Pahoehoe is a swift liquid stream of molten rock that can travel as fast as thirty-five miles an hour down a mountainside. These lava tubes are left by a stream of pahoehoe lava that is hotter and faster than the other lava in its same flow. The slower lava cools and congeals around the long hollow tubes, making our Hawaiian lava tube caves."

Emily trudged over the uneven floor, her flashlight tracing the shiny black coils of a ledge that ran like a smooth low bench along one side of the tube. The ceiling was cracked, and fine clusters of threadlike roots hung down from whatever grew above. The tube turned and twisted. Emily no longer had any sense of direction. There was darkness ahead of them, darkness behind them. Only the fragile white string unwinding from the cone connected them with the way back.

"Look at those colors in the lava!" Mrs. Fergus admired a congealed ropy cascade of lava falls several feet high. There were white lichenlike patches, glimmers of rusty red and brown, stains of sulfur yellow, streaks of red and amethyst-hued lava, with hints of olivine green.

Emily could tell by her mother's voice that here was something she wanted to paint. Emily wished she herself had some kind of talent. Her mother was an artist. Her father was a born doctor and loved the practice of medicine. Beener was good at finding things and making useful gadgets out of junk. All I'm really good at, Emily thought humbly, is being scared. She didn't know anyone more timid than she was, inside.

"Low bridge!" called Mr. Minetti.

Emily bent as the size of the tube compressed. They had to walk along with hunched backs as the ceiling slanted lower. Soon, they had to get down and inch along like worms — flat on elbows and bellies, scraping along with their knees.

"I wouldn't like Pele to choose now for an earthquake!" said Emily.

"Don't even mention it!" Dr. Fergus' voice was muffled. He didn't sound as enthusiastic as he had at first.

"Beener," Emily heard her mother say anxiously, "are you all right up there?"

"Just this one bad place. Then we're in the clear," called Mr. Minetti. His voice seemed to come from a great distance.

"Wow!" Emily heard Beener exclaim.

Ahead of her, her father grunted and looked as if he were stuck. He squeezed through a constriction in the tube. Emily squeezed behind him.

"Wow!" she exclaimed too.

The cave opened from a tube barely two feet in diameter into a chamber whose ceiling was thirty feet high. It was an underground room as spacious, it seemed to Emily, as the huge airport waiting room in San Francisco.

"We call this Grand Central Station," Mr. Minetti said as he pointed to the galleries above. "There's a triple level of lava tubes, but the upper ones have such a thin shell of floor that I don't want to take the youngsters up them."

"I had a few misgivings about that last section of tube," said Dr. Fergus. "Ten pounds more on my waistline, and I couldn't have managed!"

"Em, how'd you get through?" Beener teased.

Emily made a face at him. She wasn't really fat, just at a shapeless, waistless stage in growing up. To ignore Beener, she pretended to be interested in a low, stone platform built along one wall of the chamber. But, as she looked more closely, she forgot Beener and what he had said.

The platform was not natural. Someone, long, long ago, had brought in beach stones and built it here. There was a litter of bits of shell and fine pieces of coral and bones on the chamber floor. Against the wall, near the platform, was a black smudge of charcoal.

"Was this what you call a living site?" she asked Mr. Minetti.

"Bravo, Emily!" Mr. Minetti came alongside of her. "Ancient Hawaiians lived in this room, while they were hiding from enemies or in a time of war. They slept on that stone platform. They cooked on the floor, on a tiny fire. See that charcoal stain on the wall? One of the ambitions of the museum, when funds are available, is to get a carbon dating on Ohia Cave from the deepest layer of charcoal in this fire site. From a carbon dating in a fisherman's cave at South Point on this island, we found Hawaiians had been there in 125 A.D., some six hundred years earlier than we had guessed they came from Tahiti in their big double canoes looking for new islands where they could live more comfortable lives."

Beener stretched out full length on the stone platform. "Ouch! I'd need an air mattress. Those old Hawaiians must have been tough!"

Emily squatted and searched the loose debris of the cave floor with her fingertips. "Are these bones from something they ate?"

Mr. Minetti nodded. "Dog or pig. The Hawaiians ate dog and enjoyed it. Many Filipino and Hawaiian people eat dog today. They say it is sweet meat."

"We ate horsemeat during the Korean War," said Dr. Fergus. "Animal protein is animal protein — dog, pig, cow, horse, deer, or sheep — whatever's your custom and whatever you can get."

"I couldn't think of eating Aka!" protested Emily, thinking of Alix's little dog. She picked up a sea shell shaped like the shell of a clam. "What's this?"

"*Opihi,* another favorite Hawaiian food. It's a mollusk that grows on rocks below high tide along the ocean. It's very similar to what New Englanders call a whelk. Mr. Minetti squatted next to Emily. "No telling what's hidden in this cave. An assistant of mine once found a cache of nearly one hundred fishhook-making tools in this same room!"

That was all Beener needed to hear. And Emily's eyes and fingers searched the debris of the chamber floor, too.

"How did they see to get down here, those ancient Hawaiians?" she wondered aloud.

"With these," Mr. Minetti picked up a handful of blackened nutshells. "The kukui nut, which is native to Hawaii, is very oily. The Hawaiians made torches by threading a dozen or so nuts on a strand of bamboo. As one nut burned, it ignited the next on the strand, and the burned husk fell off. It would not be too bright a light, but enough to see one's way. There is a cave in Kohala called 'Nine Kukui Nut Cave' because, according to Hawaiians who know that cave, it took the burning of nine kukui nuts to get from the entrance to the cave's end."

"If this cave is five miles long, or whatever you said, it must have taken a thousand kukui nuts! How could they carry them all?" Beener asked.

"The advantage of Ohia, for a place of refuge, was its many exits and entrances," explained Mr. Minetti. "I know of six in this section of the cave, and none of them are too far apart."

Emily, as she explored the huge chamber with the others, imagined how it had looked, maybe a thousand years ago. She could imagine a stout *tutu,* who had found it hard to squeeze through the narrow tube, sleeping on the stone platform on a cover of tapa, the papery cloth the ancient Hawaiians made by pounding the bark of a native bush.

She could also imagine the mother tending a smoky fire, while the father worked on a bone fishhook, and babies crawled on the cave floor, smoke drifting into their eyes.

There was a Hawaiian girl of her own age, dressed in a tapa skirt. The girl would be tending the babies, crooning to them to keep them from crying. Maybe — even though this was her home island and her father's refuge cave — that Hawaiian girl of long ago would have been just as uneasy and fearful and scared of all the shadows around her, as Emily had been crawling up the narrow lava tube. Emily closed her eyes. The cave scene of her imagination was so vivid, she almost thought she could smell that smoky Hawaiian fire of long, long ago.

"Hey!" Beener's yell ended Emily's reverie.

"The lantern!" Mr. Minetti sprinted to the pressure lantern, which he had left in the middle of the chamber, on a level place on the floor.

The smoke was not Emily's imagination, nor was the smoky smell. There was a spreading blue haze in the room. The lantern was on fire!

The mesh mantle inside the glass shade of the lantern was aflame. Flames licked up and blistered the paint on the lantern's cap. The hissing sput-t-t of explosive fuel in the lantern's base was a truly ominous sound now.

Mr. Minetti yanked the bandanna off his head and used it to grab the flaming lantern by its bail handle. "We're close to an exit I know! Follow me but keep your distance — and run, everybody! Run!"

9

Safe

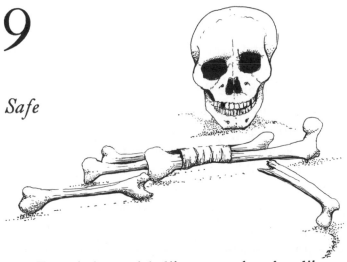

Emily's knees felt like water, her feet like two clumsy blocks of wood, as she ran behind Beener and her mother, with her father behind her, into the dark maw of a lava tube.

Mr. Minetti kept just far enough ahead so that, if the lantern exploded, flying glass and flames would not hit the others in the party. Yet they had to keep as close to him as they dared to find their way out of the cave. There was no way of telling how much fuel had already escaped from the leaking fuel can, or whether a potentially explosive collection of it was in the cave.

The cone of string was left, abandoned, in the living chamber. Smoke flowed up the exit tube on air currents that, to Emily's alarmed imagination, seemed tainted by the smell of gas.

"Turn here!" yelled Mr. Minetti.

A cautious distance behind, Dr. Fergus led his wife, Beener, and Emily into a side tube that veered off to the left. For fifty feet they sprinted up, up, up on a steady grade that left Emily gasping. On a ledge along this short length of tube, as she hurried along, Emily caught a glimpse of a grinning skull propped on a pile of whitened human bones.

"Yikes!" said Beener, noticing these, too.

He ran twice as fast, with Emily stumbling behind him. She fell on the rough floor, skinned her knee, and tore a long rip in her blue jeans. Before she could say "ouch!" her father had scooped her back to her feet and helped her around a bend.

Ahead was the most reassuring sight Emily had ever seen — a broad beam of daylight filtering into the cave.

Mr. Minetti's feet were disappearing at the top of a long stone ramp. "All clear!" he called back. Then they could hear him running across the ground over their heads.

Emily followed her father up the ramp. She took a deep breath and plunged fearfully between a maze of spider webs and half a dozen yellow jackets hovering at the mouth of the tube. She stuck her head and shoulders up into the hot bright world of Kona, just in time to see Mr. Minetti set the flaming lantern down on a stone pile thirty feet away.

The glass shade was black. The paint was

burned off the lantern's metal cap. The bandanna protecting Mr. Minetti's hand was charred, but he had not been burned.

"In this situation, whatever I could do was wrong!" he said. "I never traveled a longer hundred feet in my life!"

They all stood at a safe distance and watched and listened while the gas hissed out in a last violent sputter. The mantle flamed to extinction.

"Whew!" Mr. Minetti mopped the sweat from his grimy face. "Dr. Fergus, my deepest apologies. I had no idea I would expose your family to anything like this!" Mr. Minetti shook his head. "No more lanterns like this one underground for me!"

"No one can predict this kind of accident," said Dr. Fergus. "I'm just thankful you knew where this exit is!" He too got out a handkerchief and mopped at his damp, dirty face. To her surprise, Emily saw her father's hand was shaky. His color was unnaturally pale. Her mother had sat down abruptly on a nearby boulder, and she, too, looked unlike her usual self.

Even Beener, out of breath, had flopped down and taken Albert from his pocket and put him on the hot surface of a rock. Albert thrust his head out of his shell and looked cautiously around.

"Hey, Albert!" said Beener. "You almost got blown up down there!" Beener sat up suddenly. "And I know why! Those bananas! You can't eat up trouble, that's what. Bananas *are* bad luck!"

"If we're looking for reasons," said Mr. Minetti, "I neglected to do what I've always done in the past. I didn't leave a ti leaf and beach rock sign at the entrance. That's Hawaiian custom, a signal to the *akuas,* the spirits who are supposed to guard the cave, that we mean no harm inside."

In the still, hot sunshine, Emily suddenly felt cold. "You believe in *akuas,* like Mr. Fraser told us about the other day?"

"Believe? That's not the word, Emily." Mr. Minetti paused. "Respect is better. I like to respect any culture's superstitions because sometime, in the past of a people's myths, those superstitions arose from a very practical cause. I just feel better leaving a ti leaf and rock at a cave entrance. And I don't know why I missed on that today!"

"Aaaaah!" said Beener, retrieving Albert. "It wasn't that. Those bananas brought us trouble in the cave. That darned old Mrs. Price!"

It was sunset when they arrived at the museum cottage — a fiery sunset that tinted the ocean dark gold and crimson and left the edges of the sky a pale green.

"Nighttime in Honaunau is special," promised Mr. Minetti.

As soon as their supper was eaten, and they had helped set up cots and sleeping bags for the night,

Emily and Beener went outside into the warm starry stillness to see just what he meant.

Somehow, it felt more like being in Hawaii to Emily to be here on the beach on such a night. Torch fishermen walked along the rocks in front of the cottage. Their lights were an uneven, wobbly procession marking the shoreline. For a long time, Emily and Beener watched the fishermen go by.

Next door to the cottage, Mrs. Dacuycuy was pole fishing with a kerosene lantern propped on the rocks for light.

"Look!" exclaimed Beener, as Mrs. Dacuycuy pulled in a catch. "Red fish!"

"Menpachi," Mrs. Dacuycuy smiled. "Here. I give you fish for your breakfast. Okay?"

"Thank you!" said Emily. She looked with interest at the translucent scales and bright red sheen of the menpachi. They gave a lively flop in the rice-sack creel.

"Scat!" Mrs. Dacuycuy threatened, and an interested cat disappeared into the darkness.

Emily knelt on the ledge of lava overlooking the water. Only a few feet below, the waves lapped at the rocks. The tide was coming in. Black crabs with hairy legs stood motionless, wary of the flashlight, until the next wave came and washed them off the rocks again.

Emily's eyes adjusted so she could see occasional shapes swimming past in the water below.

"Snake!" she suddenly cried out, almost knocking the rice bag of fish into the water in her hurry to get back out of reach.

Mrs. Dacuycuy's line sang taut. Her bamboo pole jerked down to the surface of the waves. "No snake. No snakes in Hawaii. That was an eel," she said to Emily. "*Puhi*. He has sharp teeth, can tear off your fingers if you don't watch out! Keep your hands and feet out of the water at night!" She hauled in her catch, another bright red fish with enormous eyes.

Beener took the fish off her hook. Emily held the rice bag open for him to plop it in.

"Em," said Beener unexpectedly, "you were pretty brave when that lantern almost blew up in the cave this afternoon. I guess maybe you aren't as much of a scaredy cat as I thought you were!"

Emily did not dare look up at him. It was the nicest thing Beener had ever said to her, and she could not bear to let him know it wasn't true.

10

Honaunau

Kona schools ran on a coffee schedule, from November to August, so that the schoolchildren could help with the coffee harvest, Emily had learned yesterday when she asked Mr. Minetti about the children she saw walking home from school with armloads of books. In Sacramento and in Kohala, July was vacation time.

"I'm glad we don't live in Kona," said Beener. "I'd have missed vacation this year!"

There were no sugar mill whistles at half-past five in Kona's coffee country, but Emily had awakened then, as usual. In the gray dawn, she could hear outboard motors chugging into the bay and the call of someone feeding a pig. Next door Mrs. Dacuycuy's roosters were crowing.

Emily heard someone else up, so she tiptoed

past Beener, past the camp beds where her mother and father slept, then downstairs and out of the cottage for her first daylight look at Honaunau.

Coffee orchards climbed in contoured green bracelets along the mountain slopes above. Emily had seen her first coffee trees driving into Kona yesterday. They were small, slender trees with a glossy leaf the size and shape of holly leaves. The coffee cherries grew in green and yellow and ripe red beads along the branches.

Above the coffee orchards was the deeper green of high forests, and above them, loomed the barren volcanic peak of Mt. Hualalai.

Emily could see rooftops and water tanks of the villages and farmhouses on the upper main road. She could see the umbrella shapes of monkeypod trees in the dry brush jungle that was Kona's ranchland in the arid belt between the coffee lands and the beach.

Mr. Minetti was the other early riser. He was building a fire in the lava-stone fireplace in front of the cottage. He set a pot of coffee on the grate to boil. Then he and Emily went down to the rocky ledge overhanging the water to clean the fish Mrs. Dacuycuy had given them last night.

Mr. Minetti pointed across the bay with his fish knife. The ocean was a shimmering blue-green mirror this morning. The air was fresh and cool. "Over there is where we'll start our tour this morning,

Emily. I have some measurements to check and some old photographs to compare."

Emily looked across the bay at a rampart of towering black lava rock walls enclosing a palm grove. The coconut trees thrust their lazy green fronds sixty feet and more up into the pink and blue morning sky.

"Those walls look big enough to hold a small city inside!" said Emily.

"And City of Refuge is one name for it." Mr. Minetti looked up from scaling a fish. " 'City of Refuge,' 'Place of Refuge,' *Puuhonua,* in Hawaiian, It was more like a small village inside those walls in ancient times. Only a temporary population, though, because the Place of Refuge was strictly a sanctuary for those Hawaiians who had broken a *kapu.*"

"*Kapu?* Like a tabu? The same word we see on fences and private roads around the island now?"

"Exactly," Mr. Minetti nodded. "*Kapu* is the Hawaiian word for tabu, which is a Tahitian word almost everybody knows. It means forbidden, but it was also the word to describe the rules by which Hawaiians lived in ancient times. For you, Emily, it would have been *kapu* to ride in a fishing canoe or to eat a certain kind of banana or enter most temples. Girls and women couldn't play certain games. There were also special rules for the men and rules of behavior for commoners and chiefs.

"The punishment for breaking one of these strict

rules was usually death. But, no matter which *kapu* you broke, if you reached the walls of the Place of Refuge before you were caught, you were safe. After a few days, you could leave the sanctuary and go safely back home without fear."

"What if you were a little girl and broke one of these rules?" Emily asked.

"I'll tell you a true story," said Mr. Minetti. "There is an account by one of the first missionaries who came to Kona in 1820 in which she writes about meeting a Hawaiian woman who had just one eye. The other eye had been gouged out, when she was five years old, as punishment for having eaten a kind of banana that was *kapu*."

"Wow!" Emily shuddered. "I thought Hawaiians were gentle and kind!"

"Emily," said Mr. Minetti, "remember your European history? And American history? Governments have always used harsh punishments to insure their laws would be kept, and the world is still full of cruelty today.

"The Hawaiians rebelled against their harsh *kapu* system by 1819. A year before the New England brig *Thaddeus* sailed into Kailua Bay with the first American Christian missionaries aboard, the Hawaiian people had changed from their old ways. Their own queen set the example. She sat down one day with the men to eat, which was forbidden. She ate pig, which was *kapu*. She ate bananas. The priests warned that terrible things would now happen to the queen — and to Hawaii — but nothing did. So the people rose against the priests, who made these rules of *kapu*.

"They tore down the wooden gods and burned them. They tore down the temples. That was when this Place of Refuge at Honaunau stopped functioning. It was not destroyed, but other places of refuge around the island were.

"Imagine, Emily — no coffee orchards, no ranches, no hotels up on that mountainside. Imagine twenty thousand Hawaiians living in Kona. Village after village of grass houses and stone wall boundaries and palm groves and taro and banana plantations. Open air temples. The Place of Refuge busy with people. Right here. One hundred and forty years ago — not too long a time as history goes!"

It was still early, and Emily still had Mr. Minetti's picture of ancient Kona in her head, when they all left the museum cottage for the day. They carried canteens of water, lunch, a roll of museum maps, a manila envelope of old photographs, cameras, and, as usual, Beener had Albert and his lucky Kalakaua dime.

There were a dozen small tin-roofed houses, built up on stilts in the fashion of most island dwellings, along the beach road near the bay at Honaunau. The houses were set wide apart, with old stone walls between. Fishing nets were spread in lacy patterns to dry. Old truck parts, washtubs, coconuts, and piles of boards were scattered about the yards. Small, sturdy, muscular gray pigs with sharp ears and blunt snouts and coveys of chickens wandered along the roadway.

In every houseyard, was a wooden water tank, for Kona was dry country. Every drop of precious rain water was caught and saved in the runoff from the corrugated roof of the house, through the eaves troughs and downspouts to the storage tank for the family's water supply.

"Hi, Noelani!" called Mr. Minetti as they passed the last house before the white sand shingle of Honaunau Bay beach.

Emily stared at the dark-eyed girl sitting on a stone wall under the shade of a plumeria tree.

She was no taller than Emily and about the same age. Her face was pretty — smooth bronze skin, straight dark eyebrows, a shy smile that revealed flashing white teeth. Her hair was gathered into a loose ponytail at the nape of her neck and festooned with a garland of yellow plumeria blossoms. She was one of the heaviest girls that Emily had ever seen — heavy and solid. But, instead of slouching and looking embarrassed about her size, as did Jasmine Price, this Hawaiian girl stood with a proud, queenly posture, her head high. Her quiet poise reminded Emily of Princess Kalani McBryde.

"Noelani," said Mr. Minetti, "I want you to meet my friends from Kohala. Dr. and Mrs. Fergus, Emily and Beener." He nodded to them. "This is Noelani Ching. She's kept me company, she and her brother, all this week on some pretty hot trips back into the bush."

"My brother went to Hilo this morning," said Noelani, "so only myself coming with you today."

For the first few minutes, Emily and Noelani walked along side by side, letting the grown-ups do the talking.

They skirted the beach, with its rows of outrigger canoes pulled up on the sand. Some children were playing in the shallow water — the smallest ones swimming in their smooth brown skins.

"See that rock in the middle of the bay?" said Noelani. "That's Safety Rock. The best swimming is out there. We dive off it. Good fun!"

"That rock used to be far more than a good diving place, did you know that, Noelani?" asked Mr. Minetti. "In the old days, anyone fleeing to the Place of Refuge who reached that rock, was considered safe."

Noelani looked shyly at Emily. "My grandmother remembers her grandmother telling her that white tapa flags used to fly from the top of the walls. Outside the big wall — there — " Noelani gestured, "beside the bay, was *Hale o Keawe,* the House of Death, where all the kings' bones were kept.

"One time, my grandmother's grandmother was here and saw them. The queen brought a *haole* lady to visit Honaunau and took her inside the House of Death. She showed her all the gods there, with their feathers and pearl-shell eyes, and the bones of the old kings, in tapa and sennit. Then the queen ordered the men to take the House of Death down and to send the bones of all the kings to Honolulu so she could have them buried there, *haole* style.

"The men promised yes, but when the queen went away, they took the bones of the kings to secret caves and hid them. No one knows where."

Beener was listening, with that speculative look of his. "I bet I could find those royal bones, if I keep hunting in caves this year!" he boasted. Emily knew he was thinking what she was thinking, wondering about those bones they had seen on their dash out of Ohia Cave yesterday.

"You'd better not try, Beener," said Mr. Minetti with a quick glance at Noelani.

Emily wondered if it was her imagination, or did Noelani's expression relax after Mr. Minetti said that?

They walked in silence again, on through an opening in the wall and inside the palm grove that covered an area four hundred feet wide and over seven hundred feet long, flanking the waterworn pahoehoe lava flow that ran out into the sea.

A sea breeze and the shade of the palm trees

cooled the air inside this Place of Refuge. The ground was moist gray sand. There was a brackish pool that had, in ancient times, been a fish pond.

There was so much to see and learn about inside the great walls and on the beach beyond, that Emily's imagination worked overtime.

She and Noelani looked for petroglyphs, primitive stick figures of men, spears, canoe paddles, and dogs, carved deeply into the smooth surface of the waterworn beach pahoehoe.

Noelani searched for bait holes gouged in the rock by Hawaiian fishermen of the past.

They found *konane* boards etched on the lava — nine rows of nine pits each — to hold the black and white stone pieces of a game played much as checkers is played now.

Emily saw hollowed stones which had been used to catch and evaporate salt from the sea and tapa dyeing basins made from great rocks.

Back in the thorny brush, inland, they measured stone house sites and stone walls and checked locations on Mr. Minetti's maps. This was the only uncomfortable part of the trip. Swarms of cattleflies followed them. Tiny black mosquitoes seemed especially attracted to Emily's sunburned skin. Beener swatted and scratched, too.

"Too much hot in here!" said Noelani, and Emily heartily agreed.

"A breeze at last!" said Dr. Fergus, as the trail

emerged at the base of a steep sea cliff. A lava stone paved road, wide enough for four people to walk abreast, was built ramp-fashion up to the cliff top.

"Yikes!" Beener took Albert out of his pocket to look down at the surf leaping up almost to the height of the fitted stones of the road. "What a cliff!"

"*Pali,*" said Noelani.

"*Pali?*" Emily repeated. In her head, she linked the two words. *Pali* meant cliff. "Steep *pali!*" she said, pleased with how quickly her Hawaiian vocabulary was growing.

"Do you really speak Hawaiian?" she asked Noelani.

"At home we do," Noelani nodded. "My mother is pure Hawaiian. My father is Hawaiian-Chinese."

"You speak Chinese too?" Emily was impressed and envious.

"No, no!" Noelani laughed. "I can understand Chinese, a little bit, is all."

It was Noelani's Hawaiian grandmother who had told her the story about how the stone road was built to scale this cliff. King Kamehameha, the first Hawaiian king to rule over all the island, in the early eighteen hundreds, had the road built so that wagons could haul salt over it.

Ships from many countries came into Kona in those days — whaling ships, ships in the fur trade from America to China, ships carrying sandalwood from Hawaii's mountains to the Orient.

Before the days of this road, there had been only a bamboo ladder to mount the cliff. A Hawaiian *kahuna* had charge of it. When he saw travelers coming, he asked for offerings before they could use his ladder. Sometimes, if the people had offended him in some way, he would pull out the ladder when they were halfway up the cliff, and they would fall to their death on the rocks in the sea.

"Can we go show Emily the *puka* halfway up the cliff?" Noelani begged Mr. Minetti.

"Oh, yes, please!" begged Emily, too, without any idea of what a *puka* might turn out to be.

Only Beener stayed behind. "Albert's a little tired, I think," he said. He sat in the shade of a haole koa tree, letting Albert exercise.

Noelani led the way. Emily was next in line, up the King's Road over the cliff. Noelani stopped halfway up and disappeared into a niche between two big boulders on the land side of the road.

"Oh!" Emily's excitement changed to dismay. She hesitated.

"Come on! It's only a small *puka* — no need for a flashlight!" Noelani urged from inside the niche.

The grown-ups were waiting for her to follow Noelani so they could follow in their turns.

A *puka* is a cave Emily realized with dismay. This was one Hawaiian word she wished she'd known before, and she'd have stayed back with Beener.

Puka, meaning hole, was also the word for a hole in the ground. Less than twenty-four hours after Emily had made up her mind never to go undergound again, here she was!

11

The Cockroach

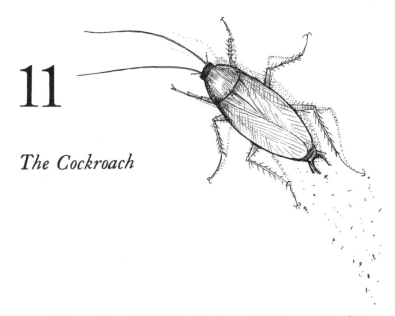

"Come!" called Noelani, as Emily walked in behind her with a fearful feeling, remembering yesterday.

The tube was lighted from the entrance for the first twenty feet. Then, the passageway curved. Emily forced herself to follow Noelani on into the dark. She could hear, but no longer see, her mother behind her. She could hear, but not see Noelani ahead. Emily walked with blind, groping steps.

Something whirred and landed with sharp scratchy legs on the back of her neck. Emily screamed and batted at her neck with her hand and screamed again as the thing flew down her shirt.

"Emily!" Mr. Minetti rushed up to her in the darkness and struck a match.

A large brown cockroach flew off Emily's

shoulder and disappeared into a crack on the tube ceiling.

"Emily Ann. Honestly!" said Mrs. Fergus.

"You scared of one cockroach, Emily?" Noelani looked surprised. She stretched her hand out and took Emily's. "Just this one place where we can't see," she reassured her, as she led Emily around another sharp curve.

Light showed ahead. The lava tube had led them through the cliff, under the King's Road, and opened onto a sheer thirty-foot drop-off above a surf that foamed and pounded and roared as if it would tear the base of the *pali* away.

Uneasily, Emily wriggled forward to look out over the edge of this drop-off. "I — I don't like crawly things very well," she said, ashamed for having allowed a common cockroach to give her such a scare.

"That's all right," said Noelani. She nudged Emily and giggled. "You like a swim?" She pointed to the rough water below. "Good fun to dive!"

Emily looked carefully and saw Noelani was teasing to help her forget about the cockroach. "Good fun!" Emily echoed, and wished that Honaunau and Kohala were closer so she could see more of Noelani Ching.

"I had no idea there were so many caves in Hawaii!" said Dr. Fergus. "I'm intrigued. I'd like to arrange a trip into that Kohala cave you and Phil

Fraser mentioned the other afternoon," he said to Mr. Minetti.

"You know Uncle Phil?" Noelani interrupted. "Tuki Fraser is my aunt!"

"She is! Then maybe you can come visit her when your school is out next month. Please, Noelani?" urged Emily.

"If you do," promised Mrs. Fergus, "we can plan that trip to Red Hill Cave for when you come. You know so much about these old Hawaiian places, Noelani, it makes them more interesting for us."

"Thank you," said Noelani solemnly. "This small kind *puka's* enough for me, but I'd be scared to go into Red Hill Cave. That one's too big! Too many things still left inside! I might come visit Aunt Tuki in August; she's going to have the birthday luau she meant to have for P'lipo making one year old."

"But P'lipo's sixteen months old!" said Emily.

"A year. Sixteen months. Have a February birthday in August. No matter!" Noelani giggled. "That's what we call Hawaiian time!"

"I like Noelani Ching!" said Emily as they drove along the narrow beach road from Honaunau on Sunday afternoon.

It was such a short drive from Honaunau to Captain Cook's monument and the spot where he was murdered, that the Ferguses decided to see that, too, since they were in no hurry to get home.

There was no road to the slender white monument on the far shore of Kealakekua Bay, but they could see it clearly from the edge of the shady beach village of Napoopoo.

This spot was a regular stop for sightseers driving through Kona, and lei sellers were set up in small homemade stands around the parking area at the end of the Napoopoo Road. The lei sellers were Hawaiians, mostly older people — the women in muumuus and one man in a newly woven palm frond hat.

"Where you from?" one of the women asked Emily, as she and her mother stopped to look at the handsome seed and shell leis.

"Sacra — I mean Kohala," Emily said.

"Kohala? Nice place, no?" smiled the lei seller.

Emily smiled back. She hoped the woman thought she'd been born in Kohala. To be an island girl, really an island girl, as were Alix and Dorothy and Noelani, was one of Emily's desires.

While Mrs. Fergus bought leis, Dr. Fergus took pictures of the Cook Monument and of the nearby high platform temple where Captain Cook had been worshipped by the Hawaiians as a god borne across the sea in the white bird of his sailing ship.

Beener was too tired to get out of the car, so Emily and her father went alone for a quick look into the ancient Hikiau *heiau*.

Here again, high above the blue waters of the bay, Emily imagined she could look down and see the ancient Hawaiian girl of her imagination, wading ashore from a great double canoe. She would be a newcomer to this island, as Emily was a newcomer, and like herself, that girl of ancient times would be eager to explore the new fire-breathing green island that she hoped to call home.

This afternoon, Emily filled the double canoe with family and friends, chickens and dogs; with seed coconut, breadfruit seedlings, banana shoots, and taro corms. This is what the canoes had carried on the long voyage from Tahiti a thousand years and more before Captain Cook sailed into this bay.

It must have been a scarey trip, Emily thought. Far worse than having to plunge for refuge into an unknown cave. Almost as bad as having to run for your life to the high walls of the sanctuary when you had broken a *kapu*.

The Pacific was such a big ocean. There would have been no maps, no loran, no radar, no radios — nothing but the stars to steer by, and the winds in the sails, and the strong paddles of the men.

Her father startled Emily out of her thoughts by putting his arms around her shoulders. "You're really enjoying this trip, aren't you, Em?" he said fondly. "Except for that cockroach!" he teased.

12

Kapu Trail

The only flaw for Emily in the day of roundup and riding at Kalahikiola Ranch, two weeks later, was that Jasmine Price had to be along.

In the morning, they watched the branding operation in the big corral above the Kohala Mountain road. Beener, Ryan, and Kazu were draped over the fence, their eyes glued to the cowboys, their faces enthralled. Emily, Alix, Dorothy, and Jasmine leaned against the rails of the corral to watch.

Dust blew in red clouds down the chute through which the cowboys drove the calves, *pipi,* into the branding corral. As each animal reached the corral, a cowboy roped it. Two cowboys held the calf with ropes and knees. The male calves were castrated and dehorned. A black tarry mixture was daubed on the horn stubs. Both steers and heifers were given injections to protect them from disease.

Outside the corral fence, another cowboy kept branding irons hot in the low coals of a fire. When the cowboys holding the *pipi* signalled, he grabbed two hot irons. One cowboy burned the brand "K" on the flank; the other branded the year on the animal's hip.

The cowboys loosed the rawhide rope, slapped the calf, and shouted to get the protesting animal on its feet, and it ran as fast as it could through the exit chute.

Cowboys kept riding back and forth, Mr. Williams, the ranch manager, riding hard along with them. A constant noisy bawling went up from the *pipi* being herded into the corral — from the wild-eyed ones being branded and injected, and also from those who had already been released into the freedom of the pasture beyond.

Almost every time, a calf was roped on the first try. Once in a while, though, the rope slipped, and the *pipi* lunged to its feet with a cowboy straddling him. Then there were shouts of laughter while the cowboy hung on for a wild ride.

Kalahikiola Ranch is not large, compared with neighboring Parker Ranch, the largest individually owned ranch in the world. Parker Ranch includes three hundred thousand acres of the Big Island. Kalahikiola has thirty thousand acres, six thousand head of cattle, and five hundred horses. By island standards, it was a ranch of moderate size.

"Are all of you good riders?" Mrs. Williams, the ranch manager's wife, asked after lunch. Lunch had been stew, poi, and rice served from a chuck wagon near the branding corral.

Jasmine shook her head. "I never was on a horse yet, but I'd like to try!"

"I'll tell Mr. Kaimana to give you Kuipo. She's a gentle old horse for a beginner. And how about the rest of you?"

There was a confident chorus of "Can!" from the boys, Alix, and Emily.

"I can't, but no matter," Dorothy Fujita said.

Emily walked very straight and proud, carrying herself the way Noelani Ching had at Honaunau, as she walked with the others to a small corral behind the ranch house. Emily had had six riding lessons at the Spur 'n Saddle Club stable in Sacramento last winter, and so she announced.

"But have you ever ridden a Hawaiian horse?" Alix asked.

"No." Emily looked puzzled. Hawaiian horses looked like mainland horses. The cowboys rode them as easily as the cowboys she had seen in westerns on TV.

"I can ride any horse, though," Emily said with confidence. "You learn a lot in six lessons."

Alix and Dorothy looked at her, and although they were her best friends, they laughed at her. Five minutes later, Emily understood why.

"No, thank you!" Dorothy declined a second time with a smile. "I don't like horses. I never did ride one, and I'm not going to try now." She laughed with the same frank, untroubled expression Emily had heard from Noelani Ching. "I'd be too scared!" she added, as she made herself comfortable on a corral rail from which she could watch the rest ride off.

Jasmine Price was scared, too, Emily guessed, but she seemed determined to do whatever Alix and Emily did. The boys were waiting impatiently for the girls.

"Okay?" said John Kaimana doubtfully, tightening Jasmine's stirrup length for the third time. He was a handsome elderly Hawaiian, white-haired, with keen dark eyes and flashing white teeth.

"Eh," he questioned Emily, "you the new doctor's daughter, Kohala, the *haole* girl went around with my granddaughter at Honaunau?"

"Noelani, you mean? She's your granddaughter?"

Mr. Kaimana nodded. "*Kolohe,* rascal, that Noelani," he said, but his eyes twinkled.

"She's coming to visit this summer. In August," said Emily, "when Kona schools get out."

Mr. Kaimana nodded. "I know," he said, looking pleased.

He slapped the gray and white flanks of Jasmine's old horse with a leafy end of a branch.

"Kuipo," he commanded, "you no *kolohe* now! Walk the *haole* girl nice!"

Kuipo whickered. Her ears cocked at an angle, she looked as if she knew she had a frightened greenhorn on her back. Jasmine hung on with one hand dug into Kuipo's mane, and the other clutching the saddle horn.

"Let's try her first, once around the corral," said Mr. Kaimana. "You walk your horse, Alix. Kuipo will follow."

Alix, who rode very well, started her horse in a circle around the inner fence. Kuipo followed, but she moved with a rocking chair motion so that Jasmine bounced up and down in the saddle with each sway. Poor Jasmine's face was pale and puffy with fright. Her glasses slid down almost off her nose. Strings of loose hair dangled in her face. She made a whimpering sound at each bounce.

"You'll be okay," Mr. Kaimana said reassuringly when the horses stopped after one time around.

Jasmine was too winded to say anything. She looked sideways over the top of her glasses at the other riders and then enviously back at Dorothy, who was sitting astride the corral rail.

"You want to go along or stay here?" Mr. Kaimana asked kindly, holding Kuipo's bridle.

Before Jasmine could answer, Kuipo whinnied and snorted, and then, abruptly, she bucked!

Jasmine slid sideways off the saddle. One foot

stuck in the stirrup as she landed with a thunk in the dust of the corral. Her glasses flew off.

John Kaimana yanked her foot free. Jasmine's pale blue eyes swam with tears. Her face and neck were as scarlet as her bandanna. Her mouth twisted with the effort not to cry.

"You hurt?" Mr. Kaimana asked, as he led Kuipo out of the way.

Jasmine shook her head. She got up and tried to wipe the dust from the seat of her jeans.

Dorothy slipped down from the fence and darted out among the horses to retrieve Jasmine's glasses. "Here," she said sympathetically, and in her quiet, understanding way, she let Jasmine pick herself up and get herself together, put the dusty glasses back on, and hobble to the corral fence.

"Poor Jasmine!" said Alix, as they waved to the two girls left behind. "Something like this always happens to her!"

"Poor Jasmine!" echoed Emily, but she began to feel envious of her and Dorothy.

Emily was posting, as the Saddle 'n Spur Club instructor had taught her. Jasmine is right, she thought, knowing exactly how Jasmine had felt. There was something wrong between Emily's posting rhythm and the rhythm of the horse. When she came down, the horse came up.

"Just sit easy and dig in with your knees!" called Alix.

"Like this!" said Kazu, riding alongside Emily and demonstrating for her.

"Why you jump up and down on the horse all the time, Emily?" Mr. Kaimana wanted to know.

Emily had never ridden such a powerful, fast animal. Desperately she tried to hold reins, mane, and saddle horn all at the same time. The horse jolted and jostled. Emily felt as if her vertebrae were shaking loose.

"Hold the reins tight!" Ryan shouted.

Emily expected at any minute to catapult to the ground. She dug her knees against the horse's side. She bent from the waist, crouching to the angle of the horse's neck.

"You kids like to ride to Ginger Pool?" Mr. Kaimana asked.

"You bet!" said Alix.

"Oh!" Emily exclaimed as she jounced along. She hoped fervently that Ginger Pool wasn't far.

The horses stretched to a gallop, as they thudded across the range and over a rise, their manes and tails streaming in the wind. The air was cool and exhilarating.

Jolt! Jolt-thump! Jolt! Emily gripped with her knees and held firmly to the reins. Then, without knowing quite how she did it, she fell into the rhythm of her horse. She was a part of him and a part of his motion. She knew, and the horse knew, she had control.

They rode for a mile up into the high ranch country, through grass that was lush and green and as tall as the horses' knees.

Mr. Kaimana led them through a gate and around the base of a hill. The horses' hooves went slop-slop now, slowly, on the wet ground. Ferns grew among the grass. They were now riding near the edge of the forest. A stream plunged in cascades of bright water down over a high rock falls.

"There," Alix reined in her horse, "is Ginger Pool!"

At the bottom of a valley, beneath the falls, was a natural swimming pool, in the shape of a perfect circle. Its rocky grotto was rimmed with ferns and ginger foliage. The fragrance of yellow ginger blossoms filled the air.

Emily slid from her horse.

"Can we?" asked Beener eagerly.

"Why do you think Mr. Williams said to bring you here?" Mr. Kaimana smiled. He tethered the horses, and the children raced down to the pool.

"Last one in's a monkey's uncle!" called Alix. She dove, clothes and all, into the clear deep waters of the pool. Beener, Kazu, and Ryan were in like three lithe, blue-jeaned fish.

"I'm the monkey's uncle, I guess," said Emily, as she jumped in. The water was icy, shocking, terrible, and wonderful all at the same time.

They swam in a wild, fast game of water tag.

They played minnow and whale. Emily followed Alix's example. Picking a head of low-growing red ginger and crushing it to a soapy pulp between her palms, she lathered the ginger soap into her hair. Then she and Alix stuck their heads under the waterfall to rinse off the shampoo.

Mr. Kaimana went off to check a waterline, and the boys went with him, exploring the valley into the forest above.

"Hungry?" asked Alix, as the two girls climbed out of the pool and stretched on warm flat rocks in the sun.

"Am I!" Emily thought of the stew, rice, and poi left on her plate at lunch. She could have eaten the whole pot of leftovers now!

Together they scrambled downstream over the rocks to a quiet eddy where a stunted guava tree dropped yellow fruit and cast its deep shadow over the water. Alix made a container of her shirttail. With agile cupped hands, she scooped into the darkest shadows of the stream.

"*Opae!*" She showed Emily her catch and demonstrated how to eat them.

"Hawaiian freshwater shrimp," she said, as she popped the tiny gray creatures, live, into her mouth and crunched with relish.

Emily took one, tentatively. "Oh — yum!" she said, minding only the queer, scratchy feel of the shrimp on her tongue.

"When you boil them, they turn bright red and taste saltier," said Alix. "I eat them that way — like popcorn."

She fished for another handful and divided them with Emily. Emily tried catching *opae* herself, but with no luck.

"You'll learn!" Alix encouraged. "Anyway, you learned to eat *opae* today!"

When they mounted their horses for the trip back, their clothes were still damp, but dry enough so they would not get chilled.

"We go a different way now," said Mr. Kaimana. "I have to check one more line for the boss."

He rode with Alix and Emily, and the three boys rode together, galloping easily down the mountain slope. Emily was at ease on her horse now, and she could enjoy the scenery. She liked the smells of this mountain country — the sweet bruised fern, the fragrance of ginger blossoms, the smell of molasses grass that was just as good as the name implied.

Near a lichen-splotched stone wall that ran down across the ranch lands, Emily noticed a faint trail in the tall, wind-bent grass. Feeling proud of herself for finding the way, she rode ahead, toward that trail. A lovely new fragrance rose from beneath the horses' hooves, a fragrance that smelled for all the world like vanilla.

"Eh, whoa!" Mr. Kaimana rode up and turned

119

Emily's horse aside before she was a length ahead of the rest of them.

"We don't ride that trail up there, ever!" he said sternly.

Emily wondered why he should sound so cross about it, but obediently she turned her horse back.

"What's the sweet smell — like vanilla?" she asked.

"Maile." Mr. Kaimana's eyes were guarded, his expression queer.

"But no *maile's* growing here!" said Alix.

"No *maile* ever grows here." Mr. Kaimana's look was even queerer.

"*Maile?* What's that?" Beener demanded.

"A green vine that grows up in the forests. People gather it to make leis, very special leis," said Alix. She looked at the old trail and glanced at Mr. Kaimana. "In Hawaiian times, the chiefs always used to wear *maile,*" Alix said. The same queer, guarded expression settled over her face.

Mr. Kaimana led them off, parallel with the old faint trail, but a distance from it.

"Why can't we ride that trail?" Beener wanted to know, for the going was much rougher where they were.

Mr. Kaimana turned and looked at Beener, and then turned and looked at Emily. His look was that combination of patience and impatience one uses with strangers who ask too many questions.

120

"It is for the old ones, that trail."

"The old ones?" It was Emily's question.

"*He poe uhane,* spirit people," said Mr. Kaimana.

Emily stared at him. Then she stared across the long grass at the depression of the old trail. Over there, the wind still hinted at the elusive fragrance of *maile*.

"You mean that trail is for ghosts?" asked Beener, a cautious hand in his pocket to check if Albert was still along.

It was Alix who shushed Beener this time. Mr. Kaimana looked straight ahead, as if he did not intend to hear.

"Where's Red Hill Cave?" asked Beener. "That's on this ranch, too, isn't it? Plenty ghosts in there, I betcha. Boy, that's where I'm waiting to go!"

Mr. Kaimana gave Beener a sharp, unfriendly glance. That was one of Beener's troubles, Emily thought. He had to be told outright. He had no sense about what was wrong or right to say.

"You want to know about Red Hill Cave, any cave, ask the boss," said Mr. Kaimana gruffly. "If Mr. Williams wants you to know, he'll tell you. That's his business, who he takes in there!"

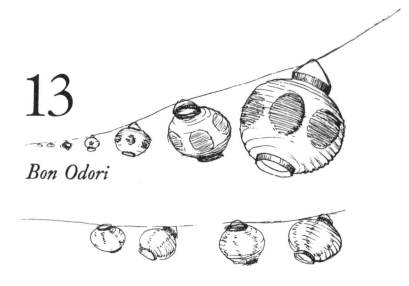

13

Bon Odori

One afternoon Alix, Dorothy, and Emily were sitting on the Fujita's veranda. They were eating boiled peanuts and watching Beener, Ryan, Kazu, and a boy named Tony Guzman trying to teach Albert to walk a straight line.

"There's a good movie at Hawi tonight," Emily said. "Let's all of us go!"

"I can't." Alix made a face. "We're invited to dinner at Jasmine's house."

"I can't go either," said Dorothy. "Tonight is the Bon Dance at the temple." She looked at Emily. "That would be something for you to see! Can you come with us?"

A dance at the Buddhist temple would be interesting. Emily had been intrigued by the glimpse of brass and rich carvings and color that could be seen beyond the open doors of the temple the Fujitas attended. It was a square, yellow, wooden building set back from the government road, flanked by trim green lawns, hibiscus hedges, and a small cemetery, with the headstones lettered in Japanese.

"Please come with us, Emily!" Dorothy urged. "You can stay at our house overnight. My father will take us down to Mahukona Sunday morning to watch them put the spirit boats out."

"Spirit boats?" Emily was still wary after that *kapu* trail at Kalahikiola Ranch last week. "What kind of dance is this?"

"Bon Dance — *Bon Odori,*" Dorothy explained. "First there is a service in the temple, a memorial service to honor the spirits, or memories, of all the people who died during the year. Every family decorates its graves in the cemetery. They hang *cho-chinn* (paper lanterns) on the graves, inside the temple, and around the lawn. After the service, everybody dances — Japanese and Okinawan folk dances — the rest of the evening.

"The more you dance, and the more you enjoy yourself, then the more honor you do the memories of all the people who have died!"

"And those boats you talked about?"

"You'll see them on the altar at the temple," Dorothy promised. "I have a kimono I can lend you to wear for the dance. I wish you could come, too, Alix. Remember what fun we had last year?"

123

Alix nodded and chuckled, "I liked that fast dance, where we all joined hands and went back and forth and yelled."

Emily had been seeing herself only as a spectator.

"You mean we just don't stand there and watch?" she queried anxiously.

"Don't worry. You'll learn quickly!" Dorothy encouraged.

"And while you're there," said Alix, "think of me, sitting and listening to Jasmine play all her pieces on the piano and looking at her scrapbooks of movie stars."

"Jasmine could come," said Dorothy. "I think she would like to. Only, her mother — "

"Her mother!" agreed Alix and Emily in unison.

A warm misty rain was falling that evening when the Fujitas and Emily turned off the highway and drove into the temple grounds.

"Hawaiians say when it rains — good luck!" said Mr. Fujita, backing into a free place in the rows of cars parked at the edges of the temple grounds.

A wooden tower, roofed, with open sides and a tiny open room at the top, stood in the center of the lawn. It was draped with purple and white cloth in a lotus design. The base was decorated with cut green stalks of bamboo laced with hundreds of vanda orchid blooms. At one side of the lawn were booths where the members of the Young Buddhist Association were selling hot dogs, soda pop, coffee, and barbecued meat on sticks.

The temple building blazed with light. People swarmed up and down the steep wooden steps and along the roofed passageway that connected the temple with the priest's house.

"One of Reverend Ota's daughters will be in our class at school," Dorothy told Emily. "See that tall, slender girl in the blue and white kimono? That's Sueko Ota. You'll like her."

Emily stood close to Dorothy, feeling strange and, at first, ill at ease. The smell of hot dogs and barbecue sizzling over charcoal, and the colored lights winking over the lawn, added a carnival atmosphere. They were American and familiar.

The spectacle of the temple, with its magnificent, bright interior, the people walking back and forth in Japanese kimonos, were all so different and exotic, that Emily felt as though she had been suddenly transported to the Orient.

In the cemetery, orange blossoms of light burned through tasseled paper lanterns that were hung from slender bamboo sticks over the graves. People knelt in the cemetery, holding paper umbrellas against the rain, while they arranged displays of food and flowers and lighted incense.

Mother would like to paint that, Emily thought. The small cemetery framed itself in her mind into a misty, hazy picture of swaying lanterns, curls of blue smoke from the incense, and colorful piles of ripe mangoes, bowls of rice, all kinds of flowers, and small portions of food.

"You're wondering why the food on the graves, eh, Emily?" Mr. Fujita guessed. "Let me tell you a story. Once there was an American student invited to visit a friend in Japan. While he was at his friend's home, the grandfather died, and the American student attended the funeral.

"The custom in the Orient is to put fruit, food, drink — whatever the dead person was fond of — in token amounts on his grave as a symbol to please his spirit. The American student felt as you must feel now, Emily. He asked his Japanese friend, 'You say you're educated, yet you put rice and cake and tea on your grandfather's grave. Do you think he's going to rise up from the dead and eat that?'

"The Japanese student said, with a smile, 'My grandfather will eat the food on his grave when your dead grandfather smells the flowers on his!'"

Mr. Fujita grinned. "Just a difference in custom. Some people like to show respect one way and some another. No custom is really strange if you try to understand the reason for it."

"No, I guess not," Emily agreed.

She looked with sympathy at a tiny plate of cookies and an orange on a child's grave. It was an old grave, but someone still loved the memory of that little child dearly enough to remember the cookies and orange that pleased it when it was alive.

A memorial service had sounded to Emily, as if it would be very solemn indeed. Yet, everyone she saw here tonight was happy and smiling. People bustled back and forth, calling greetings. Boys and girls, too little to sit through the service, ran around outside the tower and the big drums set up at the tower's base. They yelled and played hide-and-seek and tag.

Emily mounted the temple steps with the Fujitas.

She, too, left her slippers in the forest of shoes, slippers, and boots that were spread in neat pairs over the temple porch.

Inside, it was similar to any other church. The floor was varnished hardwood. The wooden pews were in rows, with flat white cushions to add comfort, if one desired.

The altar was decorated with silk-tasseled paper lanterns, vases of orchids and anthuriums, plates of oranges, mangoes, and pineapples, lacquered statues of Buddha, carved hardwood screens, small tables with silk cushions on them, brass gongs and bells. Ir one corner of the altar were two small wooden boats painted white. Each was three feet long, filled with flowers, fruit, and strips of paper printed with Japanese characters.

At the altar, dressed in a loose white kimono with a narrow gold embroidered scarf at the neck, was Reverend Ota. He was a short, plump, bald-headed man, with rimless glasses and a good-natured face. He struck gongs and chanted. Several people came forward to light incense. The service was in Japanese.

"I don't understand much of it," Dorothy whispered to Emily. "This is for the old people, this way. In Sunday School, we have our lessons in English."

Emily noticed, as she looked around, that whenever someone noticed her, he smiled, as if glad she had come.

When the service was over, they went out on the temple porch, and Mr. Fujita looked at his watch.

"We're running on Hawaiian time, as usual! It's eight o'clock. We put in the paper that the dance would start at seven-thirty. Oh, well," he looked out at the crowd waiting around the parked cars, "people come and go all evening. Being late is good this time, it's stopped raining. Look! There comes the moon from behind the clouds!"

Emily found her slippers less quickly than Dorothy found hers. The girls had worn skirts and blouses. The kimonos Dorothy had talked about were neatly folded under Mrs. Fujita's arm.

"Come, girls," she said. "I'll find someone to help you dress."

Emily followed, across the covered passageway, into the Otas' living room, where the girls and women stood in all stages of undress. Once again, she left her slippers outside the door. This would be a good custom for Sacramento houses, too, she thought, to keep all the dirt of the street that stuck to one's shoes outside the house.

"*Oba-san!*" Mrs. Fujita hailed an elderly woman who was pinning the bow of an elaborate silk *obi* for a young woman who was one of the plantation office secretaries.

"When you finish, would you help the girls, please?" Mrs. Fujita opened the kimonos. "I am no good at this," she laughed at herself. "We'll let Mrs. Otani help. She's an expert!"

"Ah. *Haole.* Doctor's girl," old Mrs. Otani said, bowing old-fashioned Japanese style.

Emily took off her blouse and skirt and stood in her nylon slip. She stretched her arms into the stiff cotton sleeves of the kimono. It was a white material, with a gay pattern of red and blue fans. There was a wide red *obi* for the waist.

Emily was dressed, and Mrs. Otani was tying Dorothy's *obi* when the powerful, slow rhythm of drums sounded outside. Music came from the loud-speaker system hooked to the wooden tower.

Dorothy clapped her hands and waited impatiently for the *obi* to be finished.

"*Arrigato gozaimasu, oba-san.* Thank you very much!" she said hurriedly to Mrs. Otani. "Come, Emily! Let's go!"

Outside, a long single line of girls and women

in bright kimonos, and men and boys in kimonos or short *happi* coats worn over their ordinary trousers, moved in the quick rhythms of the coal miners' dance. Their butterfly sleeves bent to an imaginary shovel, lifted the coal to an imaginary basket, gaily thrust the shovel over their shoulders, and marched on to repeat the task in a few steps.

"You keep your eyes on the person opposite you in the circle. Just do what she does, and you'll soon see how. It's easy — and fun!" Dorothy told Emily.

Dorothy motioned Emily to take her place in the line, ahead of her. Feeling awkward and self-conscious, Emily waved her hands and stepped first to one side and then to the other in imitation — but usually the wrong way.

She was too much aware of the spectators watching her, but the second time around, her feet began to do what they should. She kept her eyes on Sueko Ota, across the circle, mimicking Sueko's every move.

"Good!" Dorothy encouraged from behind her. "Oh, Emily, I'm so glad you came!"

Emily loved to dance, especially folk dances.

"Hey, there's Em!" She heard a familiar voice. Her parents and Beener had come to watch the dance, too.

"That looks like such fun!" Emily heard her mother say.

At ten o'clock, there was an intermission.

"Ryan and Kazu like this part of the evening best," said Dorothy as she led Emily into the supper line.

Trestle tables were set up on the temple lawn. There were paper plates and disposable wooden chopsticks. Dorothy showed Emily how to serve herself with chopsticks — working them like a combination of tongs and knitting needles so that they would pick up potato salad, pickled cucumbers, rice balls, *chop sui,* a rich smelling stew that Dorothy called *nishime,* and even red wedges of watermelon. Mr. Fujita offered the girls soda pop from cases at one end of the serving tables.

They sat on white pillows in the wooden pews of the temple to eat. People were eating and chatting both inside and out, and altogether, it was the jolliest, friendliest church supper to which Emily had ever been.

Kalani McBryde's Hawaiian phrase popped into Emily's happy head.

"Oh, Dorothy," she said, as the two of them rejoined the circle of dancers. "*Kohala no ka oi!* Bon dances *no ka oi!* Thank you for inviting me to come tonight!"

14

Mrs. Price Again

Outside Dorothy's bedroom window, the first thing Emily saw Sunday morning was a cardinal balancing on the branch of a plumeria tree.

"How-are-you? How-are-you?" the cardinal inquired. He was a saucy flash of red against the pink petals of the tree.

It was a beautiful, breezy morning. Below the acres of green cane, below the intermittent red and green rooftops of houses, the ocean glittered a dark blue, laced with white. It was so clear that it seemed to Emily that if she stood on the sea cliffs a mile below the Fujitas' house, she might reach across and touch the island of Maui, twenty-six miles away.

"I wish I had sisters, instead of brothers," sighed Dorothy, as they washed and dressed.

"Me, too!" said Emily.

The neighborhood was noisy with the sounds of a Sunday morning anywhere — radios playing, cars being washed, people driving out to church, the loud noise of power mowers — and the smell of freshly cut grass was being blown into their room.

The one Sunday morning noise unfamiliar to Emily was the musical Ilocano of a crowd of Filipino bachelors gathered three houses up from the Fujitas for what Mr. Fujita explained, with a broad grin, was a "practice" chicken fight.

"Ilocanos are natives of Luzon, the largest island in the Philippines," he told Emily. "Many of our Hawaiian Filipinos are Ilocano, but some are Visayan, and there is one Igorot man in the district. Filipinos are good people, but you'll find some islanders who look down their noses at the Filipino population because they were the last big group of immigrants brought in to help work in the cane fields."

Emily liked Mr. Fujita. He reminded her of Mr. Fraser, who also treated her like a grown-up and told her so many interesting things.

"All kinds of people. All kinds of religions in Hawaii," said Emily later, as they drove past the Mormon and Catholic churches on their way to Mahukona.

"And all of us, who are different from one another, try to respect each other. That's what makes Hawaii a good place to live!" Mr. Fujita said.

The wharf was crowded with cars and people this morning. Several boys were swimming off the boat-launching ramp, splashing, shouting, and riding the big easy swells of the surge.

A car and boat trailer were backed up at the small boat hoist on the edge of the wharf, next to a launching ramp. A loop of chain with a strong hook, operated by an electric crank on a steel boom, lifted a fiberglass boat in slings from the trailer, out over the wharf, and down into the sea. Twin outboard motors were tilted in brackets on the boat's stern. The name stenciled on the bow was "Lulu P."

"Oh! Oh!" said Emily, as she and Dorothy got out of the car.

Mr. Rowland Price, a heavy man with sandy hair and a patient, badgered expression, was holding the *Lulu P.* away from the side of the wharf and trying to unfasten the slings.

"Hello, Shigeru!" he called to Mr. Fujita.

"Hello, Rowland. Going fishing?"

"Thought we'd see what's out there," said Mr. Price, and he smiled.

Mrs. Price and Jasmine stood at one side of the trailer. Jasmine was carrying a red food cooler. Mrs. Price was dressed in slacks, a long-sleeved shirt, and a baseball cap. She had sunburn cream lathered in a white film over her face.

"Hello, Emmy. Hello, Dorothy," said Mrs. Price. "Good morning, Mrs. — " She stopped and looked with dismay at Dorothy's mother. "Dear me, I can never remember your name! These Japanese names are beyond me anyway!" she laughed.

"Fujita," said Mrs. Fujita courteously.

"Of course. I should remember! I've known you off and on for fifteen years!"

She reached over and poked Jasmine. "Jasmine, say hello to the girls!"

"H'lo," said Jasmine. Her head was bent; her shoulders slouched, and her hair hung down in limp curls on her neck. She was wearing a polka-dotted bathing suit with a ruffled skirt.

"I certainly didn't know we'd run into this commotion!" said Mrs. Price, her eyes on the quiet group standing along the ocean side of the wharf.

Reverend Ota was there in a dark suit, with a narrow gold brocade scarf over his collar. The ladies of the Buddhist temple choir were in street dresses, holding small triangles with bright silk tassels in their hands. They were all people Emily remembered from the Bon Dance last night.

"What's going on here this morning?" Mrs. Price asked suspiciously.

"Our church is having a special ceremony, part of the Bon services. We are sending the little spirit boats out. It's a custom we haven't observed for years," said Mrs. Fujita, still with a pleasant smile.

"Oh." Mrs. Price managed to convey her disapproval in that one word. "Emily, did your mother

135

give you permission to come to this?"

Emily resisted the temptation to be rude.

"Yes, Mrs. Price. In fact, she was sorry she couldn't come down to see the service with us."

Mrs. Price's pencilled eyebrows went up and down as she repeated, "Oh?"

"Rowland!" she called down to her husband. "I'm waiting. Hurry up!"

Mr. Price was having trouble loosening the last sling.

"All right. All right. Just a minute," he called up.

Jasmine leaned over to see what her father was doing in the boat. Her glasses slipped and fell off.

"Da-dee!" she wailed, as they disappeared under the crest of a wave.

"Dive in, Rowland, quick! Those glasses cost forty-two dollars a pair!" Mrs. Price yelled.

"I can't do two things at once, Lulu!"

With one hand, Mr. Price tugged at the sling he was trying to free, and with the other hand, he was trying to keep the boat from bashing against the wharf.

"No *pilika!* I get 'em!" yelled one of the Hawaiian boys on the ramp.

He dived, with a flip of sturdy brown legs into the air. Emily could see his gliding shadow diving down, down, down to the rocks and coral heads of the bottom.

He brought up Jasmine's glasses on the first try.

Mrs. Price leaned down to retrieve them from his hand.

"Lulu! Watch out!" Mr. Price shouted, both hands still busy with his boat.

Mrs. Price had reached out too far. There was a loud splash and a scream as she fell in.

"She can't swim!" Mr. Fujita exclaimed.

Clothes and all, he dived off the wharf, put a strong arm around Mrs. Price, and swam her to the safety of the ramp.

She hobbled up the ramp, coughing and choking; salt water streamed from her wet clothes and hair. Her face was red with embarrassment.

"Rowland!" she said angrily, as if both mishaps had been his fault. "I'm certainly not going out in that boat with you now!"

"All right. All right," said Mr. Price. "Thank you, Shigeru," he said to Mr. Fujita. "Mrs. Price is no swimmer. I think we may as well go home. This doesn't seem to be our lucky day!"

Jasmine had crept away from her mother and stood beside Dorothy and Emily, as interested as they were in watching a second boat which was hove to off the end of the wharf.

Mr. Yamamoto, who had been a drummer at the Bon Dance last night, was at the wheel. In his boat were the two painted spirit boats that Emily had seen on the temple altar. They were filled with the offerings Emily had seen in them last night, and their bows were garlanded with flower leis.

At the quiet end of the wharf, as calmly as if he were secluded in some faraway temple, Reverend Ota began to chant. The ladies of the chorus responded in the five-toned scale melodies of the Orient, striking their silvery high toned triangles with little metal hammers.

When the chanting was finished, Mr. Yamamoto brought his boat alongside the wharf, and the priest jumped down into it. Mr. Yamamoto chugged past the can buoy where Alix and Dorothy and Emily usually swam.

Across the harbor, on the opposite bluff, was the whitewashed beehive shape of an old lighthouse. Kiawe trees danced gold and green in the intense sunlight, their delicate leaves and branches quivering and creaking in the lightest breeze. On that opposite shore, too, were the shells of abandoned warehouses and the rusty siding that had once been the first sugar railroad on the island of Hawaii — all that remained of the sugar port Mahukona had been. Now trailer trucks drove the bulk sugar from Kohala Mill to the big deepwater harbor of Kawaihae for shipment to refineries in California.

The crowd on the wharf thronged to the edge to watch in respectful silence as the spirit boats were lowered from Mr. Yamamoto's boat. They bobbed along on long slender lines in its wake.

Emily shaded her eyes with the palm of her hand. She looked out over the glare of the sun on the water, watching the two tiny boats for as long as they were in sight.

"When they are a mile or so offshore, they cut the little boats adrift," Mrs. Fujita said.

"Do the spirits really eat the food?" asked Kazu.

"No, not really," said his father.

"Then who does?" asked Ryan.

Emily could sense that Jasmine was listening, and Mrs. Price, who was standing behind her, was listening, too.

"The fish eat it, I guess," Mr. Fujita said. "Whoever finds it when the little boats capsize. It's a token ceremony, boys. A custom we follow because it has a meaning of respect and reverence for the dead, whose memory we honor especially at *Bon Odori*. You boys have never seen this custom before — you either, Dorothy!"

Mrs. Fujita explained why. "After Pearl Harbor, we Japanese Americans wanted to forget — right away — all the Japanese and Buddhist customs we had. We wanted to be all-American, all the way, to show our fellow islanders that we *were* loyal Americans. In those war days, there were no Bon dances. There were no services in the temples. The Buddhist priests, who were Japanese citizens, were sent to the mainland to relocation camps.

"Now the years have passed, and we can celebrate some of our old customs, because we have proved ourselves in the islands. It's part of being American, to me, to be proud of who you are and what you are, and to let your children know and celebrate the customs, traditions, and beliefs of their grandparents."

Emily looked cautiously at Mrs. Price, because she knew it was for Mrs. Price's benefit that Mrs. Fujita had told all she had.

Mrs. Price cleared her throat loudly. She turned toward the crane where Mr. Price was hauling out his boat.

"Jasmine," she said, "go over and help your father. Don't stand and gawk! It's not polite!"

Jasmine flushed scarlet. "I never knew all that before!" she said to Mrs. Fujita. She smiled shyly and then went to help her father with the boat.

"That Mrs. Price makes me ashamed to be a *haole,*" said Emily indignantly, as the Prices and their boat trailer drove away.

The crowd had dispersed. Emily and the Fujitas were alone on the wharf.

"Emily," said Mrs. Fujita gently, "there are people like Mrs. Price in every group — people who don't like or don't want to try to like — anyone different in background from themselves. Mrs. Price is very frank about how she feels. But you know old Mrs. Otani — the lady who dressed you last night? She is a Japanese Mrs. Price. She is too polite to ever let it show to you, but she distrusts *haoles* as much as Mrs. Price distrusts anyone who isn't white.

"Mrs. Otani is old-fashioned and stubborn. She won't ever change. I don't think Mrs. Price will change either. Both these women spend their lives in a place they don't like.

"Mrs. Otani came as a picture bride from Japan fifty years ago and has never gotten over being homesick. She has never accepted nor tried to understand life here. Mrs. Price came from Kansas twenty years ago to marry Mr. Price, whom she met in college. Mrs. Price still thinks of Kansas as 'home,' just as for Mrs. Otani, home is still the Japanese town of Gifu."

"Emily," said Mr. Fujita, "you and your family have been here a short time only, but I give you credit! You are more *kamaaina* already than either of those two women will ever be."

"*Kamaaina?*" repeated Emily.

She knew that Hawaiian word. Princess Kalani had used it. It meant old timer — a person who has become Hawaiian in his heart and ways, as well as by the length of his stay. Poor Mrs. Otani! Poor Mrs. Price!

"Me? *Kamaaina?*" Emily smiled at Mr. Fujita. It was the very nicest compliment that anyone could pay her.

141

15

Beener's Experiment

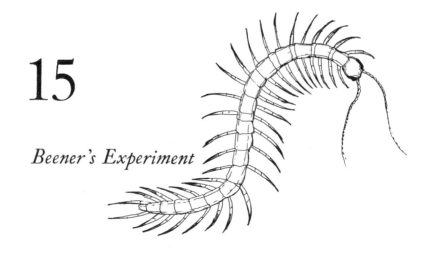

"Another ten days and school starts. There is one last big trip I want to take before then," said Dr. Fergus, "Red Hill Cave!"

It was the middle of August. Kona schools had just closed for their summer vacation. Noelani Ching had arrived to spend a month at the Frasers and to help her Aunt Tuki get ready for seventeen-month-old P'lipo's long overdue first birthday luau.

Emily had made up her mind that she wouldn't go along to Red Hill Cave. Ohia's flaming lantern and the cockroach in the Honaunau *puka* had been enough spelunking to last her a while. She planned, instead, to stay home with Noelani, Alix, and Dorothy. But when the day came, Emily couldn't bear to run the risk of missing anything. She was up at half-past five with everyone else, and the first one ready. They left by station wagon for the first stage of the trip — the drive to Kalahikiola Ranch.

At the ranch, they were joined by Mr. Williams and Mr. Minetti. It was seven-thirty when they started out cross-country in one of the ranch trucks.

"Albert all secured?" Dr. Fergus shouted as they jounced over a hump in the dirt road that almost sent the three of them flying. Beener, Emily, and Dr. Fergus were riding in the truck bed.

Beener grinned and patted his jeans pocket.

"Aren't you hot in that sweat shirt, Beener?" asked Emily.

Beener was wearing the bulky sweat shirt that had been his winter play outfit in Sacramento. It was a hand-me-down from a cousin and still several sizes too big. There were hand-warmer pockets across the front. The sleeves were rolled up in a bulge at Beener's wrists. The bottom of the sweat shirt draped to the crotch of his jeans.

"I'm like Albert. Cold-blooded," said Beener, averting his eyes from Emily's. "Besides, it's going to be real, real chilly in Red Hill Cave."

Emily kept on staring at her brother. His face was sweaty. He looked uncomfortable to her. There was something suspicious about that sweat shirt, and about the way Beener was acting today.

"Still with us back there?" Mr. Williams called out. He stopped and got out of the truck cab to open and close a cattle gate. "If you keep watch

143

the next mile down, you may see some goats," he said. "The Hawaiians brought pigs and dogs to the islands, but it was an English explorer and an American sea captain who brought in the first ancestors of the wild goats and sheep around here. Lord Vancouver left a pair of cattle and a pair of sheep at Kawaihae for King Kamehameha. He made them *kapu* — allowed them to run wild on the island — and the result is, good Big Island sheep and goat hunting today.

"There used to be wild cattle herds, too. So many that Spanish cowboys were imported from Mexico to round up and kill the wild cattle a hundred years ago. The Hawaiians called these Spaniards *paniolos,* which is the Hawaiian name for all cowboys now."

Along the rim of a deep gulch, a while later, they saw a herd of wild goats racing away.

"Boy, Dad! I wish you'd brought the twenty-two!" yearned Beener.

It was six miles over the rough dirt ranch roads to the base of the big cinder cone known as Red Hill.

"It is red!" exclaimed Emily, as Mr. Williams parked the truck in a gulley, near cattle-damaged ruins of old Hawaiian stone walls.

"That red dirt, which is rich in iron, was Hawaiian medicine in the old days," Mr. Minetti told her. "The *kahunas,* who were doctors, used to mix it with poi and give it to patients who had anemia."

Dr. Fergus listened to this with interest. "Many

of those ancient Hawaiian medicines were remarkable," he said, "and I'm impressed by how much those *kahunas* could do. They were expert bonesetters. Before a *kahuna* could practice on anyone else, he had to break the arm and leg bones of one of his children and reset them so that they healed."

"Holy kasmoley!" said Beener. "I'm glad they don't make doctors in Hawaii pass that kind of a test anymore!"

It was a hot half-mile hike on toward the beach from where the truck was parked. Emily was glad for the protection of her crew hat against the bright morning sun.

Over her shoulder she carried her own knapsack today. In it were her flashlight, a canteen of water, a snack-size box of raisins, a chocolate bar, and extra socks.

In a shallow draw, Mr. Williams held up his hand. "This is it! The entrance is around here somewhere. As many times as I've been to this cave, it still takes me a while to find it. We like to keep the cave mouth camouflaged, as it was in ancient times, to discourage any visitors who have no business in there."

From the far side of the draw, on a pile of dusty reddish rocks that looked no different from half a dozen other rock piles around, Mr. Williams finally gave a halloo. "Here!"

The men lifted the rocks aside to uncover a

narrow slit in the ground. Just inside the slit, the ends of two long poles were visible.

"Carrying sticks," said Mr. Minetti. "The Hawaiians used them in comparatively recent times. Oh — perhaps fifty years ago, to carry bodies down into the caves."

"Bodies?" asked Beener.

"This cave was used for refuge and burial," said Mr. Williams. "There are some fairly modern burials in canoe-shaped coffins, but most of them are the old tapa-wrapped bundles of long bones and skull."

"Good!" said Beener, with a smug, secretive grin.

Emily watched Mr. Williams lie down on his back and squeeze down through the cave entrance slit. Beener went next. Mr. Minetti followed him.

"Em?" said Dr. Fergus.

"Okay!" said Emily, feeling brave today.

"I'll go first, Emily," said her mother. She groaned as she squeezed through. "No more *pupus* for me!" came her muffled voice.

Emily sat down and slithered feet first into the opening. The entrance to Red Hill Cave was a narrow, dusty airless tube. Emily slid and wriggled at a forty-five degree angle down to a tiny, dim chamber that connected with another narrow downward chute. Her father's body blocked the light from above, when Emily reached the first chamber. The others had gone on down. Below, she could hear Beener's distant voice.

Emily turned on her flashlight. She twisted her body into the second passageway. Instinctively, as something brushed the top of her crew hat, she looked up. The dusty ceiling of the tube was six inches above her head.

Hanging on a short length of spider web from the ceiling was a long, brown centipede. His body swayed in an air current, toward Emily's upturned face. She ducked and screamed. "Daddy! Help! Eeeeeeeeeeee!"

Dr. Fergus came sliding down the entry tube in a rumble of loose dirt and stones.

"Centipede!" moaned Emily. She couldn't move for fear the centipede would swing at her again.

Dr. Fergus looked at it and at her, and shone his flashlight directly above.

"A dead one. Long dead. For heaven's sake, Emily! I thought you'd at least broken your neck, the way you screeched." Dr. Fergus brushed the dead centipede to the tube floor.

"Oh — " said Emily in a very small, shamed voice.

Mr. Minetti and Mr. Williams had heard her, too. They came crawling back up the second chute. Mr. Minetti's face showed his concern. "What's wrong, Emily? Are you hurt?"

Emily shook her head, too ashamed to make more of an answer. Her father's disgusted voice was enough. "She was frightened by a dead centipede. No *pilikia.* Sorry!"

The two men turned and went back down. Emily wished she were anywhere but here right now.

"Let's go, Emily!" said her father crossly.

Emily hesitated. Jasmine Price could never have felt more miserable than she did now. She scrunched sideways in the narrow chute. "I'm going back outside and wait, Daddy. Okay?"

There was a long annoyed silence. Then her father said, "I'll go on out with you, Emily, just in case."

"But you'll miss seeing the rest of the cave." Emily felt worse than ever. "That wouldn't be fair! I can wait outside alone. Please, Dad! You can trust me. I'll stay on that pile of rocks. I won't move!"

Dr. Fergus backed up, and Emily followed him, wriggling up out of the slit entrance to the cave.

She sat on the pile of rocks beside the slit, her hands hugged around her knees, her chin on her chest, ashamed to meet her father's gaze.

"All right, Emily," he decided. "But stay here! It's too easy to get lost in this rough country. Don't get the notion, no matter how long we're down, that you're going to try to find your own way back to the truck!"

"Daddy, please. You can trust me!" Emily sniffled and tried hard not to cry.

She sat on the rock pile in the sun, and watched her father disappear into the slit in the ground. Tears and sweat ran down her dusty face.

"Oh, darn bugs anyway!" wept Emily.

Soon, her seat ached. The sun seemed to bore a hole through her crew hat and into her skull.

"I'm not really moving far," Emily said aloud to herself. She bent down and put her white handkerchief under a nearby rock to mark the entrance slit. Then she got up and walked to the shade of a single kiawe tree a few feet away.

Next, she decided she needed the energy of her chocolate bar. The melted chocolate left such a sweet taste in her mouth that, sip by sip, she soon drank all the water in her canteen.

It seemed hours later, the longest wait of her life, before she heard sounds from the cave entrance.

She rushed over, in time to greet her father's head and shoulders emerging from the rocky slit. His skin and clothes were coated with red dust. The back of his shirt was torn. He looked anxiously — and at the same time peevishly — at Emily. "You still all right up here, Em?"

"Oh, sure," she lied. "But you were down there a long time! Do you have any water left, Daddy?"

Dr. Fergus handed her his canteen. "Thanks to you, Emily," he said, "we cut short a most remarkable and interesting trip. It would not be wise to leave you out in this hot sun for more than the hour we allotted ourselves."

"Well, Emily." Mrs. Fergus was next out of the cave.

"I know. I'm sorry!" said Emily, miserably. Her mother didn't have to say anymore.

Mr. Minetti came out, followed by Mr. Williams. Beener emerged last.

Emily expected, and knew she deserved, a teasing from her brother. Beener's eyes glinted with mischief. There was a wicked grin on his dirty face. He was still wearing his ridiculously bulky sweat shirt, and it certainly gave him a funny shape.

"Albert okay, Beener?" asked Mr. Minetti.

"You bet!" Beener took Albert from a pocket and set him down on a rock. Albert looked healthy and quite himself, his head thrusting curiously out of his shell.

"What a turtle!" Mr. Williams laughed. The men began filling the cave entrance with the rocks they had removed before they went in.

Emily wandered over to the kiawe tree and picked up her empty canteen and her knapsack. She wondered about Beener. He had paid no attention to her! He was busy spitting on and polishing his Kalakaua dime and watching Albert.

When no one else was looking, Emily saw him take a quick furtive glance at the hand-warmer pocket of his sweat shirt. He patted it. Then he put his dime in one pocket, his turtle in the other.

The cave entrance was plugged.

Mrs. Fergus walked ahead with Mr. Williams. Dr. Fergus and Mr. Minetti walked together. Beener ran along by himself.

Emily lagged at the rear. No one paid any attention to her. They were all talking about what they had seen below. Emily sighed, listening. She had missed the best cave of all!

She turned and looked back toward the entrance. Her handkerchief! It was a flash of white under its rock!

Emily opened her mouth to say something, and then decided not to. "We don't want to mark the cave entrance," Mr. Williams had said. If she called out now, the men would have to go back that hot quarter mile, or else wait in the sun while she did. Everyone had had enough of the dusty dry heat. The handkerchief may blow away, or it will blow full of red dust and no one will notice it if they come by, Emily hopefully made up her mind.

She followed the others around a clump of cactus. They started to climb up out of the draw and around the base of Red Hill.

Emily paused, and a second time, she looked back. The rock pile, the entrance to the cave, and the telltale white handkerchief were no longer in sight.

16

Cave-sick

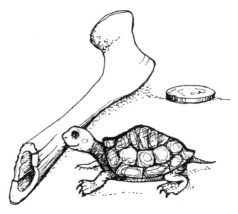

Emily woke in the middle of the night. Something was yanking at her bedclothes! She sat up, fearfully, and groped for the switch to her bed lamp.

"No, Em. Please!" begged a weak, shaky imitation of Beener's voice.

Emily tried to see in the dark.

"Shhh!" Beener implored. "No light, Em. I don't want to wake Mom and Dad yet. Please help me, Emily. I'm sick, really sick. I'm cave-sick like that Norwegian doctor Mr. Fraser told us about!"

Beener thrust a long, hard, smooth object into Emily's hands. "I'll never experiment in a cave again. Those old *akuas* have plenty of power, and they're mad at me! They're making my leg bone hurt, Em, and I'm so hot I think I'm going to burn up."

Emily stifled a scream. She dropped the object Beener had given to her onto the bed.

"A bone! Beener Fergus, you took a bone from Red Hill Cave? That was what you had hidden under your sweat shirt! That's why you wore that awful big sweat shirt in there!"

"I took it," Beener's whisper was penitent. "I wanted to see what would happen if I did. You know. A scientific experiment, Em. Mr. Fraser said, if you take bones out of a cave, you'll get cave-sick. You won't get well until you put the bones back."

Emily could feel the heat radiating from Beener's body, through his pajamas. "Beener!" she said. "Let me call Daddy. You're sick is right!"

"Wait!" Beener's hot hand clutched her. She could feel him shaking with fever. "I don't care how you do it, Em, but promise. Please, please, please! Will you put that old leg bone back in the cave for me?"

"Me?" Emily gazed at her brother in the darkness.

"And don't tell anybody. Don't say one word about my experiment to Mom or Dad. Just put that bone back. Borrow a horse and ride down there, Em. You know the way!

"Cross your heart and hope to die. Keep it a secret and put it back for me, Em?"

"Gosh, Beener — " said Emily.

Then he gave a gasp, and let go her hand.

Emily caught him as he collapsed in a faint.

"Oh, Beener! Cross my heart and hope to die, I'll help you!" she whispered. She held his hot, limp body on her lap. With one hand, she shoved the leg bone under her bed.

"Mother!" she shouted, and turned on her bedlight. "Mother! Daddy! Come quick!"

"One hundred and five degrees." Dr. Fergus read the thermometer he took from Beener's mouth. "Let's wrap him up in a blanket, Helen. We'd better get him to the hospital!"

Emily pulled the blanket loose from the foot of her bed. She helped her mother wrap Beener in it.

Dr. Fergus parked the station wagon at the front steps of the lanai. Then he came in and carried Beener to the car.

Mrs. Fergus sat in the back seat, holding him. "You're not afraid to stay home alone for a while, Emily?"

Emily felt the emptiness of the big house behind her. The stars overhead were bright, but the great branches of the monkeypod trees spread the lawn and the house with the darkest of shadows.

"I'm not afraid!" said Emily. Impulsively, she ran down the steps to the car. "Wait, Daddy!" she said. "Do — do you think Beener could be cave-sick, maybe?"

This wasn't telling Beener's secret — it was

just making a suggestion — that was all!

"Cave-sick? Oh, for heaven's sake, Emily!" said Dr. Fergus in the same tone of voice he'd used when he found the dead centipede.

"Emmy, go on back to bed, dear!" her mother said. "And don't worry. Beener will be all right! He may be getting the measles. The Guzman boy next to the Fujitas' broke out with them yesterday."

"It's not measles," said Emily, but not so that she could be heard.

She watched until the twin beams of the station wagon headlights dissolved out along the road, and the driveway bounced back into darkness. Then she sat down on the topmost lanai step. She didn't feel like going back inside yet, with that old bone hidden under her bed.

Not a breath of wind moved the branches of the monkeypod tonight. Not a rooster crowed. Not a dog barked. Cave-sick, Emily thought. Poor Beener, and after her cowardice today in the cave, how could she ever borrow a horse from the ranch and ride down to Red Hill and put the leg bone back?

The shadows on the lawn seemed to move and change as she watched them. Emily thought she could hear something moving at the side of the house. A small stone rolled over and clinked against another stone on the driveway as something passed by.

Emily stood up. A small black shadow separated itself from the shadows of the bamboo palm flanking the driveway.

"Aka!" said Emily. She laughed aloud in relief. Alix's little dog walked up the lanai steps and stood, ears erect and stumpy tail wagging. "Oh, Aka!" said Emily gratefully. "You're home alone and lonesome and afraid of the dark, too!"

Together, Emily and Aka walked into the house. Aka's toenails made a reassuring brittle click-click on the bare floors.

Emily went into Beener's room. Yes, Albert was safe in his plastic bowl. The Kalakaua dime was in its nest of cotton, in its screw top jar, on Beener's nightstand.

In her own room, Emily got down on her hands and knees and reached under the bed. Aka looked at the leg bone with interest, and sniffed it.

"No," said Emily, slipping the bone into her long cardboard treasure box. It just fit! "I wish this was an ordinary old bone for you to chew on, Aka. But it's not!"

Emily and Aka kept a wakeful vigil the rest of that night. For extra company, Emily brought Albert into her room.

At six in the morning, Mrs. Fergus came home and brought Fumiko to stay with Emily. Then she went back to the hospital again.

At ten, Dr. Fergus came home for breakfast, a

shower, and a shave, and a brief rest.

"If it weren't for his sore leg I'd suspect he was incubating measles," he told Emily and Fumiko.

"His leg hurts?" Emily questioned. "His left leg?"

"Was he complaining about it to you? I asked him if he had hurt it in the last few days, and he said no." Dr. Fergus frowned.

"You still don't think he might be cave-sick?" said Emily, in a small voice.

"Emily!" said her father, with a slightly exasperated voice.

Disconsolately, Emily watched him return to the hospital.

The neighborhood was quiet, with the Frasers, Leiths, Noelani, and Alix gone. The house was quiet, with only herself and Fumiko in it.

At noon, Emily went to lie on her bed in her room and think about how she was going to return the bone.

Four hours later, Noelani's voice at the back door woke her up.

"Noelani!" Emily woke up, sat up, and remembered — all at once.

Noelani was Mr. Kaimana's granddaughter. Mr. Kaimana was ranch foreman at Kalahikiola. Through him, without Mr. Williams knowing about it, Emily might be able to borrow a horse. Red Hill was a prominent landmark on the ranch — and once she had a horse, Emily was certain she could find the way.

She hurried to the kitchen where Noelani waited, talking with Fumiko.

"Oh, Emily! You should have come with us to Hapuna!" said Noelani. "We had the best time!"

"I should have and so should have Beener," said Emily glumly. She gave Fumiko an apologetic glance. "Noelani, please, can I see you in private a minute — outside?"

"Can you keep a secret? A terribly important secret?" Emily asked, when they were settled on the grass under the monkeypod tree.

"I guess so. Sure!" said Noelani.

"It's Beener's secret really. You heard from Fumiko how sick he is? He's cave-sick, Noelani, and it's my responsibility to do something about it."

Quickly, Emily told Noelani the whole story of Beener's experiment in Red Hill Cave.

Noelani's dark eyes shared Emily's worry. "I'll ask my grandfather, when he comes down to Aunt Tuki's for supper tonight," she promised. "But I don't know — he doesn't like the idea of anybody going in those old caves. Maybe he'll *kokua* — maybe he'll help you, and maybe not — "

That evening, Emily saw the Kaimanas' car go in, and much, much later drive out of the Frasers' yard, but then the Frasers' lights went out early. No word as to whether Noelani had asked her grandfather or not.

Again, her parents stayed with Beener all night at the hospital. He was very sick, still with a high fever, and complaining his leg was worse. Emily spent the night at Alix's house, but it was not the fun it ordinarily might have been.

Next morning, she was at the Frasers' back door before seven o'clock. Noelani sat on the steps, holding P'lipo in her lap, and feeding him a breakfast bowl of poi.

The eighteen cats and seven kittens sat waiting to see if Noelani would give them a bite of breakfast, too.

"Will he? Did you ask him?" said Emily anxiously.

Noelani gazed at Emily in her slow, calm fashion. "That's bad. That's very bad what Beener did, but my grandfather said yes, he'll *kokua* for you. Aunt Tuki is driving up to the ranch anyway, so we'll go for that horseback ride with Grandfather this afternoon."

Emily threw her arms around Noelani and P'lipo. The bowl of poi went flying and all the cats after it.

"Thank you!" she cried, sure now that Beener was as good as cured.

17

Emily Goes Alone

It turned out to be the worst possible kind of day for what Emily had to do.

By noon, rain splashed noisily on the broad-leafed surfaces of ti and banana and giant ape. Rain dripped in a steady bright fringe from the eaves of the corrugated iron roof. Rain puddled the lawn and the driveway.

The wet world of Kohala was bounded by towering clouds above the cane fields and a curtain of storm that blanketed any view of the sea.

Mrs. Fergus sounded confused at Emily's plans. "There's nothing you can do about poor Beener," said Mrs. Fergus, "so I guess if you really want to go up riding with Noelani at the ranch this afternoon —"

For a moment, Emily was tempted to confide in

her mother. It would be a relief to her to know Beener was going to be better today.

"Mother —" Emily began. Then she changed her mind. "I'll bet you something about Beener!" she said, instead. "I'll bet you he'll be all well and home and at P'lipo's birthday luau Saturday night!"

Mrs. Fergus sighed. "I hope you're right, Emily. But your brother is a very sick little boy. If he's not better by tomorrow morning, Dr. Wong and Daddy are going to ask a specialist to fly over from Honolulu to look at him."

Emily put her arms around her mother. "They won't have to! He'll be better! I know!"

Emily was wearing her oldest blue jeans, a long-sleeved blouse, and her crew hat. The bone, her flashlight, extra batteries, a canteen of water, a ball of string, a candy bar, and a package of matches were in her Girl Scout knapsack, all bundled into an extra sweat shirt so no one would ask questions as she went through the house and out to the Frasers' car.

"I don't know about you two going riding today," said Aunt Tuki dubiously as they drove over the mountain road in the rain. "If I hadn't had to pick up things for the luau from Uncle John today, I'd not have come out at all."

Every gulch had a stream gushing down over rocks and crashing down the mountainside in waterfalls. The cattle stood in miserable drenched clusters,

161

their backs turned to the wind.

But, when they arrived at the ranch, Mr. Kaimana had the horses saddled and ready. He wore a heavy slicker and had an extra poncho ready for each of the girls. The brim of his battered hat was turned down, the petals of its crown flower lei wilted and torn from the wind and rain.

Emily draped her poncho over her head and shoulders. Noelani rode along bareheaded in the downpour, her face aglow, her black hair glistening. She sang a high, sweet, melancholy-sounding song in Hawaiian as the horses plunged through the mud and waterlogged high grass, down across the mountain road.

Noelani loved the mountains and horseback riding. She loved the cool, blustering wind and rain. It made Emily more courageous about what waited at the end of her ride, to see Noelani with her back proud and erect, a circlet of yellow plumerias around her damp black ponytail.

"No more rain by Red Hill. Always dry at the beach," Mr. Kaimana promised.

He was right. As they dropped in elevation, the hard heavy rain eased to a shower, and lower still the showers sprayed off into a light mist.

Rainbows glistened on the cinder cones. One great double rainbow arched from the black, ground-sweeping clouds behind them to the glimmer of surf-tossed, sunlit, blue sea now visible below. That was

162

one of the advantages of the Big Island. If you didn't like the weather where you happened to be, you got in your car and in an hour's drive — or often less — you could change from hot to cool, or from wet to dry.

The horses made the trip down much more quickly than had the slow, four-wheel-drive truck. There was no need to hike this afternoon either, for the horses could walk where the truck could not go — on around the base of Red Hill and into the shallow arid draw.

Emily stifled a cry at the sight of her white handkerchief fluttering like a signpost near the rocks that covered the entrance to Red Hill Cave.

Mr. Kaimana saw the handkerchief, too. "How come?" he exclaimed. "Anybody can find this place now! Always before I look maybe half an hour for the entrance. The boss do that, I wonder?" He scowled.

Emily dismounted, hobbled her horse the way Mr. Kaimana and Noelani fixed theirs, and walked to the rock pile. She yanked the handkerchief from its rock weight, and stuffed it into her jeans pocket. "I — I left it here Saturday. I forgot it," she said, ashamed.

Mr. Kaimana looked at her with a long, resigned look of disgust, but he said nothing.

"I'm sorry!" Emily apologized.

The two girls helped lift out the rocks that

plugged the cave entrance.

Noelani peered curiously at the dark slit, and the protruding ends of the carrying sticks. "Spooky!" she pronounced. "I never was this place before."

"Last person they put in here was one old lady," Mr. Kaimana recollected. "She died when I was a small boy. Most of the people down in there, though, they're old ones. From long, long time ago."

Emily got out her knapsack. She pulled out her flashlight and her ball of string. Her heart was thudding like Kalani McBryde's ghost drums of Keokea must sound: a rapid, frightened boom-boom in her chest. Her throat was so dry she couldn't swallow. Her hands were clammy.

"Okay?" she said, trying to sound calm. She turned her flashlight on and off, checking the batteries. She waited for Mr. Kaimana or Noelani to lead the way into the cave.

"Sure. Okay. Go ahead. We wait for you," Mr. Kaimana said.

Emily looked at him.

"Emily," said Noelani. "You sure are brave. I wouldn't go in that cave for anything! Not even to help my brother, I think!"

Emily stood helplessly beside the carrying sticks. "I've never been down in this cave. I waited outside on Saturday. I — I — all alone, I don't know where to go!"

Mr. Kaimana squinted at her. "Easy place to

get in. Easy place to find," he said. "First you slide down on the *okole,* the seat of your pants, for maybe six feet. Small room. One more time, slide down a narrow place again. Then, looks like one dead end. But no. You climb over one big rock. A place in the ceiling where you lift yourself through. Then you walk maybe thirty feet and you come to a big room. No way to get lost. No place, unless you fall over your own feet, where you can get hurt."

Emily still hesitated.

"Humbug your brother taking that bone!" said Mr. Kaimana gruffly. "He ought to know better! That's why I stay out here. I don't want anything to do with taking something out of a cave, and I don't want anything to do with putting it back!"

"Neither do I," said Emily, feeling shaky and queer. "But I promised Beener — and there's no other way — "

She gripped her flashlight. She tied one end of the ball of string to an end of a carrying stick. The only part of Mr. Minetti's cave rules that she must disobey was not to go alone and yet, she supposed, it was almost observing that rule to have Mr. Kaimana and Noelani waiting and watching for her out here.

Emily got down on her haunches. She paused to take a last look at the three horses browsing and stamping their hooves, and at Noelani's grave face, and Mr. Kaimana's impatient one.

165

"Don't you fool around looking at things down below, eh?" said Mr. Kaimana.

"Don't worry!" said Emily. "I won't!"

She closed her eyes and clenched her teeth.

"Brave, yuh?" Emily heard Noelani say as she slid down past the carrying sticks.

In the first tiny chamber, Emily opened her eyes. She coughed, from a cloud of dust that had followed her slide down. She snapped on her flashlight. The beam played on the hard shiny back and waving feelers of an enormous cockroach, twice the size of the one that had frightened her in the *puka*-by-the-sea. Gingerly, Emily scuttled past him. Ahead of her, the steep rocky chute where she had encountered the centipede led on below.

Emily kept her eyes open, and the knapsack, string, and flashlight all in a firm grip this time, as she skidded on her *okole,* down-down-down. The chute ended in a bubble chamber just big enough to stand up in and turn around, and suspect — as Mr. Kaimana had warned her — that you had reached a dead end. There was a huge boulder between Emily and the flaking red dirt wall of this bubble. "Climb over it," she remembered. She did.

It took her a few minutes to find the opening out through the ceiling, and it was no easy task to hoist herself up and through it.

The passageway into which she scrambled was nothing like the fresh, burnished black lava tubes of

Kona caves. The walls, ceiling, and floor of this tube were scaling, dusty rock that shaled off at a touch. Kohala, Emily remembered Mr. Minetti telling, was the oldest part of the island, in geological time. It seemed to her that here in Red Hill Cave, she could sense the age of Kohala, could almost feel the difference of thousands and thousands of years that had passed since this particular lava tube cave — and the Kohala that lay out in the sun above it — was formed.

The flashlight stabbed ahead, throwing eerie shadows into the contoured emptiness of great cracks and piles of rock debris. A good thing Pele didn't walk often or very heavily through Kohala, for Red Hill Cave didn't look as if it would survive too strong a shake.

Emily kept paying out a slack length of string behind her. She kept the flashlight trained on the floor of the passageway so she could avoid the only danger Mr. Kaimana seemed to think she might encounter — stumbling over her own feet. Emily grew indignant, thinking about what Mr. Kaimana had said, and about him and Noelani sitting up above ground letting her venture into this cave all alone.

Still — Emily tried to put herself in their place. She had asked their *kokua* to keep her secret, and Beener's, and to get her down here. Both Noelani and her grandfather, Emily was sure, had a stronger fear of and respect for the "old ones" and the *akuas* of this cave than she herself perhaps could realize.

Emily thought of the day she had almost ridden up the *kapu* trail. She remembered that mysterious fragrance of *maile* where no *maile* grew. She remembered the flare of hostility in Noelani at Honaunau that Saturday when they mentioned the old bones in Ohia Cave.

Emily put one cautious wary foot ahead of the other up the passageway. No! She did not blame Mr. Kaimana and Noelani for staying outside. After all, her errand to Red Hill was family business, a matter between herself and Beener, something that she had personally felt it her obligation to do.

The passageway, after the thirty feet of Mr. Kaimana's directions, opened into a room as big in area as the living chamber of Ohia, where the lantern had caught on fire. Emily paused on the threshold. Here, in the heart of Red Hill Cave, she needed no exercise of the imagination to wonder how this had looked in ancient times. Red Hill had been off the track of passersby, carefully hidden for all these intervening years. Those who had visited it — almost all — had come with enough respect and discretion to leave everything exactly as it had been.

The major use of the big room was, obviously, for a living cave, a place of refuge in time of war. Against one charcoal-blackened wall was a hearth site, with piles of dried *pili* grass still beside it to use for kindling. A midden of *opihi* shells and bones was on the floor near the hearth site. On the rough natural niches in the chamber walls were calabashes, gourds for storing water, carved wooden bowls almost two feet in diameter for keeping poi and other food.

On the cave floor, in the deep dry red dust that rose in choking clouds at every step, Emily saw a broken nose flute discarded among the husks of burned *kukui* shells and the pieces of a broken stone poi pounder.

At the rear of this room, blocked off from the living area by a low stone and earth wall, was a deep alcove with a ceiling that dropped to less than her own height.

Emily walked slowly, fascinated, to this wall. She leaned on it and shone her flashlight into the alcove.

Near her, immediately on the other side of the stone barricade, a dozen canoe-shaped wooden coffins were jammed side by side on the earth floor. An ancient black opera hat was on top of one coffin. A pair of high-heeled, high-buttoned ladies' shoes with pointed toes were visible through the split end of another coffin.

Emily gasped and swallowed and stared on beyond.

The floor of the alcove was spread with bundles of bones: ancient tapa-wrapped bundles; bones, still more ancient, whose coverings had desiccated and turned to dust in the dry air. Their contents were freed into a jumble of long bones and the grinning teeth and leering eye sockets of skulls.

It was all Emily could do not to scream and run. With shaking fingers, she unfastened the straps of her knapsack and took out the bone. She had to climb over the barricade, pick a careful foothold by stepping over one coffin at a time to get back to the jumble of bones where Beener had stolen this one.

Emily tried not to see the glimpses of mummified shrunken fingers, a still lustrous switch of black hair, the crumbling edge of a tree-fern pillow used to cushion some long dead head. The gaping split boards of the coffins showed her much more than she wanted to see.

Emily poised the leg bone over the scattered bones at the rear of the alcove. Now she actually was here, so close to the reality of all these "old ones," she was no longer afraid. Here was death as it came to everyone.

Emily looked with wonder at the skulls — big ones with strong, perfect teeth and powerful jaws, small skulls of children, skulls with the two upper front teeth knocked out — which was an ancient custom of showing grief on the death of a king.

Gently, respectfully, Emily put the leg bone Beener had taken down on a tattered shred of tapa cloth, near a lonely looking skull.

"My brother is sorry for what he did," she whispered. "Please forgive him!"

Emily turned around. She clambered back over

the coffins and over the stone barricade. She picked up her knapsack and her ball of string. She fastened the knapsack to her shoulders, and began to rewind the fine white web she had spun into Red Hill Cave.

Now that she had done what she had to do, even though she was alone, Emily wished she could stay down here longer. The calabashes, the gourds, the *pili* grass, the broken nose flute, the pieces of poi pounder, gave her the feeling that if she waited in this room for just a little while, the ancient inhabitants of Red Hill Cave would return.

Emily sighed. After this, she might never have another chance to visit a Hawaiian cave, and Emily was beginning to feel quite at her ease, quite comfortable here underground.

"Don't you fool around looking at things down there, eh?" Mr. Kaimana had warned her.

Emily appreciated his words now. She knew how hot it was outside and how time dragged when you waited for someone.

She took a last look around the living chamber. "Good-bye, old ones!" she said in a soft voice.

Her flashlight stabbed ahead of her, out into the passageway and through the passageway to the chute. The climb out was not as easy as the slide in — but Emily made the first one. She pulled herself up into the bubble chamber and wound her string up after her. There was the enormous cockroach — or his cousin. This time, she passed by without quite so much fear. She felt pleased with herself.

She scrabbled up the steeply slanting chute toward the entrance. She turned off her flashlight and wriggled past the carrying sticks and untied the end of her string.

"Emily!" Noelani hailed her.

"I did it," said Emily, wiping her dusty sweaty face on her sleeve. "I —," she paused, noticing a ti leaf and a water-smoothed beach stone placed ceremoniously beside the entrance to the cave. Those had not been there when she went down! Mr. Kaimana must have hesitated to let her see him put out the traditional notice to the *akuas*.

Emily looked at the ti leaf and beach stone. She looked gratefully at Noelani and her grandfather. "Thank you!" she said.

18

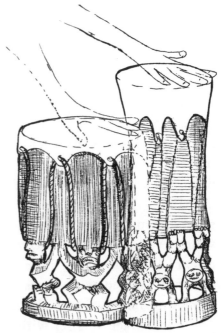

Ghost Drums

Keokea Park was on the lush windward coast of the Kohala district, on a grassy, palm-sheltered delta where the mountain stream from Keokea gulch flowed into the sea.

Red cliffs towered on either side of the park, and on one of them, its ruins choked in a wilderness of lantana, was the Hawaiian *heiau,* the ancient temple Princess Kalani had told Emily about. And tonight, Emily remembered, there was a full moon! Maybe she'd get to hear those ghost drums herself.

She agreed with the Frasers. Keokea was a perfect place for P'lipo's birthday luau.

The park pavilion, an open-sided shelter with a concrete floor, was decorated luau style. Emily, Alix, Dorothy, and Noelani had been helping with this all day. Each post of the pavilion was wrapped with large leathery green leaves of monstera, the *puka* plant of the islands, and into each hole in these leaves, the girls had thrust a bright hibiscus flower.

Ferns, sprays of orchids, plumeria blossoms, hundreds of rainbow colored hibiscus, were strewn down the centers of the ti-leaf-covered picnic tables.

Pineapples were cut so that their shells and spiky green tops were a serving dish for spears of yellow fruit. Paper plates covered with a broad green ti leaf held white cubes of *haupia,* a pudding of coconut milk cooked with cornstarch until it was thick enough to be eaten with the fingers.

Each place was set with paper plates and cup, a spoon, and a napkin-wrapped cardboard cup of poi. The centerpiece was a birthday cake three feet square, with one big candle on it.

"Happy birthday, seven months late, P'lipo!" Emily laughed.

"He'll have more fun opening his presents now than he would have had when he was one year old!" said Noelani. She was in charge of P'lipo tonight. He was wearing a red carnation birthday lei.

This was like no birthday party Emily had ever seen, for the Frasers had invited over a hundred guests, young and old!

Mr. Fraser, Mr. Leith, Mr. Fujita, and Mr. Kaimana were busy with shovels and hoes behind the pavilion where, early this morning, they had dug and prepared an earth oven, an *imu.*

Dr. Fergus had his movie camera along.

"Come on!" he urged Mrs. Fergus and Emily. "Let's get some pictures of this pig."

Emily stood with Noelani and P'lipo at the edge of the pile of fresh, moist earth the men had shoveled from the top of the pit. They were busy now stripping off tarpaulin and canvas bags, wetting their hands before they plucked out the steaming hot rocks that had covered and cooked the food.

"Ouch!" said Emily.

"If they work fast, and wet their hands every time, they don't get burned," Noelani said.

A delicious mouth-watering odor rose with the steam.

"Ummmm!" said Alix hungrily. "*Kalua* pig!"

"Nothing better!" Dorothy exclaimed.

The men lifted the whole roast pig onto a long, metal-lined, wooden trough fitted with carrying poles at either end.

Mr. Fraser and Mr. Fujita posed long enough for Dr. Fergus to get a good shot of them with the pig on a board. Then they cut the meat into small pieces, mixed it with as much hot water as the meat could absorb, and seasoned it with Hawaiian salt. Then, using the carrying poles again, they took the carved roast pig down to the pavilion.

"Better find yourselves places at the table, girls!" advised Mr. Fraser.

Emily, Alix, Dorothy, and Noelani sat down

175

together, across from Jasmine and Mrs. Price.

"Hi," said Jasmine with a shy smile.

"Happy birthday, P'lipo," said Mrs. Price. "We brought you a birthday gift. I'm sure you'll like it better than anything else you get!"

She reached across and chucked P'lipo on his fat dimpled chin. A roguish look came into P'lipo's eyes. He bent his small head, opened his mouth, and bit!

"Oo! Ouch!" cried Mrs. Price. She jerked her hand back across the table. She held up her finger and rubbed the red tooth marks on the flesh.

"Noelani, I think you'd better let his mother take care of him!" she complained.

Noelani smiled. "He's sorry. Aren't you, P'lipo? *Kaukau,* P'lipo?" she asked, opening his cup of poi. She twisted a spoonful of the thick purple paste and popped it into P'lipo's mouth. He ate with gusto. "See? He was hungry!" Noelani looked calmly at Mrs. Price.

Food cooked in the *imu* had a distinctive, sweet, smoky flavor, Emily discovered. She sampled everything. *Opihis* and familiar *opae, Kalua* pig, limu (Hawaiian seaweed), breadfruit, which tasted like a cross between a sweet potato and a pineapple and was the size and shape of a small pumpkin. There was lomilomi salmon, raw salmon which had been rubbed with salt and cracked ice, and mixed with onions and fresh tomatoes; tender tree fern shoots, *Imu* baked

176

bananas and yams.

"Poor Beener!" sighed Emily. "At least, his leg got all better. Now if it weren't for his measles, he could be here!"

The sun slipped below the horizon while they were eating. A rosy afterglow tinted the sky, which then deepened to a darker and darker blue, until the first pale stars of evening winked overhead.

"Let's go down on the beach," suggested Alix when they had eaten all they could.

"Oh, let's!" Emily took her empty plate and poi and juice cups, and followed the others' example, putting them into one of the rubbish cans at the edge of the pavilion. There was no dishwashing after a luau!

Noelani returned P'lipo to his mother so he could blow out the candle on his birthday cake.

"Jasmine! Come with us," urged Noelani, as Alix and Dorothy were excusing themselves.

Jasmine looked pleased. "Okay, yuh?" she asked apprehensively of her mother.

"May I, you mean, Jasmine," corrected Mrs. Price. "Yes, but be careful if you go near the water, dear!"

Down on the beach, the girls roamed through the wet cane trash that was washed like straw on the beach from waste flumed out by the sugar mills. This cane trash was a good place in which to find glass balls that the Japanese fishermen used as floats.

It soon grew too dark to beachcomb. The five girls climbed up on a big rock at one end of the beach. They sat quietly together, watching the stars come out and the patch of milky light on the horizon where the moon would rise.

The men lit luau torches — tin cans filled with rolls of paper saturated in kerosene. The smoky orange flames ringed the pavilion with light.

Somebody brought his autoharp from his car, and somebody else brought out a guitar. These were soon joined by a ukelele and a bass viol.

"Pretty soon, I go up and dance a hula for P'lipo's birthday," Noelani said.

"I brought my gourds and my split bamboos," said Alix. "I promised Aunt Tuki I'd hula too."

"I brought my ukelele to play," Jasmine volunteered.

Emily sighed again. P'lipo's luau was perfect, all but for one lack that she wouldn't have minded a month — or even a week ago.

"Poor Beener!" she said.

"I hear he has the reddest face and the worst measles rash anyone ever had in Kohala," Dorothy said.

Emily nodded, "No fever, though. It went down Monday night, after Noelani and I came home."

"And his leg doesn't hurt him anymore!" said Noelani.

178

She and Emily exchanged secret glances. No one else knew. No one else ever would.

Beener had sent Emily his thank you note from the hospital, insisting she accept a gift that their mother still couldn't understand.

"But, Em," she protested, "his special lucky Kalakaua dime! And he wants you to have it for your collection — no strings attached — just like that!" Mrs. Fergus looked bewildered, but pleased. "I think you children must be soaking up the Hawaiian spirit of aloha at last!"

"What more could you do for a brother?" said Noelani philosophically, now.

Emily fingered the pocket of her muumuu. She held up her hand — Beener's small turtle felt smooth and cool and his tiny legs brushed gently against the skin of her palm.

"Albert's been everywhere else, so I promised Beener I'd see Albert got to this luau too!"

"I thought you were scared of creepy, crawly things," said Alix.

"I was," Emily smiled, "and I still am — some. But not of Albert anymore."

"You're lucky, you know that, Emily?" said Jasmine in a wistful voice. "You live here in Kohala only one summer, and already you're more *kamaaina* than me — more island than me — and I've lived here all my life!" Jasmine sighed, "If only my mother'd let me do some of the things I want to do!"

"You ever make a wish on the evening star, Jasmine?" asked Emily.

"No use, for me," said Jasmine disconsolately.

"Oh, Jasmine!" said Noelani, as she put a friendly arm around Jasmine's shoulders. "Don't say that!"

I'll make a wish for her, Emily thought with compassion. Better yet, I'll make a wish for her mother!

Emily gazed at the tip of the moon rising and the stars paling beside it. I wish, she said to herself, that Mrs. Price and Mrs. Otani, and anyone like them, anywhere, could open their eyes and their hearts and their minds to Princess Kalani's and my Hawaii.

I wish the whole world could know what aloha means, and try to live that way. I wish everybody would be proud of who they are and proud to be friends and try to understand anyone who looks or lives or speaks differently.

I'm a *haole,* Emily thought. The word no longer offended her. She was not ashamed to be *haole,* as Jasmine's mother so often had made her feel. She was a *haole,* as Alix was part-Hawaiian, as Dorothy was of Japanese descent, as Noelani was Hawaiian-Chinese, as Mrs. Dacuycuy at Honaunau was Filipino. As Beener's friend Tony Guzman was Puerto Rican, and as Mrs. Ferreira, the postmaster, was Portuguese.

180

These names were only labels that told other people what part of the world you were proud to have your ancestors from.

"Hey! We're missing the music!" said Alix. "C'mon, Jasmine! Noelani! Dorothy! Em!"

Only Emily stayed behind on the rock. "I want to wait here a while," she said. "You go. I'll be up later on."

Alone, with Beener's turtle for company, Emily stayed on the rock until the full moon hung its light well up in the sky. She gave Albert a view of the moon floating a track of brilliance over the high surf and across the bay.

"Oh, Albert," she whispered, "this is going to be much too short a year! *Kohala no ka oi. Hawaii no ka oi.* Hawaii's the best!"

Tonight, with the ordeal of Red Hill Cave behind her, and all the summer's adventures, and all she had learned — about herself and others — Emily did feel *kamaaina,* Hawaiian in her heart like a real island girl.

Best of all, the longest part of her Hawaiian year still lay ahead. I'll bet by Christmas, Emily thought, I'll be able to look a cockroach in the face — close — and not run away!

The music from the pavilion was high and sweet. The surf was a close rhythmic thunder. Emily strained for another sound, her eyes on the moonlit ruins of the Hawaiian temple on the cliffs above.

181

Was it her imagination — or could she really hear what Princess Kalani had hoped she would — the faint boom-boom of ghost drums in the night?

Emily listened — and smiled.

Glossary Follows

Glossary

Hawaiian is a beautiful, ancient language still spoken by many people in the islands. Many Hawaiian words have become anglicized and are in wide, everyday use by all islanders. Here are a few rules for pronouncing the Hawaiian words in the proper, ancient Hawaiian way.

Every syllable and every word in Hawaiian ends with a vowel. Each vowel should be· pronounced separately, with the exception of certain vowel combinations such as *au* (ow), *ai* (eye), and *ei* (ay). Aa is pronounced ah ah.

Some Hawaiian words have only vowels, but most have consonants. The consonant always begins a syllable. For example: *pi-li-ki-a* (pee-lee-KEE-ah).

The accent of most Hawaiian words falls on the next-to-the-last syllable: ah-LO-hah. The first syllable of a two-syllable word is accented: PU-kah. Words containing five syllables are stressed on the first and fourth syllables.

Here is a simple guide to help you in pronouncing Hawaiian vowels:

A	as in father	
unstressed E	as in bet	
stressed E	as in way	
a final E	is also pronounced *ee* in some anglicized words; e.g. *hoale*.	
I	as in see	
O	as in no	
U	as in true	

aa (ah-ah) rough, stony type of lava from volcanoes which moves very slowly and looks like heaps of clinkers or slag.

akua (ah-KOO-ah) God, gods.

aloha (ah-LO-hah) affection, love, sympathy. It is a greeting which can mean hello or good-bye. *Nui* means great and *loa* means very or long, so *aloha nui loa* is a greeting of very great affection. *Oe* means you or thou, so *aloha oe* means aloha to you or farewell to you.

ape (AH-pay) a large-leafed plant, about eighteen inches high, common in Hawaiian gardens.

Hale o Keawe (HAH-lay o Kay-AH-vay) House of Keawe — the name for the enclosure where the remains of King Keawe and other ancient Hawaiian kings were kept in what we would now call a royal mausoleum.

haole (HOW-lee) originally a stranger or foreigner, now means a Caucasian or white person.

haole koa (HOW-lee KO-ah) small, scrub tree used for cattle forage. Has a similar leaf and appearance to the native koa tree. The seeds are boiled and strung into leis.

hapa (HAH-pah) fraction or part. *Hapa haole* means part-white or part Caucasian.

haupia (how-PEE-ah) a pudding of coconut cream (made from squeezed fresh grated coconut mixed with boiling water to melt the rich "cream" from the coconut meat. This is done in a cheesecloth bag and the "cream" squeezed out and allowed to stand until it can be skimmed from the top of liquid). It is then cooked with cornstarch until thick enough to be cut into cubes and eaten with the fingers.

heiau (HAY-ow) an ancient Hawaiian place of worship. Some *heiaus* were elaborately built stone terraces and others were simple earth platforms. Most of them were built on hilltops or points of land that jutted out into the sea.

He poe uhane (Hay PO-ay oo-HAH-nay) Hail, spirit people! *He* is the word for hail, *poe* is assemblage or company, and *uhane* means souls.

hibiscus (High-BIS-cus) Hawaii's state flower. It is much like our hollyhock, but grows on a bush instead of a single stalk. Hibiscus grow in a rainbow of colors. Each flower lasts only twenty-four hours.

humu-humu-nuku-nuku-a-puaa (HOO-moo-HOO-moo-NOO-koo-NOO-koo-AH-poo-AH-ah) the big name of a small multicolored reef fish which has a pig-shaped snout.

imu (EE-moo) underground oven, a pit lined with hot stones in which food is cooked by the heat from these stones.

kahuna (kah-HOO-nah) priest, doctor, sorcerer; expert in any profession, for instance there were canoe-building *kahunas*.

Kalakaua (Kah-lah-KOW-ah) family name of King David Kalakaua who ruled Hawaii from 1874 to 1891. He used the European style on the design of his coins, calling himself Kalakaua Rex. Rex is the Latin word for ruler or king.

kalua (kah-LOO-ah) to bake in the underground oven or *imu*. *puaa kalua* means, literally, baked pig, but the common island expression is *kalua* pig.

kamaaina (kah-mah-EYE-nah) land-child, native-born. Also the name given to one who lives and becomes as a native-born in the islands. To be called a *kamaaina* is a great compliment, especially for a newcomer.

kapu (kah-POO) prohibited, forbidden, taboo.

kiawe (kee-AH-vee) the algaroba tree, a legume from tropical America first planted in Hawaii in 1828, where it has become the most common of trees, especially along the dry lee coasts.

Kohala no ka oi (Ko-HAH-lah no kah o-ee) Kohala is the best.

kokua (ko-KOO-ah) help, assistance, to help.

kolohe (ko-LO-hee) mischievous, naughty.

konane (ko-NAH-nee) ancient game resembling checkers. It is played with pebbles placed in even lines on a stone or wooden board called *papa konane*.

kukui (koo-KOO-ee) candlenut tree. In ancient times, the oily nuts were strung on bamboo splinters or palm frond midribs and used as torches. The nuts are often polished and made into handsome jewelry, or the meat of the nut is ground and used as a relish at luaus.

kuleana (koo-lay-AH-nah) property belonging to a family or any subject in which one has a special interest.

lanai (lah-NAH-ee) porch, veranda, or open-walled roofed addition to a building.

lauhala hat (laü-HAH-la) a hat woven from pandanus leaves which have been dried, split, softened in water, and sometimes bleached in the sun before weaving. The pandanus tree is known as the hala tree in Hawaii.

lei (lay) garland, wreath, or necklace of flowers, shells, seeds, or nuts. Leis are given as a token of affection, usually to guests, and especially to friends and relatives who are leaving on or coming home from a journey.

lilikoi (lee-lee-KO-ee) passion fruit.

limu (LEE-moo) seaweed. Many kinds of seaweed are gathered, cleaned, and eaten in Hawaii.

lomilomi (LO-mee-LO-mee) salmon or other fish, usually raw, mixed with chopped raw onions, chopped tomatoes, and salt. The meaning of *lomilomi* is to massage, and this dish is prepared with the fingers.

luau (LOO-ow) a Hawaiian feast, also the name of the leaf of the taro plant which is used as one of the main foods and food ingredients at these feasts. For example, chicken luau is chicken stewed with these greens and coconut milk.

maile (MY-lee) a native vine with shiny, fragrant leaves used for decoration and leis, generally only on very special occasions of importance or for very important people.

malo (MAH-lo) loincloth worn by the men in ancient Hawaii.

muumuu (MOO-oo-Moo-oo) the loose gown designed for the native women by the first missionary women who came to Hawaii from New England in the 1820's and 1830's.

okole (o-KO-lee) buttocks.

opae (oh-PAH-ee) shrimp.

opihi (o-PEE-hee) limpet, a popular variety of seafood picked off the rocks at the tide line and eaten raw. They are like clams but stronger in flavor.

pahoehoe (pah-HOY-hoy) smooth, unbroken lava; the type which flows in a swift, riverlike stream that may travel as fast as thirty-five miles an hour and cools to the appearance of a wrinkled asphalt road.

pali (PAH-lee) cliff, precipice, or steep hill.

paniolos (pah-nee-OH-los) cowboys. The first cowboys in Hawaii were Spanish and called themselves *espagnol*. The Hawaiians pronounced it *panioli* and then adapted it to mean cowboy.

pau hana (pow-HAH-na) finished work. *Pau* means finished or eaten and *hana* means work.

pili (PEE-lee) a grass that was used for thatching houses.

pilikia (pee-lee-KEE-ah) trouble of any kind, great or small.

pipi (PEE-pee) beef cattle (from beef or *bipi*).

pipi kaula (PEE-pee kah-OO-lah) long, thin strips of beef which have been salted and dried in the sun and then broiled before eating.

poi (poy) the staple of the ancient and modern Hawaiian diet. It is a purplish gray or pink paste made from cooked taro corms (and sometimes breadfruit). The cooked taro is pounded to a paste and thinned with water to the consistency of thick gruel. It is a very nutritious food and is becoming as popular a baby food on the mainland USA as it has long been in Hawaii.

puhi (POO-hee) eel.

puka (POO-kah) hole, cave, door, gate, opening.

pupus (POO-poos) small bite-size pieces of food served as relishes or hors d'oeuvres.

tabu (tah-BOO) forbidden.

tapa (TAH-pah) a thin papery cloth which is made by pounding the bark of the paper mulberry plant. Tapa cloth was used in ancient Hawaii to make loincloths for the men, for bed-coverings, and in any way that cloth might be needed. The tapa was pounded with a carved beater to make patterns and designs and dyed various colors.

ti (tee) a common plant in Hawaii. It has a tall stalk,

usually three to twelve feet high, with long, thick, glossy green leaves growing in a single tuft at the top. Ti leaves are used to make hula skirts, to wrap food, and as a table covering at luaus.

tiki (TEE-kee) carved statue of a god.

tutu (TOO-too) grandmother.

The following words are not Hawaiian, but they are commonly used in the cosmopolitan islands of Hawaii where every language has contributed a few words that have been adapted into common, everyday usage. There are no accented syllables in the Japanese words.

arrigato gozaimasu (ah-ree-gah-toe go-zy-mah-soo) Japanese for thank you very much.

bon odori (bone o-do-ree) the dance part of the Buddhist Bon ritual held in midsummer to commemorate the memory of the dead. It has a deep, traditional religious meaning, but is as well a popular and gay part of the Hawaiian Bon celebrations.

cho-chinn (cho-chin) Japanese paper lanterns (literally, hanging lights).

chop sui (chop soo-ee) the same as chop suey on mainland USA.

geta (gay-tah) Japanese wooden clogs worn outdoors.

happi (hah-pee) originally the name of the hip-length kimono worn by construction workers in Japan. One could tell the kind of gang the wearer belonged to by the symbol or sign on the back. They are now popular as lounging coats, artists' smocks, beach jackets, and are worn with capri pants by the teenagers at Bon Dances.

Ilocanos. Ilocano. (Ee-lo-cah-nos) Natives of a region on the island of Luzon in the Philippine Islands. They speak a language called Ilocano. Many Ilocanos have settled in Hawaii, and the language is still commonly heard on radio and TV programs and seen on signs in banks, post offices, and plantation company offices.

kaukau (KOW-kow) food, to eat. Island pidgin and derived from the Chinese. It may have the same origin as the army expression, chow.

kim chee (kim-CHEE) Korean pickled vegetable relish, usually made from Chinese cabbage or sliced cucumbers. It is highly seasoned with chili pepper, garlic, and ginger.

mempachi (mem-pah-chee) a small red fish generally caught at night. This is the Japanese name for *u'u* or squirrel fish.

nishime (nee-shee-may) a delicious Japanese stew made of chicken or pork, seaweed, and vegetables seasoned with shoyu and simmered together until tender.

obaa-san (o-bah-san) grandmother; also the term used by younger women when speaking to an older woman. It is a polite Japanese expression.

oba-san (o-bah-san) aunt.

obaki (o-bah-kee) Japanese word for ghosts.

obi (o-bee) the wide sash worn at the waist of a Japanese kimono.

sakura (sah-koo-rah) Japanese card game.

sashimi (sah-shee-mee) thinly sliced raw fish. This is a Japanese delicacy, but the ancient Hawaiians, and most modern islanders, also enjoy eating raw fish.

Where Cross The Crowded Ways

Gary Forbes

A Case Study In Effective Urban Ministry

C.S.S. Publishing Co., Inc.

Lima, Ohio

WHERE CROSS THE CROWDED WAYS

Library of Congress Cataloging-in-Publication Data

Forbes, Gary L., 1939-
    Where cross the crowded ways / by Gary L. Forbes.
        p.   cm.
    ISBN 1-556-73]34-9
    1. First United Methodist Church (South Bend, Ind.)   2. South Bend (Ind.)
— Church History.   I. Title.
    BX8481.S733F67 1988
287'.677289 — dc19   87-33006
                                                                CIP

8819 / ISBN 1-556-73034-9   PRINTED IN U.S.A.

Table of Contents

For the people of First United Methodist Church in South Bend who are experiencing dying traditions and discovering new ones.

For my family and friends who ministered God's grace to me, when life seemed lost.

For Jerry, my friend, wherever you are. May God watch over you.

For L. G. Sapp, Bob and Ruth Jackson, and Bishop Ralph Alton who incarnate in their lives personal and social concern for the unwanted and wounded.

Preface

The impetus for this book comes from the suggestion of a colleague that what has missionally evolved in the ministry of First United Methodist Church in South Bend, Indiana, should be put in writing, so that similar congregations might be motivated to seriously consider their contexts of service in order to become creative catalysts of Christ.

After the first and second drafts of the book were finished, and had remained on my desk for a year, I suspected that this book might only add clutter to already existing case studies. However, what appears here does have a directional word for the "sleeping giants" in the center of many cities. I pray that this case study will provide impetus for those who are simply waiting for pastoral leadership that will give them missional permission to be let loose to love for Christ's sake.

A major contributing factor to the book's year long hibernation was the fact that one is hesitant to make public the dark side of one's private existence. But, in the final days of deciding whether or not to offer my manuscript to the reading public, it was this very fact, in light of the unfaced dark sides of many pastors which impede their creative contributions, that was the driving dynamic behind the offering of these pages. Dark sides faced openly and honestly can become symbols of hope for pastoral ministry. When the dark sides are confronted, they can become positive factors for fulfilling one's calling. Naming the demons can issue in personally productive periods of ministry.

Personal vignettes are shared with the hope that they depict the fact that authentic evangelism is, more often than not, more diverse and ambivalent in its process and outcome than polished, packaged evangelism programs would have us think it is. When persons are involved, the one constant which is continually present is that relational evangelism cannot be programatically packaged for the sake of insuring positive numerical results.

You read here only the recorded events that came about as a result of the dedication of hundreds of First Church lay people. They dreamed. They dared. And they directed ministries that went far beyond what any of us could have anticipated.

In addition to this multitude of ministers, appreciation must go to Reverend Phillip Emerson who suggested the writing, to Scott Shoaff, who through his own ministry, kept before us the vision in order that many might not perish, to Ruth Lapp who typed the original manuscripts, to Connie Lovejoy who assisted in writing chapters ten, eleven, and twelve, to Linda Dolby and Shari Schap who helped with the editing, to my family whose vacations were shortened by the work, and to a compassionate and supportive staff who ever had as the priority of their ministry the creation of a climate where the uprooted could find "a rest upon the way."

Gary Forbes
September 3, 1985
Lafayette, Indiana

All names of chapters one, eight, ten, eleven, twelve, thirteen, fourteen, and fifteen have been changed to protect the identities of the real people.

Foreword

My personal acquaintance with the author of this quite remarkable book makes his request that I write a foreword both appreciated and challenging. This is the story of one minister's personal struggle and its influence on his pastoral leadership of one congregation to which he was appointed. The resulting development of a congregation's ministry to its community in particular ways is a challenge to every Christian congregation to be aware of its opportunities and responsibilities as an agent of the Christian Gospel to serve the needs of people who live in the church's vicinity. The narration of the author's experiences helps us to be sensitive to the human nature of all persons, even ministers of the Christian church. The narration is a revelation of the ways in which God can use such human instruments for the fulfillment of God's purposes as revealed in the ministry of Jesus Christ.

This book is like a mystery novel, in that its early chapters raise the question of what prompted the writer to lead his congregation in the development of the particular ministries he describes with justifiable pride. The book also reveals why he was impelled to put the description of those ministries and his involvement in them into written form. There is an obvious passion in his writing that is not explained by mere literary interest. The reader will sense an emotional compulsion about the subject matter that is more subjective than objective. Then one arrives at the chapter in which the writer describes with amazing candor his personal struggle with alcoholism and the concurrent emotional and spiritual agony that accompanied the acceptance of his condition and his dealing with it. The chapter, "Witness from Weakness," answers the earlier inquiry It is as though the writer realizes at that point that his narrative requires this identification of his personal motivations, and it illustrates the way in which God can use whatever life crises we may each have to make us sensitive to people with similar struggles.

Perhaps, only those who have experienced the same or similar life experiences can fully appreciate the intensity of the urgency that motivated the author's challenges to his congregation, his personal involvement in the programs he helped develop, and his interest in the persons served, some of whom he identifies in short biographical descriptions in the closing chapters of his book. But all of us can be inspired by the way in which he accepted the guidance of God, through his experiences, to urge the church he served to minister to those whose needs he particularly recognized.

There is a basic premise in this book that merits special comment.

It is that the true test of every congregation's commitment to the Christian faith is not so much what happens in the church as the influence of its mission on those who are outside the fellowship. By inference, the purpose of this book is not to say that every congregation should develop the same ministries as are described herein. It can be truthfully asserted that in every community — even the most rural — there are persons who need such ministries. But there are other human needs that may be more typical of some communities. In any case, the challenge to the Christian congregation is to identify those needs and to answer the question, "What can we in the name and spirit of Jesus Christ do to help people to deal with their life crises?" It is to that kind of ministry that Christ calls his followers, whether that is identified by ministers or congregations. This book is a worthy and inspiring narrative to encourage us to that end.

Ralph Alton
Retired Bishop of the
United Methodist Church

A Successor's Surprise

It was two months after being appointed as the Senior Pastor of the First United Methodist Church of South Bend, Indiana, that I saw Gary Forbes. He had given me a copy of the manuscript of his new book at Annual Conference and I had just completed reading it. I said to Gary, "I am used to ministers over-exaggerating as they describe their programs and the great crowds involved, but your book is a tremendous understatement of all that is going on at South Bend First United Methodist Church. I don't know of any downtown church that has as many human service programs in their own church building as does First Church. It is a wonderful mission which I hope that we continue, but it is also a tremendous amount of work that is almost overwhelming at times." He just smiled with a knowing look that said, "You don't know the half of it."

The first day I walked through the church I was amazed with the scores of people associated with the various community service programs taking place. I learned immediately that some of these programs continue with very little time from our church staff, and others would consume all our time, if we let them. I am proud of the involvement of our members in their support of these ministries, and appreciate their patience when there is a conflict of time and space with the more traditional congregational activities. Some of the service projects will change as the needs of our community change, but I am sure that our service to others in the name and spirit of Christ will not change.

One month before coming to South Bend I attended a conference in Nashville, and a lay person from Niles, Michigan, was present. I told him I would be coming to First United Methodist Church of South Bend as their new pastor. He answered, "Oh, I know which church that is. That's the church that does so much for other people." That's a great reputation for any church to have, and it certainly fits First Church.

Allen Byrne
First United Methodist Church
South Bend, Indiana

Chapter One

You Have the Story Wrong

"Let him who is without sin among you be the first to throw a stone at her." (John 8:7)

The call from the jail came in the early afternoon. Brother Terrance, the chaplain, asked, "Gary, remember Ben from the A. A. meetings at the jail?" I remembered Ben well. Our relationship started while he was living at First United Methodist Church, where I had been the pastor for nine years. The relationship had continued for seven months as we participated together in the A. A. meetings at the Saint Joseph County Jail. He had lived in the Church's Upper Room temporary housing program before going to jail for child abuse, an act he had committed while intoxicated.

"Ben has a church which would pay his bail if First Church would take him back." There was no hesitation on my part because, regardless of the low esteem in which a child molester is held, by both the prison population and society at large, Jesus Christ loves and died for the child molester; and, therefore, we are under commission to extend Christ's love to the molester through the accepting ministry of the church.

Shortly after the chaplain's call, Ben walked the three short blocks from the jail to the church, carrying only his meager belongings and a very gracious spirit. After seven months in jail he was exuberant about his release and extremely remorseful about the incident of child molesting. He said, "I did what I did while I was drunk. I am so very sorry for what the little girl and her family had to go through and the memories with which they have to live."

I gave him a hug and took him upstairs to the Upper Room. I thought he would never let go when we embraced in the accepting love of God.

In outreach ministry one of the constants is the myriad of obstacles encountered. With Ben, for the first few hours, all obstacles seemed to be removed and there were no complications. Then, the expected happened.

As Ben sat in the day-room with the other residents, passing the time enjoying the first hours of freedom from incarceration, another resident read the evening newspaper. On the front page was the announcement of Ben's release. Ben must live with the searing memory of his crime. But must the media release it as public information? I still do not yet understand why that must take place.

Ben went home with me that evening, met my family, and then we attended an A. A. meeting together in a nearby city. The meeting had no sooner started when I was asked to come to the telephone, something which almost never happens at a meeting. That which we had hoped would not happen was beginning to transpire.

The director of the Upper Room was calling. "The entire residency has come to my home to voice in unison their opposition to a child molester living with them." Thinking fast, I told her that I would meet with all of them after the A. A. meeting.

When I returned to the meeting, Ben looked at me with eyes which reflected deep rejection and defeat. Somehow he knew and asked, "Is there trouble at the church?" My response was one of anger and brokenheartedness, "Yes." And then I said, "You will not have to go back to jail. We will discuss it after the meeting."

The remainder of the A. A. meeting was for Ben a complete loss. He was wondering where he would spend the night. (Homeless people, although they spend endless nights sleeping in the streets, do not want to do so if they can sleep elsewhere.) Even though I had said he would not have to go back to jail, he still was asking himself, "Will I have to go back to jail for an unlimited stay until my trial?" Could he get into the mission this late at night? Would they take him if they knew the situation? I remember touching his arm in a supporting gesture and saying, "You can stay at my house if things do not work out at the church." He heaved a deep sigh of relief. No more jail.

When we returned to the Upper Room, all of the residents were in the day room, sitting in a circle. I told them the meeting would not last very long, and then I shared with them my personal pilgrimage of recovery from alcoholism.

I began by telling them how the people of First Church had given me loving support as I started the recovering process. I explained to them that they had a place to stay that night because the church had witnessed my recovery and wanted the same opportunity for anyone who had personal problems.

As the conversation continued, I shared with them that I realized how difficult it was for them to change their attitudes about Ben, but that they had to know that members of the church at the beginning of the Upper Room had been adamantly opposed to the venture that was now housing them. These First Church members had a very difficult time changing, but some of them were presently supporting the ministry with their time and money. I pointed out that the Upper Room residents now have warm beds, food, and financial and emotional support because the people of First Church were open to God and were willing to accept them.

Although most of the residents responded lovingly and positively to this message, one continually voiced her opposition. "All I can think of is how he laid in that jail cell for seven months thinking about little girls."

This antagonist was the very person who had called me three months earlier, asking if she could come from Atlanta and live in the church so she could be in the same community with her children. If she had a place to live in South Bend, she thought she could begin a new life. Beth's feeling toward Ben serves as an incessant reminder of how the recently liberated can become so quickly oppressive.

I had known Beth before she called to ask for housing. I met her initially at an A. A. meeting where I had spoken. After the speech she said, "I am coming to your church this Sunday." She came the next Sunday and many of the following Sundays.

Subsequently, I discovered that Beth was cross-addicted, supporting her habit by prostitution. She turned cheap tricks just a few blocks west of the church. I had come to know Beth very well, as she attended several A. A. meetings with me. Knowing her as well as I did, I felt free in the resident's meeting to ask her to share how it happened that she was living in the Upper Room. She said, "I could not tell them that!" I pushed her hard. "Go ahead, Beth. Tell them how you called from Atlanta. Tell them what you were doing in Atlanta. Tell them how you were welcomed with no questions asked. Tell them how you support your habits turning ten-dollar tricks."

Before Beth could respond, an eighteen-year-old boy who was sitting opposite her in the circle, a person you would not assume knew anything about the Bible said, "You've got the story all wrong. You are the whore throwing the first stone."

There was a stunned, but holy silence. In that moment the Holy Spirit came, the group was one in purpose, and even Margaret, (whose children had been victims of molestation by their father, who was serving out his sentence in a Texas prison), with tears streaming down her face, said, "He deserves a chance and we should help him make it back."

I polled the circle, asking each person what they felt about Ben living there; and, to the person, including Beth, they said, "Let him live here." Winston said it best. "The church has given me chance after chance. [He was back in the Upper Room for the fourth time.] I have lied. I have stolen from them, conned them, torn up church property; and, yet, they still welcome me back. Who am I to say Ben cannot live here?"

Then the beautiful happened, something one is not fortunate enough to see in the church very often. The director had Ben come into the room. The residents, one by one, walked toward him, embraced him, and welcomed him home. Beth and Margaret grew tremendously in that moment. As they embraced Ben they felt the touch of grace in their own lives.

Going home that evening, I gave thanks to God for the presence of the Holy Spirit that brought the group together as a reconciling community. I could go home and rest easy — for one night. The next day at the church, the day-care director wanted to see me. She had read the paper the night before; and, now, she informed me of an Indiana law which stated that a child molester could not be present on the same premises as a day-care center.

Why is it so difficult to do God's work? Ben was working in the building. I found him and informed him of the new development. Once again fear registered the deep defeat that had been his constant companion throughout life.

I assured him we would work on the problem together. There would be no more jail for him. The question was: How would we work on the jail problem? The alternatives were narrowing. When the director came home that evening, I shared the day's complications with her. She immediately responded, "I do not know why I did not think of it last night. Ben can live at my house."

Once again God was at work. There were no other complications. Ben began the long way back. He worked long hours on an ice cream route, and then he found a new job, driving trucks across the country.

Months later I walked out of my office, and there was

Ben. He was a few pounds lighter. He had a sober glow about him. He was immaculately dressed. He had not had a drink in over a year. He had made amends with the family of the little girl he had molested. He gave me a big hug and we talked for awhile. The defeat in his face was gone. He was truly alive! It is so very important to get the story straight. That was his story — but there was Beth.

Wouldn't it be wonderful if the story could stop there? It did for Ben, but not for Beth. A few months later she was arrested. She had smoked pot and had drunk "mad-dog hootch" for an entire day. Later the policeman told her that, while she was in that condition, she had stabbed an old wino and taken twenty dollars from him. The stabbing was serious and put the man's life in danger — a life in grave danger for twenty dollars. But addicts care little for life, theirs or anyone else's. The addict demands satisfaction for the moment and often at unbelievable prices. For Beth the price was twenty years in prison, a year for every dollar.

Because Beth was experiencing one of her periodic blackouts, she did not remember stabbing the old man. In her jail cell, a few days after her arrest, she was very alert, but the night of the stabbing was completely gone from her memory. To this day, as she is serving time, she does not remember the event leading to her arrest and incarceration.

I will never forget her trial. None of her family was present. Her estranged husband was not there. She had been forsaken except for one of her procurers and her pastor. I will never forget the look on her face as she turned to me and said, "Twenty years! Twenty years is a long time. My two children will be grown when I get out of prison."

During my many visits to the local jail after the trial, while she was waiting to be transferred to the state prison, she talked to me about her relationship with Christ. While in jail, she had accepted Christ's love for her. As she writes me now from the state prison she asks about Ben. She tells me she loves me and instructs me to take care of her "street people."

She has the story straight now, but what direction would her life have taken had she understood the story sooner? For Ben's successful pilgrimage, I rejoice. For Beth I weep. She haunts me. Does she haunt you? There are people like her in your surroundings. O God, let us know the urgency of getting the story right. Entire lives depend on it. Tell it! Tell it! Tell it!

Chapter Two

The Call That Changed My Life

And they went through the regions of Phrygia and Gala-
tia, having been forbidden by the Holy Spirit to speak the
word in Asia . . . Come over into Macedonia and help us.
(Acts 16:6, 9)

Let me now tell you how this climate of compassion
came into existence. First, let me say that the people who
share in the ministries described in this book were already
present. They had been faithful to the claims of Christ over
the years. Their faithfulness, fired by a new vision, was
going to lead them to a place of mission which they could
not possibly have envisioned. I, as their new pastor, could
not have known where our new relationship was going to
lead.

The journey began in another city one hundred miles
to the south. In 1976 I was thoroughly enjoying the third
year of a pastorate that held nothing but exciting horizons
for me. The Frankfort church was one where you could
build a personal kingdom and continue to have your messianic propensities stroked. The Frankfort church was the
epitome of what any United Methodist pastor could want,
and I owe much to that wonderful group of Christians.

Frankfort is a county seat town. The church had one
thousand members and the colonial style sanctuary had just
been newly constructed. Every Sunday morning the sanctuary was overflowing and chairs were brought in for the
crowd. We went to two services, new members were uniting with the church, study groups were being formed,
money was no problem, and pastor-people relationships
were spontaneous and deep. "What more could I want?"
I asked myself. And then the telephone in the church kitchen
rang.

I remember the night of the phone call vividly. We all

have a tendency to remember those times when God's purposes take precedence over our precious plans. The Administrative Board that evening had just voted to build a new parsonage (my family and I had never had the privilege of living in a new parsonage); and, in addition, had decided to give me a sabbatical to work on my doctorate, and also, a four-week vacation. Not a bad night's work for an Administrative Board. On that same evening we were finalizing plans to take fifty youth to Florida; and then the church secretary said, "The District Superintendent wants you on the phone." It was the moving time of year. I had only been at Frankfort for three years. What would he want with me? I was soon to find out.

He said, "The Bishop wants you to go to South Bend First Church." Immediately a whole scene and conversation which had taken place the previous Sunday flashed before me. At a district conference being held at the Frankfort church, I had been talking to a pastor before the convening of the conference. He related that a dear friend of ours had been appointed to First Church in South Bend. I remember saying, "I am glad it is his appointment. I would not touch it with a ten-foot pole." The pole was getting shorter. Obviously my friend's appointment had not materialized. Now I was being asked to pastor a church that in no way that I could imagine held any of the promise that the Frankfort appointment provided me.

"I do not want to go." What a ridiculous response, when I was being given the privilege to pastor one of the great and historic churches in the state. The District Superintendent said, "You go home and think about it." That usually means, "Call me in the morning and give me your decision." Well, my decision in the morning was going to be, "No," just as it was "No" in that moment.

I went home that night in a numbed, stunned state. "Stunned" is the only word that described my very confused state, and "stunned" does not begin to describe the intense confusion taking place inside me at that time. Really no words describe the suggested detour in my life that had been put before me that evening.

After a thorough discussion with my wife, the "No" was clearer than it was the night before. I told the Superintendent I wanted to stay in Frankfort. My family was happy. My work at the church was just beginning. The Superintendent said, "You could at least talk to the South Bend Superintendent. Drive up and see the situation." I agreed to the suggestion.

The drive north held no anticipated excitement for me. I really wanted to be back home. The farther I drove, the more acute the uncertainty became. The city scared me. The immensity of the building convinced me I did not belong there. The Superintendent's lurings did not lessen my personal ambivalence. The next day I called both of the Superintendents involved and strongly reiterated my negative response. Both said, "Give it more time."

The following weekend I conducted a preaching mission in Winimac, Indiana, which is near South Bend. One of the fine lay persons from Frankfort accompanied me on the mission. While we were in Winimac, I asked him if he would like to drive up to South Bend and see the church the cabinet had asked me to pastor. We left for the north.

When we walked into the church, there were three people in the hallway of the educational building. The building of eighty-one rooms was virtually empty. I knew for sure this place was not for me. The sanctuary and its expansiveness only further convinced me that an emphatic, "NO!" was the right decision. But the promptings of the Spirit are not easily thwarted by our fears nor our final decisions.

That evening at Winimac I was at peace — for a while. I was preaching a mission, something I love to do. My best friend was with me. I was going to stay at Frankfort. All was well. So I thought, but God had other plans.

Before the evening service at Winimac, I went into the chapel to pray, a dangerous practice to pursue when you are running from God. The windows of the chapel were named after various saints. One of the windows was named Saint Matthew, the name of the church in Frankfort. The next thing I noticed was the united fellowship banner which carried the words, "Christ Above All." Did that mean Christ above Saint Matthew's in Frankfort? "Oh no, Lord. You are not going to do that to me. Such a coincidence cannot be a message from you. I do not believe you work that way. It is just some unresolved residue from the indecision of the past days. It will go away." But it did not.

In the service that followed, the opening hymn was "Praise To The Lord Almighty." The fourth verse contains the words: "Let the amen sound from the people again . . ." Could this mean that old First Church could come alive again? Sure it could mean that, but someone else could be the catalyst for such a happening. I was comfortable with my conclusion, but God was not of the same thinking.

The following week at home was one in which I was more than certain of my decision. I was glad the struggle had subsided. Things were back to normal. There would be no "farewells." My four sons would not have to leave the town and friends they loved. Sunday came with its usual uncanny regularity. I would leave for Florida in the afternoon.

I was standing at my study window watching the stream of cars coming early, so the people could get a good seat for the worship service. They had repeated that ritual for three years. As I watched them drive in, I thought to myself, how could I have ever entertained the idea of leaving such a fine situation? What I was really saying was: "How could my ego stand the absence of such recognition?"

The sanctuary was packed again. People were listening on the radio. (The church in South Bend did not have a radio broadcast and still does not have one.) I was preaching the sermon; and, *then*, God spoke to me. In the sermon a word came to me, a word which was clearer than anything I was saying to the people in that moment. I do not know to this day whether it was a voice direct from God. (I do not discount such experiences, but they have not been normal or recurring happenings for me.) I do not know whether it was a fleeting thought, but I did know without a doubt that it was a personal prompting — the strongest, most undeniable prompting from God that I had experienced up until that moment. The word that came was: "Gary, you really do love these crowds more than you love Me, don't you?" The struggle was over. I knew I was beginning the final months with the wonderful people who were listening at that moment. The time had come for me to do something for the church and not always be concerned about what the church could do for me.

That afternoon I told my wife, Marilyn, what had happened in the morning service. In her own loving manner she said, "I will go where you have to go." If we had known in that moment what the leaving was going to mean, perhaps she would not have been so willing. But D. T. Niles is exactly right when he says in his book, *The Message and Its Messengers*, "The devil always shows you the distant scene; he hides the precipice at the end of the road. God, on the other hand, makes only the next step plain."[1]

I called the Superintendent that afternoon and said I would go to the church in South Bend. That was the beginning of a journey that was to hold more than you could ask or think. Needless to say, the initial phone call weeks earlier instigated a "call" that would shape my calling for the years to come.

Chapter Three

The Darkness Where God Is

The light shines in darkness, and the darkness cannot put it out. (John 1:5)

I shared God's call with the Frankfort congregation. "It is time for me to go where the church calls, rather than follow my past pattern of letting the church always do for me." They graciously understood.

I detailed for them the situation and said it was certainly not going to be an easy situation. Parenthetically, let me suggest that incumbent pastors can do a great service for their successors by sharing forthrightly that they are going to move because they have chosen to do so, and not because of pressurized extenuating circumstances that are beyond their responsive control. Open honesty diffuses feelings that the congregation may possess as to the incumbent pastor being manipulated without consideration for his or her own desires. Such candidness prepares a healthy atmosphere for the congregation's relationship with the succeeding pastoral leadership.

Following that worship service in which I pictured the challenge and certain difficulty of the situation to which I had been called, Dr. William Briggs, one of the associate pastors, shared a word of wisdom which has sustained me more than once in present and future pastoral pressures. "There is a text in Exodus which states: 'Moses went into the darkness where God was.'" And then he said, "I would rather be in the darkness with God than in the light without God."

Usually when a person follows the clear call of God, the ensuing story is saturated with success episodes which leave the impression that the providence of the church issues in continual serenity of spiritual harmony. Would that this to be so. I did not realize how dense the darkness could become, partly because of erroneous leadership decisions on my part, partly because of an addiction that led me into the abyss, and partly because of an attempt to be faithful to the mission of Christ with its accompanying conflict which one would sooner not have to experience. However, the inevitability of conflict is inescapable.

Not being able to find the First Church building on the night we were to meet the pastor-parish committee was the first experience with the darkness. The stores and used car lots surrounding the building were well lighted, but only their reflection made it possible to see the foreboding silhouette of the place which was to be the context of my ministry for the next nine years.

But light does shine in the darkness, because inside was a small remnant who had a vision of what they thought the people of God in that place could become. They had no idea, nor did I, what the becoming would entail or mean in the years to come as the hopes began to become reality.

The directives from the initial meeting were clear. The committee said, "We want the building to be opened as a channel of witness to the city. We want the pastor to be a biblical preacher. We want the pastor to call on the people." It was indeed a challenging charter for any pastor.

In the months to come, after my arrival, in order to begin realization of these hopes, the Council of Ministries met in retreat for two days. After receiving input from the entire congregation, the Council shaped a missional purpose for the body of Christ in that locale. Nine years later the purpose still appears on the front of the worship bulletin, directing the ministries of the church. The purpose reads as follows:

1. To proclaim God's love to all people as shown in Jesus Christ.

2. To provide a Christian community in which to grow.
3. To demonstrate and reflect God's love through all of our relationships.
4. To look for hurts and allow God to heal those hurts through us.

The most intense struggle in shaping the purpose came at the point of including Jesus Christ in the first statement. It astounded me, but later observations revealed that religious syncretism and Unitarian influence had permeated their theological perspectives, more than had the redemptive dynamic of Jesus Christ. (This is a stance not entirely strange to other churches.) However, in any church, there are those who understand the unique person of Jesus Christ and the importance of Christ's reconciling act in shaping the authentic mission of the church. God always has a faithful remnant in the local church. The remnant remains tenaciously committed to Christ, which results in the church coming alive when leadership recognizes their presence and subsequently frees them for faithful expression of their discipleship.

The importance of the first statement was to determine events in the years to come. The bishop asked if the church would include a black pastor on the staff. This always seemed a strange request to me: A Christian bishop asking a Christian church to act in a Christian manner, but I understood the concern that motivated the bishop's request.

If we were to proclaim the love of God to all people, a good place to start would be to evidence an open itinerancy; to say to the black people of the community that First Church takes the "all" seriously by including a black person on the pastoral staff of the church. For three months meetings were held to discuss what such an inclusion would mean to the witness of First Church. Point one of the purpose was always present in the discussions.

I remember well the first meeting in the Americana Hotel with Roger Gay, an attorney and pastor-parish chairperson, and Bill Welsheimer, a well respected funeral director, community leader, and life-long member of the church. Roger Gay, who has since died, brought the meeting to a conclusion by saying, "It will be difficult. Some people in the church will oppose the decision, but I know Jesus Christ is for it and so am I. I will support the action." Mr. Welsheimer felt the same way and voiced the same support.

The first of many changes to come was on its way. Many meetings with congregational leaders followed. Mr. Gay received numerous phone calls from people expressing opposition to the new direction, but he remained faithful to the Christ he loved. It was not by accident that Dr. Robert Dungy, now Dean of the Upper Room Chapel, became one of Roger's closest friends and was more than a faithful pastor during Roger's terminal illness a few years later.

The new senior pastor, who had been so graciously accepted five months earlier, was also receiving anonymous phone calls from those who said that the church did not think that their new pastor was going to be a "nigger lover." The darkness set in for a while and then left for a season, but in the first seasons of darkness it was very dark. But when the light of God started to shine through the "all," the darkness could not put it out.

An Administrative Board meeting was held in September of 1976 in order to take the final vote on open itinerancy at First Church. The meeting had the largest attendance of any Administrative Board meeting I had ever experienced. A large contingency of non-board members was present. After a thorough discussion, the decision to include Dr. Bob Dungy on the pastoral staff was passed. There were no dissenting votes.

Mr. J. Alvin Taylor, one of the faithful older leaders of

the congregation, said, "I have polled the non-voting members present, and we want to go on record as wholeheartedly supporting the action of the board." The "all" was permeating the people of God. Robert Dungy came to serve as a friend and loyal colleague for five wonderful and fruitful years.

All was not over, however. The night of this memorable meeting was one of the most delightful experiences of my ministry, but the morning after afforded me one of the guiding directives for my future ministry. The next morning, when I arrived at the office, there was a note instructing me to call a certain person in the church who had been present at the meeting the night before. I thought the worst. I can now gratefully say that my perspective has vastly improved. It is so much better to exhaust the positive before the negative is considered.

I knew that the person who left the note for me to call was not in favor of a black pastor. When the person answered the phone, he said, "I do not agree with the action of the board last night, but I know it was the right thing to do. I want you to know I mailed a $1,000 check this morning to go towards the new pastor's salary." What a Christian witness! If you do not agree with an action, but you know it is Christian, support the action and your growth in Christ will take on deep and lively dimensions. The "all" was beginning to work its way in one more person.

The action with regard to a black pastor could not have taken place without the thorough initiation and support of the denominational connectional structure. The bishop initiated the process. The cabinet wrote a suggested procedure by which the inclusion could happen. The local laity were faithful in tense times. And the activity of the Holy Spirit through the structure was present at every juncture.

One of the factors cared for by the structure was to

provide a percentage of the salary support. In a day when many Christians look at denominational connectional structure with more and more suspicion, this incident speaks pertinently to the fact that when the structures are open to God's leading, God does work through the connectional channels to bring about his inclusive purposes. We found at First Church that the church at large was committed to the "all" and connectional structures are still the most viable means in existence for gospel imperatives to be realized.

There were two other groups that realized the importance of the church being faithful to the all-inclusive revelation of God's love in Jesus Christ: the secular press and the black community at large in South Bend.

The following was expressed in the South Bend Tribune:

> In a time when integration is discussed by many sectors,
> but not often acted upon, First United Methodist Church
> made real what the church says it believes by welcoming
> Reverend Robert Dungy, a black pastor, to its pastoral
> staff. First Church is to be commended for this action.

Can Jesus Christ get the attention of the secular world? Isn't it often true that Christ gets the secular's attention before he gets the attention of the church? This fact should continually challenge the witness of every congregation.

The black community of the city was also influenced by the action. They believed that First Church meant business, and today through the outreach ministries, the worship services, and an inclusive membership, black people are a vital part of the church's life.

Permit me one more thought on this matter. One of the reasons the city terrified me was due to the fact that I was raised in a very small Indiana town. The question I often asked was, "How could a person from such small surroundings minister in the city, an environment which was totally foreign to him?" The large city and its related problems were frightening to me, but at one point I had been very well prepared.

God works in our lives long before we are aware there is a God who is working in us. In the town where I grew up there is a small university, and, at the close of World War II, students from other cultures comprised a large percentage of the student population. One such person was Willie Taylor, a black student from Jamaica, who was very active in my home church. Once, during the pastor's absence, the pastor had made arrangements for Willie to be an usher and help receive the morning offering. A powerful person in the church and the community refused Willie the opportunity of his appointed participation. My mother heard the conversation which took place between the man and Willie before the worship service. Following the service, without any display, this very plain and simple woman, in the presence of the city's power structure, invited Willie to our home for Sunday dinner. Willie Taylor, in the ensuing years, along with numbers of his black peers, were dinner guests in our home on many different occasions. I began to learn about and relate with black people because of my mother's belief in the "all." The emphasis on inclusiveness was realized in a church years later because of this simple woman's commitment to the Gospel of Jesus Christ. The "all" did then, and always will, endure and the gates of hell cannot prevail against it. "The light shines in darkness and the darkness cannot put it out." God is in that darkness and to that extent the darkness is giving way to the light.

Chapter Four

A Building of God

And the Word became flesh and dwelt among us . . . (John 1:14)

For God so loved the world, that he gave his only Son . . . (John 3:16)

For many people the word "church" means the church building. We must continually capture anew the image of the church being the people of God. The building is where the body of Christ gathers for worship and koinonia. Even with this admitted recognition, buildings are an inextrica-ble part of the culture of Christendom; thus, an over-riding issue confronting contemporary Christianity is whether the building will be a witnessing extension of the body, or an impediment to the incarnational principle.

"Open the building to be a witness in the city." This was an initial directive of the pastor parish committee. They did not realize, nor did I, what this was going to mean for the daily ministry of their grand old structure. I certainly did not dream of what it was to become. God only asks our obedience for the first step. The ramifications of the obe-dience are entirely God's.

The Book of Discipline of the United Methodist Church states:

> Trustees shall not prevent or interfere with the pastor in the use of any of the said property for religious services or other proper meetings or purposes recognized by the law, usages, and customs of The United Methodist Church. (Discipline 1980, paragraph 2527, page 595)

Now it is certainly true that the local church trustees have responsibility for such functional matters as building structure, insurance, meeting local safety codes, trusts and estates, but the religious witness of the structure is the pastor's responsibility. The pastor must keep the channels of communication open with the Trustees and Administrative Board, but the pastor has the awesome responsibility for seeing that the building becomes and remains a visible and viable witness for Christ in the community. Nothing is more detrimental to a church's witness and presence in a community than a building that is solely used for the narrowed parochial purposes of the local members of the church. Pastors must understand the importance of this witness, and have the wisdom and courage to implement the disciplinary directives with regard to this witness.

The issue of course revolves around the phrase, "religious purposes." What does this mean? Some pastors and people interpret the directive to mean the pastor has use of the building for worship and "spiritual matters" only. But the Christian faith does not separate worship from ministry to the world. The incarnation of Jesus united once and for all worship and the world where people live their daily lives. Worship or the spiritual cannot be separated from the daily realities of people without finding itself subscribing to the earliest historical heresy facing the church — Gnosticism.

Gnosticism can have a structural-physical expression as well as a philosophical-theological one. Gnosticism was a system of thought that considered the material to be evil; and, therefore, the spiritual could have no traffic with the material. Gnosticism is the historical heresy that sees the church as being only interested in the spiritual aspects of life. The early church in its formative years saw the dangers to the church's witness which were involved in this expression of spiritual sophistication.

The church building must not be a purveyor of this heresy. When Gnosticism is applied to the structure, the building becomes an expression of the gnostic idea that Jesus

has separated himself and his people from fleshly involvement in the world. Jesus came in the flesh. Jesus died for
the world. Therefore, the building that bears Christ's name,
many of which are far too ornate for the One who had no
place to lay his head, must be liberated from structural
Gnosticism so it can be a fleshly witness for the world that
Jesus loves.

Recently, I read an article in the *Christian Century* (June
1984). It was an interview with Will Campbell, the maver-
ick Southern Baptist preacher and author. He said in the
article:

> When I am in the North, people luxuriate in my criti-
> cism of certain southern emphases in the Christian faith.
> They enjoy it when I scathingly criticize such groups as
> the PTL Club. They applaud when I mention that the
> money coming from the poor is used to build a condomin-
> ium for the Bakkers, a house which has a room with mir-
> rors so one can see the ocean from any angle. But what
> the folk of the North do not appreciate is when I suggest
> that this is not much different from their ornate structures
> which, with closed doors, cast their irrelevant shadows
> over the unwanted who pass their doors everyday. They
> are the pimps, winos, homosexuals, prostitutes, the dis-
> enfranchised, and the broken who know they are not wel-
> come in the cathedrals of the middle class.
>
> (Paraphrase)

When a local church in its building expression does not reach
out and minister with an open building policy to those that
pass by, it is an incarnation of the earliest heresy confronting the Christian church, and such a church is far removed
from the New Testament Gospel of Jesus Christ.

The importance of the open door was brought home to
me by one of First Church's staff members, as he accidently
needed the services of one of the other churches in the city.
It was in the latter part of the day. The church was in a

suburban area. The staff person was seeking aid for an indigent person. The doors were locked and a bell was attached near the door which bore the sign, "Ring To Be Let In." Nearby was an intercom. He rang the bell and a voice came over the intercom, asking the nature of their business. Phil explained the dilemma. The voice replied, "Go downtown to First United Methodist. They are open and they care for matters like that." When Phil related the events to me, my feelings were ambivalent at best. I was sad for the church that was closed and I was overjoyed for First Church. First Church is downtown, a much more dangerous area than suburbia, but the doors are wide open for all.

Let me relate another episode. I was speaking at a conference for the aging at the Century Center, the city's convention center. After the presentation, a United Methodist lay person asked to visit the church to observe the outreach programs. Following the visit the lady called me to voice her delighted surprise that she had actually found the front doors of the church open. This is an experience now witnessed by more than 4,000 people weekly who frequent the halls of the church.

Certainly the Scripture is replete with instances where the openness of God's people and hospitality are expressions of God's love for the world. In fact Scripture has some hard words about the lack of hospitality and unwillingness to serve the world. Surely the building of God, set apart for God's work, cannot escape the direction of Scripture with regard to the fact that authentic worship results in an incarnational witness to the people of the world. 1 John says, ". . . for he who does not love his brother whom he has seen, cannot love God whom he has not seen." (1 John 4:20) The structure must evidence, and does so, either positively or negatively, the teaching of this scriptural injunction. Henrik Kraemer, the Dutch theologian, has a word for us here. He says, "Every Christian needs two conversions. The first conversion should be to Christ and the second to the world." The church's buildings need conversion to the world that they are called to serve.

The secular community knows that a church building should be an expression of the Gospel it claims to possess. The community also knows that the witness is extended or impeded by the church's willingness to open its doors to the community. The church that refuses to take this mandate seriously will not only receive the scorn of the community, but the community will soon discount what the church professes to claim. What could be a more devastating judgment on the church than to have the world respond to the fact that the church does not believe its own message. The manner in which our buildings are used sends forth a message one way or the other.

Shortly after I arrived as pastor, some lay persons and I visited key people and agencies in the downtown and its surrounding environs. Almost to the person, they expressed the concern that First Church had withdrawn from involvements in the city; they were not certain of our intent to carry out our stated intentions. After the visits, the lay persons were shocked at how the city experienced and perceived the church. Whether the observations were altogether valid could have been debated; but, nonetheless, that is how the community saw the church. Perceptions are often more determinative than realities, although in these observations the perceptions were very close to reality. The church, by and large, had isolated and insulated itself from the downtown and the immediate surrounding community. The lay persons agreed unanimously. "We must change this image." And change it they did! An open-building policy became the expression of an open, all-inclusive Gospel.

The building has eighty-one rooms and, at the present time, sixty-seven of the rooms are used daily. The least used, of course, by its very nature, is the sanctuary, although even this room is used many times a year for concerts, black revivals, and United Methodist district gatherings.

We have helped start four black churches. When the Serbian Orthodox Church burned, they worshiped in the church's chapel for a year. Before they moved into their new facility we shared in a worship service with them in First Church's sanctuary. To our knowledge it was the first Protestant-Serbian worship service ever held in the United States. I was present when they dedicated their new facility and they were very effusive in their appreciation for the ministry of hospitality which was extended to them by First Church in their time of need. A few years later when First Church was celebrating its sesquecentennial anniversary, one of the high points occurred when Father Suca, along with one of the Serbian lay persons, presented Bishop James Armstrong with a $500 check for First Church's ministry of hospitality to the Serbian church.

The church also has a relationship with the charismatic community in South Bend. This community is one of the largest charismatic concentrations in America. Their offices are located one block from First Church. We have also housed Unity and black Islam groups. I am very aware that the two previously mentioned groups are not in the mainstreams of Christian tradition, but our missional mandate is to witness to the world, and these groups are part of that world.

Other groups who find their residence at First Church are Emotions Anonymous, Alcoholics Anonymous, Drugs Anonymous, Take-Off Pounds, five classes of English as a second language, a refugee day care center, a refugee nursery school, a family-counseling center, a job-counseling center, senior citizens, a soup kitchen, a furniture repair shop, an art studio, a cello teacher's studio, forty Suzuki violin students, food co-ops, school banquets, hospital groups, a church day-care, a community nursery school, the Upper

Room temporary housing, tutoring programs, a food pantry, political forums, Laubach literacy office, Women's International League, community child co-operative, blood pressure clinics, voter registration centers, government food distribution center, senior citizens nutrition site, and a variety of community clubs. The building is also used for numerous black church events such as style shows and congregational dinners, the Michiana Children's Chorus, the Young Life Office, an addictions counseling center, and various business training seminars are conducted on the premises. Monetary charges are not exacted for the building's use. If a group can afford to help with the utility costs, contributions are accepted.

When a congregation uses its building in such a way, it can be readily seen that maintenance monies are really used in a missional sense. It is true that such services do not result in immediate evangelistic returns in the sense of increasing institutional strength. However, authentic ministry is difficult to measure, and only the Holy Spirit knows how God is using these ministries for the sake of the Kingdom of God. Knowing that God knows and is active is enough.

Detailed administration is necessary when a building is used in a missional sense. Operational policies must be written and constantly updated. Constant efforts at communication become a priority. A building coordinator and a business manager are important, and a committed and understanding staff is of the utmost importance. In fact, our people are brought on the staff when it is known they will be dedicated to these types of ministry. Needless to say, this is especially true of the custodial staff, since a horrendous amount of work is theirs as the building ministers via the incarnational principle.

Today, when I go into the building, I no longer think of a church building. My mind instead turns to a structure that houses the body of Christ in worship and is a channel of missional expression in its daily outreach to the world. Paul said, "God was in Christ reconciling the world unto Himself . . . So we are ambassadors for Christ, God making His appeal through us." (2 Corinthians 5:19-20) Certainly the building which bears Christ's name, and through which God makes a portion of his appeal, is an inextricable part of his reconciling purpose. When such is the case, it can truly be referred to as "a building of God."

Chapter Five

Into the Ground

. . . that you being rooted and grounded in love, may have power to comprehend . . . and to know the love of Christ which so passes knowledge, that you may be filled with all the fulness of God. (Ephesians 3:18-19)

In a recent telephone conversation, someone, opposed to the direction the church had taken, said to me, "You are turning First Church into a mission church. You are driving it into the ground." I can think of no greater compliment even though it was made as a caustic criticism. There is, however, one mistake in the statement. No pastor turns a local church into a mission church. Jesus did that by the very nature of his ministry and person, and mandated its continuation in the Great Commission: "Go into the world and preach the gospel to the whole creation." (Mark 16:15) The pastor and people together through the disciplines of prayer, Bible study, sensitivity to the leading of the Holy Spirit, open discussion, courage, and willingness to obey, open themselves to flesh out what Jesus had already said would be the nature of the church. In fact, the very ground of the church's existence is the willingness to allow Jesus, through us, to drive the church into his grounds for the purpose of building authentic Christian mission. Emil Brunner helps us articulate the purpose of the church when he states, "The church exists by mission as fire exists by burning."[3] The church must be driven to the ground of Jesus and become a mission church, if it is to claim the name "church" at all.

The emphasis on the mission nature of the church provides the backdrop as to the various groups that exist in the context of First Church. There are several different categories of groups. There are groups to which the church ministers by allowing the building to serve as their residence and base of operation. There are outreach ministries which evolve as a result of the church's life together. Resident-type ministries are under the diligent administration of the pastor via disciplinary directives. The outreach ministries arise from the missional planning of the congregation, as the people live under the Bible and the stated purposes of First Church.

. Each ministry described in the subsequent chapters is under the leadership of a lay board. The pastor is aware of all that takes place, but is rarely in attendance at the administrative meetings of the various ministries. Lay persons are very willing to work in these areas because they feel a sense of personal Christian investment. It is much better, as one lay person said, to be involved in concrete missional witness than to be sentenced to a commissional work area for life. So often the latter groups exist to produce programs for program's sake alone, and people feel they are being used to justify the existence of an institution. People will invest themselves in ministries which meet the needs of people and carry out the ministry of Jesus. Where there is lay involvement the program does not exit with the absence of the pastor, nor does it cease when there is a pastoral change.

Since its early beginnings, First Church has had a history of outreach in the community. As one of the oldest congregations in Indiana, First Church was established in 1831, one year after the city was founded. The first report of the South Bend mission was in the Illinois Conference general minutes of 1832. From these modest beginnings came the other Methodist churches in the city, which originally were Sunday school missions, except for one group who left over the purchase of an organ. Interestingly enough, that church now has one of the finest music programs in the city and a very fine organ too.

First Church founded the North Indiana College in the late 1850s. Until a building was constructed the classes were held in the church building. The little college, dedicated to the cause of Christian education, folded in 1866 because it was not able to survive the financial and manpower drain of the Civil War.

A black church was founded by the pastor in the 1850s. The idea underlying this action was a concern to evangelize the blacks, but it was not intended to incorporate them into the already existing congregational structures. This pattern continued until the 1970s except for one or two black families. In the late 1970s, more black people started to attend and unite with the church, and many minority people are now daily involved in the outreach programs. Recently, two black persons have chaired the Administrative Board.

From 1869 to 1913 the church experienced a growth period of outreach. The church founded the public library and also what was to become one of the city's hospitals. The hospital's establishment reveals the mission impetus of those early Methodists. In 1893 an unwed mother came to the city looking for a place to live, and soon another came. The women of the church brought two deaconesses to the city and, with that impetus, a home for unwed mothers was begun. On January 8, 1896, the Women's Society formed a corporation, and Epworth Hospital came into being as well as did the nursing school. From this small beginning of three beds came the five-hundred bed regional Memorial Hospital and nursing school which, presently, is undergoing expansion. In connection with the hospital, the women founded the Visiting Nurses Association and the city's Y.W.C.A.

At the present time, as is true with many contemporary churches, there is an intense feeling on the part of some of the church's membership that religion and politics should remain separate. This is especially the case if the political-religious views of the pastor are not consistent with the majority feeling of the congregation. If these feelings were similar, then a political-religious wedding would be acceptable. The concern that the two be separate does not find support in the historical precedent of the early history of First Church. After the Billy Sunday Crusade of 1913 the membership of the church formed the Citizen's Party. The party originated because the church people were opposed to the open platform fostered by the corruption of the Republican and Democratic parties. The Citizen's Party elected the mayor and the city judge. Historical reality has a way of challenging present mind sets with regard to ancestorial action, especially in the area of political and religious interaction.

In the 1950s two other socially significant developments emerged. There was the feeding program which was one of the first federally-funded programs of the United States, and there was the establishment of the Budget Corner, a consignment clothing store which opened its doors in 1959. The Corner is still in existence, having just celebrated its twenty-fifth anniversary.

The Corner was started by eight women who received the support of the W.S.C.S. upon recommendation by Dorothy Lindley. The Corner started in a small building and within five and one-half months had outgrown its original quarters. In 1972 the store moved to its present site which is a large commercially-oriented store.

The Corner in its twenty-five year existence has raised $414,940.96. One-third of the money is given to local and United Methodist mission projects, and two-thirds of the money is returned to the consignees. Unsold clothes are given to the Goodwill and the Upper Room.

Two-hundred volunteers, along with two paid managers, work the store. Some of the volunteers come from other churches in the city. One of the great benefits, other than the money raised, is the fellowship and meaning given to the workers, especially those people who are retired. The

Corner has been an evangelistic outreach in that people who work in the store have united with First Church. Certainly this underscores the fact that the unchurched are attracted to congregations which are expressing Christ's purpose through social missional outreach.

Let us return to the phone conversation to which we referred at the beginning of this chapter. "You are making First Church into a mission church." It is strange indeed that someone should say such a thing, especially if they had historical contact with the ministry of Jesus and the history of the church to which they belonged. Precedents for a mission church were established long ago by Jesus of Nazareth, by a group of South Bend Methodists who started as a mission, and now, in a real sense, First Church has returned to her original charter. A mainline church can be relevantly involved in mission, when it never loses sight of the fact that it, too, was a mission before it ever became mainline. Relationship with historical reality can give impetus for mainline Christianity to become a vital movement again, rather than being a lifeless monument that only considers its history, periodically, for the purpose of evoking nostalgic stirrings — which more often than not divert our attention from extending social holiness in the present age.

Chapter Six

When Yesterday Comes Home

*. . . look to the rock from which you were hewn, and
to the quarry from which you were digged. (Isaiah 51:1)*

The constant tendency of a local church with a great
history is that its members will glory in the past and neglect
the pressing mission demands of the present. Churches have
the uncanny ability to "pursue yesterday." Along with this
perspective, in a church's peak years, there is a tendency
to refuse to acknowledge trends of decline. Inclined to believe that the church can exist on the spiritual resources and
missional motivations of past generations, there is the in-
clination to assume that the cracks in the foundations are
not serious and will eventually disappear.

During the zenith of First Church's history, when the
church had in excess of 2500 members, the Administrative
Board decided the church had enough members and that no
intentional program of evangelism was necessary.

On another occasion, an occasion fraught with potential disaster, an appointed group conducted a thorough study
of emerging trends, many of which were institutionally terminal. When the committee submitted its findings, key
church officials disregarded the seriousness of the findings.
If such trends are not confronted and corrected, they will
come to their fruition. And they did!

New directions started to be realized years later, when
the leadership decided they were called to serve the present
age and surrounding community. I remember reading,
"Christians are those who read statistics with compassion."
One such lady was Dorothy Resseguie.

She had been the Christian education director for six
years. Dorothy always had a great concern for children. She

asked me one day what I thought about the church establishing a day-care center for children six weeks of age to three years old. There was no such center in the city. My response was, when you find a person like Dorothy with such a vision, you turn them loose and then stay out of their way.

After six months of intensive, thorough study and research, the Administrative Board voted to open what is now one of the largest centers in the country. The center cares for seventy-five babies, with a staff of twenty-five, two full-time directors and a budget in excess of $225,000.

The center, now in its eighth year, is administered by an incorporated board — composed of one-third church members, one-third parents of the center, and one-third people of the community. As pastor I kept in touch with their work through their minutes and director. I have only been to two board meetings in the history of the center. When lay people see the vision and have the expertise, there is no need for pastors to be omnipresent and omniscient. Every time I see the smiling faces of the children, the security of the mothers as I pass them in the halls, and the professionalism of the staff, I rejoice for lay people who see the challenge and exercise their ministry as they are freed to be faithful.

In the center there are some full-paying families, but most of the children are from low-income families and are the children of single parents. The center makes it possible for these parents to find personal dignity through work. In the time I have been associated with the center, I have not met a person who would rather be on welfare than working. The working mothers see welfare as a dehumanizing system. The mothers are thankful when their children can have a good start and good care, as they, in turn, experience what it is like to be worthwhile wage-earning people.

The association I have had with the center has made me more of a politically and economically oriented pastor than I had been before my contact with the center. Alan

Walker, in one of his books, is certainly correct when he states that in the future the Gospel will be fashioned in terms of economic witness. It does very little good to see people come to Christ and then send them back into a society where they are oppressed by pathological societal structures. The only Christian who would think otherwise would be the "cultural Christian" who enjoys and extends by their affluent life style those same systems of oppression.

Recently, at a dinner in a plush dining room on the campus of a very wealthy United Methodist University, two very well-fed United Methodist pastors, myself included, became involved in a theological discussion. My colleague said that one famous theologian contends that, in the long pull of history, such matters as the "filoque" controversy, and what one feels about such matters, may be more important than some of our present-day concerns. A few weeks earlier I had just seen a child eating out of a day-care garbage bag. My response to my colleague was: "That may be true, unless you happen to be the person who is deprived of such present day concerns as bread, bed, and work." Now, for certain, it is not a matter of either/or , but Christians need to acknowledge that theological niceties and intricacies are, more often than not, the privilege of the middle class, taking place in plush surroundings, and sitting before a satisfactory meal. The poor are pressed by more immediate concerns.

Parenthetically, permit me to share the fact that in that conversation authentic theology was taking place. It was taking place in the midst of a conversational controversy. It seems to me that such is the context of theology. Christian theology is not a specialized subject of academia. Theology is done in the heat of discussion, when the church considers the exigencies of the real world to which it is called. Theology is done at board meetings, finance meetings, trustees meetings, and in a myriad of conversations such as the one mentioned above. When theology becomes simply an academic exercise, and when the institution sees it only within the confines of the academic, whether it be the seminary or a local church discussion group, rather than an instrument to serve the world, then theology has lost its *raison d'etre.*

During the conversation with my colleague, my mind remembered the time when the District Superintendent asked me if I would attend a jurisdictional meeting on hunger which was to be held at the Abbey in Lake Geneva, Wisconsin. I said that I would be glad to attend because I had wanted to visit a monastery for some time. Honest to God, I thought I was going to a monastery for a three-day seminar on hunger and the urban church. I was to learn upon my arrival that the Abbey is not a monastery, but instead is a luxurious multi-restauranted motel complex. Luxurious is a modest description. That first night I called my wife and remember saying to her, "Honey, this is not a monastery. I do not know how many restaurants and stores this place has. I have bath towels here larger than the drapes in the parsonage, and I need a map to find my way back to the room." I said to her, "When I returned to the room this evening, after one of the plenary sessions, the sheets were turned back and there were very tasty Swiss mints placed on the pillows."

I should have known better. If I were going to a United Methodist conference on hunger it certainly would be held in ·a place like the Abbey. But you do not minister in my local context without saying some earnest prayers of repentance, when you are in such plush surroundings as you discuss the plights of the oppressed.

Humorously, I thought to myself, "Well, Gary, if you are going to suffer for Jesus, you might as well do it in style." Carlyle Marney reported a similar episode. When he went to Myers Park Baptist Church in Charlotte, North Carolina, a thought kept going through his mind as he would drive up to that elegant church structure from his luxurious parsonage. He said, "Lord, I have given it all up for you."[4] During that night at the Abbey, I longed for the huddled masses which compose my pastoral context. How can I be comfortable in surroundings like the Abbey, when I know people I minister to are sleeping in trees, culverts, and Salvation Army drop boxes?

My pastoral context has made me thoroughly aware of the present political and economic issues. It is impossible to separate the effects of federal budget cuts from real prophetic religion. Oppressive economics that cut food programs for day-care centers and decrease other monies which are integral to the support of such programs must be challenged. The Christian Gospel demands the opposite of dehumanizing people. When there are not monies for adequate day-care, single mothers cannot leave their babies in a decent place, so they in turn can go to work. When they do not work, they go on welfare; and then they are called "lazy" by the adherents of the presently accepted political context.

It is not wise to make "prayer in the schools" an issue when people do not have enough food at their tables over which to pray. It is time for the other side, the oppressed and their advocates, to continually voice their concern, so that people do not have to experience a continual hell of no work and the dehumanization which accompanies such political policies. The Bible says nothing about a trickling-down economy, but it does say that "justice should roll down like waters and righteousness like an ever flowing stream." (Amos 5:24)

When I read about the billions being spent worldwide on armaments, and watch a single mother have to take her child out of a day-care center because of budget cuts, thus forfeiting her job, I cannot help but become a Christian,

politically concerned, who must challenge such political per-
versions. The recent words of former President Richard
Nixon, spoken before the press association, ring in my ears,
"At least the Communists know what the problems of the
world are: poverty and self-determination. Only the present
administration thinks the problem is Communism." And,
in an attempt to eradicate Communism without paying heed
to the more systemic issues, the United States has histori-
cally fostered the possibility of Communism's further
growth, often becoming as devilish as the devil we combat.

This outlook reminds me of a parishioner in another
congregation. At her home for Sunday dinner, she and her
husband explained that they had lived in Cuba most of their
lives. He worked for one of the major fruit companies; and
she cared for, and helped educate, a young boy: Fidel Castro.
She told me, following dinner, that she did not understand
how Fidel, such a fine boy, could have turned out the way
he did. A few moments later she was relating how the fruit
company used to bring in boat loads of people from other
Caribbean countries to work in the fields for a yearly pit-
tance. She was totally unaware of the relationship between
the two events, and she had been in the church her entire
life. Something had gone seriously awry.

Often people in the church criticize the presence of the
day-care center in the church building because government
funds help support it. When this happens, I direct their attention to the following episode:

One day a two-year-old came to the center as usual.
When one of the workers was giving her the morning bath,
she could not bathe the child's genital area because it was
bleeding. It was obvious that someone had hideously
molested her. Government monies made it possible for the
condition to be discovered. Government monies made it possible for the child to receive psychological care, and the

government monies made it possible to investigate the conditions surrounding the situation. The child was helped, as was the parent. Multiply this over the country, hundreds of times a day, and any amount of government money which supports day-care seems minuscule. In fact, money spent in such a manner gives credence to the phrase, "government for the people" — the little people. And such monetary expenditures give concrete expression to the principle that government is to provide for the welfare of the people — one of the guarantees of the Constitution. People who are opposed to such use of monies fail to understand the basic premises of American society and the Christian Gospel, in all of their personal ramifications.

Government monies made it possible for a Vietnamese baby to be in the center. She was in the center for three years. The center was responsible for teaching her about her new surroundings, teaching her how to speak English, teaching her how to relate to a different race and nationality, and for giving her parents an opportunity to work. She is a part of the huddled masses that this nation and the Christian church have always welcomed. The little girl is one of the strangers to which Jesus refers in Matthew twenty-five. Separating faith and government is only done by those who have forgotten that they, too, were once part of the huddled masses, and whose Christianity is nothing but cultural Baalism at its best.

The center also makes it possible for Memorial Hospital to increase its nursing force, because working nurses leave their children at the center and work at the hospital which is two blocks from the church. The hospital has equipped a center room and also provides materials for the center. In addition, the center has become a laboratory observation place for Memorial nursing students, as it is also for nursing and education students from St. Mary's College, Bethel College, and Indiana University at South Bend.

Jesus said, "Let the little children come to me for such is the Kingdom of God." (Matthew 19:14) Well, the children are coming thanks to Dorothy Resseguie, monies from the government, the North Indiana Conference, and the dedicated visionary leadership of lay and professional people. Every morning when I go to my study I walk by the center. Sometimes the children are in the hall. They wave and smile at me. They are safe and secure while their parents are working and finding dignity in doing so. In those moments the conflict does not seem as present as usual; and, when it reasserts itself, the conflict is in subdued perspective. Passing by the center daily, I hear a voice from First Church past saying, "Yesterday has come home. The mission we began is continuing as was meant to be." "Remember the rock from which you were hewn and the quarry from which you were digged." (Isaiah 51:1)

Chapter Seven

Do You Have Anything We Do Not Have to Cook?

". . . for I was hungry and you gave me food . . ." (Matthew 25:35)

I had just left my car in the church's parking lot; and, nearby, there was a man going through the trash container trying to find food. Later on, I was standing in the hall, and a five-year-old had expectantly torn open a plastic bag containing the garbage from the day-care, exclaiming to his mother, "There is food over here!" Could this be taking place in South Bend, Indiana? Where had I been? Most likely, I had just come back from a dinner meeting with one of the church officials at an expensive restaurant, a meal which they had paid for, or which I would eventually voucher on my expense account.

Often there are people waiting for me following a worship service which they think has lasted too long. They wish that the service would be shorter so that they could get to the restaurants for Sunday dinner before the lines become too long — not realizing there are those who stand in longer lines every day for the only food they will eat that day, or for that matter, for several days.

"I was hungry and you fed me." (Matthew 25:35) They are still hungry. The hungry are still present. They need to be fed. They are as hungry as ever. Figures detailing how well the economy is doing do not alleviate their hunger. In fact, these figures, which often look good, simply mean that the unemployment index goes down because people who are eligible have kept the index up, and when they no longer qualify for benefits, they no longer appear in the figures. Such a variable makes unemployment appear less than it is, but the unemployed are still without jobs and food. They are still hungry, and there are as many demands on the church's food pantry as ever. There are more people joining the food co-op, and there are as many eating in the soup kitchen.

The food-for-the-hungry program of the church has been around for eleven years because of the admirable work of a former pastor who challenged the congregation to fast one day a week and to give the money they would have spent on meals to the hungry. In the beginning, one-fifth of the money stayed for local hunger and the remaining went for world hunger. That practice has since changed so that now all of the money stays for the local hunger problem except when special offerings are taken for world hunger.

The monies for the local problem are raised by weekly specified offerings, and the people give about $3,000 a year to First Church's pantry program. The children also bring food on the first Sunday of each month. One of the outgrowths of the food program is that it has served as a model for other churches; and one such church, fifty miles away, contributes food to the pantry once a month.

At the outset, people who came for food were the transients of the street, but recently, the clientele has been people who are ashamed to ask for food. But when your family is hungry, it is not difficult to swallow your pride, if that means that you will, in turn have food to swallow. When people come for the food, no questions are asked. The reason for this is that the church should be a place where people do not have to experience the impersonal, as they do in lines of the welfare office, the food stamp office, and other government agencies. I have been to these places with people; and after one day of filling out forms and walking from one agency to another, people tend to lose their dignity, and also their motivation. Multiply that experience by a lifetime, and one begins to partially understand the frustration that eventually explodes into violence, cultural cynicism, and personal denigration. I can spend a few token days in these lines, but I can never fully experience the oppression, because I know I will not have to repeat the hopeless ritual again tomorrow in order to feed my family.

But there are guidelines for First Church's food distribution. The only negative guideline listed is with reference to alcoholics who are drinking at the time they ask for the food. It is not that the church is unsympathetic to their plight, as you will see in a subsequent chapter, but many of the alcoholics sell the food on the street to support their insatiable habit. We discovered this for certain when one of the people attempted to sell food to the Upper Room supervisor. It is impossible to know who all of these people are, so some of the food still exchanges hands after the people leave the pantry. Not giving food to a drinking person is what is known in some circles as "tough love." Giving food to addicts does not help them; it only enables them to further demean their lives. I am not totally satisfied with this reasoning, because some of the addicts do eat some food before they sell the remainder. They do have to eat, and that fact presents a dilemma that deserves more thinking than just extricating ourselves from the problem by saying, "If they want to eat they will have to stop drinking."

The food programs are administered by two ladies in their autumn years, Ruth Hamilton and Bea Moore. One can readily see that the argument which says older people are opposed to such outreach cannot find support. We have discovered that the aged make possible many of the programs in which we are involved. They have the time and the experience to give, and the outreach provides them with a sense of worth and mission. They personally know what hard times are like, and they know that the dire straits in which people can find themselves are mostly due to forces and factors beyond their control.

Bea Moore, a caterer by trade, because of her contacts, her personal Christian commitment, and her dogged determinism, has made it possible for the church to be a distribution center for government surplus food. We receive hundreds of boxes of food. The food stocks the pantry, is used in the soup kitchen, provides for the people who live in the church's temporary housing program, and is shared with other distribution sites in the city.

The people want to pay for the food if they can. To make this possible, the church founded a food co-op which was started on a trial basis for three months. It started in 1980 and now has grown to over four hundred members. The co-op has two paid workers and handles its orders through its own computer.

A key person in the co-op ministry is Tom Rockwell. Tom is a shut-in. He is one of the best known chefs and culinary experts in the United States, having spent a lifetime in the food industry. He has authored several cook books and has taught culinary art at several major universities. I first met Tom when I came to South Bend. He was in the hospital and was at the point of death. Needless to say, he has recovered and spends hours each week ordering food for the co-op, using the telephone at his home.

The co-op is open to all people. Food is purchased on a wholesale basis, and people can save up to forty percent on groceries. The produce is fresh and is secured on a prepaid pre-ordered basis. The people sack their own food and pick it up on Fridays. The membership is four dollars yearly, and this fee provides the basis of operational expense. After this initial fee the personal cost depends on what a person purchases. The co-op is authorized to accept food stamps, and is an outlet for the government cheese program. Food that is not picked up is given to the Upper Room housing program, whose people often do the physical set-ups for the co-op.

The co-op is administered by a visionary group of lay people. As pastor I have never been to a co-op board meeting. Through their efforts and continued vision they have started other programs which are extensions of the co-op. These are in the senior citizen centers and other churches in the South Bend area.

When a local church dedicates itself to intentional outreach, it becomes a model to other churches and gives them the impetus and hope that they can become involved in the lives of people through outreach programs. The co-op model has been shared with others through such efforts as mission saturation weeks within the districts or various other programs.

New members come as they hear about the co-op from other members. Also, each year in July the city has an ethnic festival which recognizes and celebrates the city's large ethnic diversity. Nearly 100,000 people visit the two-day festival each year. The church has an information booth at the festival which describes the various outreach ministries, and fliers for the food co-op are distributed to the people visiting the festival.

Even with the two above mentioned food programs, there was still a group of people who were not being reached. On one occasion a person who came to the pantry asked, "Do you have any food we would not have to cook?" Obviously this meant that they did not have the appliances with which to cook; and as a result, were not receiving the nutritious meals which they needed.

In a sermon one Sunday I related this concern. Following worship eight people came to me and said, "We would like to start a soup kitchen." The people were caterers, school teachers, a hospital nutritionist, and homemakers.

The Administrative Board authorized the program to be operated on a three-month trial basis. Again, I have been to just one of their administrative meetings. The kitchen is carried on by the active involvement of lay people. They started without any seed money, without any knowledge of such matters, but they had caring, compassionate, and willing hearts. They responded, and the kitchen became a reality which has now been in existence for four years.

The media was extremely helpful in the beginning stages. Though we did not ask the media to cover the kitchen, they heard about the ministry and asked if they could come and do stories about the work we intended to do. As a result of their interest, we shared some of the needs, and people in the community responded with such items as refrigerators and their own volunteer service.

From the beginning the money for the kitchen was raised by the offerings of church people. The kitchen was not in the operating budget of the church, but $12,000 was raised by offerings and varied contributions during the first year of the kitchen's operation. In addition to these monies, a local bakery owned by a Roman Catholic family gave the kitchen day-old pastries, a dairy gave powdered milk, and a bread company provided bread. The Saint James Episcopal men's group prepared vegetables and noodles each week. The Holy Cross House sent bones, and a dear friend from another parish sent $400 a year for the program.

One night Mrs. Moore and her husband, Ray, were eating in one of the finest restaurants in the city. She had the special of the evening, which was chicken prepared in a way that only used a small portion of chicken. She wondered what they did with the rest of the bird, so she asked to see the manager; and, now, the leftover parts of the chicken come to the soup kitchen. There are places in this hungry world for "parts, just parts."

Then a strange happening occurred one day. The captain of the local Salvation Army called and asked if we could give him information on how to begin and operate a soup kitchen. Things had come full circle from John Wesley to

William Booth to the Salvation Army kitchens to First Church now helping the Salvation Army organize their kitchen. In that moment both Wesley and Booth must have been rejoicing.

The soup kitchen prepared and served in excess of fifty thousand bowls of soup in two years. It employs one paid staff member. The kitchen is operated by people from First Church and other churches in the community. People in the Upper Room also work in the kitchen as part of their commitment to the church program and the kitchen has become a community work place for people of the Metcalf House, a half-way house for those recovering from mental illness. The hospital now sends some of its psychiatric patients to the kitchen in order to afford them some on-site occupational therapy.

In addition to eating on site, many persons carry soup and other food home so that they have something to eat on the days when the kitchen is closed. The carry-out is now about equal to the on-site consumption. Various groups of people eat at the kitchen, and no questions are asked with regard to their personal situations, but they are urged not to sell the soup on the streets in order to support addictive life styles. The kitchen clientele is composed of street people, families, Upper Room residents, people passing through the city, teenagers, and aging adults. As of late, we have noticed that there is an increasing number of single parents and their families.

We also operate the Budget Corner, which brings clothes to the people so that they will have warm clothing to wear during the horrendously terrible South Bend winters. Some of the people find their ways to the living quarters housed in the church, and they also take advantage of the other services in the building, such as the blood pressure clinics, sponsored by the city's Real Services agency on aging.

My father came to the kitchen one day. As a young man just out of high school he had worked in the Civil Conservation Corps. During the ensuing years he had become an active politician, serving as a county assessor for eighteen years. The soup kitchen brought back many memories for him. The next day, following his visit, I left the city for a preaching mission in Virginia. When I returned the next week, I discovered that my father had returned to the kitchen with money and clothes. He had remembered in a short time what he had spent a lifetime trying to forget. It certainly would be well for more people to experience such moments of stirred memories. If this were to happen with more regularity, the hardened, inflexible prejudicial stances which too many people espouse toward the poor would undergo radical alterations.

The kitchen has been an entrance point into the fellowship of the church as a worshiping body for numbers of the people who originally came just for food. Their presence has provided for a rich variety in the composition of the congregation. One Sunday, during the singing of the invitation hymn, I saw a man with long hair, no teeth, a red bandanna around his head, dressed in a tank top and faded dungarees, holding hands with an executive from the Bendix company. I could not stop the tears, and there must have been a hilarious uproar in heaven over that sight which was taking place in an old traditional bastion of affluent middle-class Christianity.

On another Sunday morning, during the singing of the hymn, a man I knew well from the kitchen came down the aisle to join the fellowship of the church. He was attired in his usual conglomerate of Goodwill, Salvation Army, Saint Vincent dePaul and Budget Corner clothing, fittingly accompanied with his second-hand combat boots. He was not the usual person who presents himself for entrance into that church, but there he was. He had been welcomed at the kitchen, and he knew he would be accepted in the sacred moment that was to follow. When he met me at the altar, he kissed me as was his custom whenever he met me, because that is how people in his native Israel and Cuba did things.

Alex was born in Israel sixty years ago of Jewish and Arab parents. Because they were not accepted by the family, they moved to Cuba where he was raised. He was a pilot in Batista's air force, and had to leave Cuba during the Castro revolution. His life from that moment on had been one turbulent horror after another. There was no work in Florida; his wife could not get to the United States; there was a divorce, then seventeen years in an Indiana mental hospital, and now he was standing at the altar of First United Methodist Church in South Bend.

He is a faithful member of the church. At various times he has been a member of Bible study groups, and some of the people helped him go to Israel to visit his sister whom he had not seen for thirty years. Two days before I left the city to go to my new appointment I saw him on the street corner, and I think I began to faintly understand what Fletcher meant on his death bed when he said, "Remember my poor." He did not mean it in a possessive, paternalistic, and condescending way. He had just come to love them so much, and they had become an inextricable part of his life. Alex learned of my moving and called me on the telephone. There was a haunting loneliness and hurt in his voice, as if he had been rejected once again, but I assured him he would experience continued love and acceptance from the new pastoral team, and the ongoing support of the congregation who knew him as the wonderful person he truly is. I do have to say, however, that his call reminded me of how much I was going to miss his friendship.

When Alex came to the altar that morning, he was followed by a very well-dressed lady. I asked her what she wanted to do and she replied, "I want to be a part of a church that is willing to accept this man."

Some come only for soup, but in the process others come and find the one who is the Bread of Life; and I for one, also want to be a part of a fellowship like that!

Chapter Eight

Strangers Who Became Friends

He had no place to lay His head. (Matthew 8:20)

"I was a stranger and you welcomed me." (Matthew 25:35)

The day, an early morning on a Saturday in April of 1976, is still vividly etched in my memory. I had no idea that what was about to happen would lead to the most controversial and rewarding ministry in the church. I had just returned from a preaching mission in Griffith, Indiana. Supposedly, these missions are to be evangelistic outreaches; when, in fact, they are, at best, experiences in congregational renewal. The evangelism hopefully, emerges from the renewal efforts. Evangelism is sharing the good news with the unchurched world; and we do not execute that task with much urgency in the church today, perhaps because we have become confused between renewal and evangelistic outreach. Much of what is called evangelism is, in fact, a reclaiming of those who are already a part of the church, and a very lost unevangelized world is left untouched.

What was about to happen that Saturday morning was going to put those of us at First Church in touch with the unchurched, with a touch more reality than anything we had done under the commonly accepted categories of evangelism. As Connie Lovejoy and I were waiting for a Council of Ministries meeting to begin, Fred stumbled through the door. His pants were torn up both seams, and he was wearing an oversized frayed overcoat. His life not only manifested the ravages of the previous few days of intoxication, but also revealed the twenty previous years of dissipative drinking. Fred was forty-one-years old; by the time the day was over, he had conned another pastor. Gary Forbes had been taken in.

Fred stayed in the parsonage that evening and then lived in the church for several days. He said that he knew of others like himself. No doubt he did; and within a month there were thirty like him living on the third floor of the church building. I thought the people of the church and the staff were ready for such a ministry, but they were not. The presence of the "visitors" reminded the members of the congregation that they too needed grace and acceptance, and that they could not depend on their middle-class status as a guarantee for their relationship with God. Facing acceptance of a different class of people set up the context for conflict among our membership.

As I look back on the beginnings of the Upper Room, I can see that this ministry was started as a result of a great mistake on my part as the leader of the congregation. However, I must also say that at no time was the motivation errant. Through the beginnings of the program I learned that God works through, and is not deterred by our blunders. Again, D. T. Niles in his book, *The Message and Its Messengers*, reminds us that Ishmael was a mistake, but God made of him a great nation. In fact, if the mistake of the Upper Room had not been made, there would not have been the impetus for a program that has brought new life and meaning to hundreds of lives, and which has been the motivating factor for renewal in the congregation of First Church.

There are two dynamics that served as the foundation for the Upper Room ministry. First, a church must take seriously the people and turf which surround it even if both have been neglected for years. One of the associate pastors had spent much of his time with the unwanted. He walked the streets three nights a week, and the street people knew him as "Father Scott" because of the clerical collar he wore and because of the Roman Catholic background of the city.

Scott Shoaff would have been the last person you would

select as a street pastor. Scott is a very "straight" person. But, he was on the street because the love of Christ constrained him to be there. When one is filled to overflowing with the Holy Spirit, there are some things one does that are completely in contrast with how a person outwardly appears. When God chooses a person to do a special work, the personnel committees of boards of ministry, cannot, with all of their modern knowledge and psychological measurements, know for certain who it is that God will choose for his special work. In fact, a psychologist once told Scott that he would be out of the ministry in five years, because he was too much of a mystic. Well, he was on the staff for five years; and he is, now, a very effective pastor in a church which has come alive under his dynamic leadership. Because of Scott's dedicated concern and presence in the streets, Fred came to First Church as a result of the word that had spread through a very efficient grapevine communication. There was a person at First United Methodist who really cared.

Along with Scott I did some of the street work, but one cannot minister in the streets till the late hours of the morning and be a pastor during the day. Something had to give. The experience did convince me, however, that the mainline denominations need to make it possible for people with this special calling to have the support of the larger church. Each city within the bounds of an annual conference should consider seriously whether or not they should have an intentional presence among the people of the pavement. We should be reminded that, after all, Christianity began with its presence among the unwanted and disenfranchised. One way for us to transform our middle-class monuments into a movement again is to evangelize the world, the world we talk about, but understand very little.

God uses people and works through such a ministry. He not only touches the unwanted, but he often changes the plans of the comfortable who simply visit such ministries for the sake of awareness and observation. A group from the Wesley Foundation at Purdue University came to the church for such a weekend experience. On Saturday night I took them to some of the go-go bars in the area. As we walked into one of the places, one of the dancers, dressed in a baby-doll pajama outfit, came toward me and asked, "Doctor, may I talk with you for a moment? I would like to have my kids back." The woman serving the drinks at the bar asked if I would visit her father at the hospital. He was dying of cancer. (Later she wanted to know if I would visit her when she had back surgery.)

Following our visit, the group returned to the church to process and discuss what we had observed and experienced that evening. I was told later by the leader that there was a young man in the group who was of the fundamentalist persuasion. As Wesley went to the fields, so he went that night, very reluctantly, to the "haunts of the wicked." Going to such places was not his idea of being separate from the world, but what happened that evening altered his life and changed the direction of his future. He was a masters degree candidate in forestry at Purdue University. As a result of his contact with the world that night, he responded to the call of God upon his life and is now preparing for the United Methodist ministry.

The second dynamic foundation for such a ministry is found in a biblical theme which for centuries was basic to the church's faith and outreach, but whose importance has waned due to our preoccupation with private property, the Calvinistic work ethic, and the fear of the one not like us which stalks us on every front. I am referring, of course, to the matter of hospitality.

Henry Nouwen in his book, *Reaching Out*, has challenged the church again to take the matter of hospitality seriously. He points out that our world is full of strangers, people who are estranged from their past culture and country, from their neighbors, from their friends, from themselves, and from God. He says:

> We witness a painful search for a hospitable place where life can be lived without fear, and where community can be found. Although many, we might say most, strangers in the world become easy victims of a fearful hospitality, it is possible for people and obligatory for Christians to offer open hospitable space where strangers cast off their strangeness and become our fellow human beings.[5]

Nouwen goes on to say that the Bible is replete with instances which call us to hospitality. The Bible not only shows how serious is the obligation to welcome strangers into our homes, but it also tells us that strangers bring precious gifts with them. He says, "When this happens, the distinction between host-hostess proves to be artificial and evaporates in the recognition of a new found unity."[6] The fact is that the fear in society with regard to the stranger is intensified because strangers on both sides never meet. The healing which can overcome the paranoia that exists between peoples, a cleavage which deepens with all the political rhetoric of the present, becomes a hopeful possibility when the biblical importance of hopitality is lifted once again to the prominence it once had.

For such a healing to become a reality at First Church, there were months and years of experience which had to take place. The healing began when the Upper Room people moved out of the church into Mrs. Lovejoy's home. She was gone for a summer and turned her home over to fifteen indigent street people who were totally unknown to her, and they lived there for three months with a leader of sorts.

In the fall of 1979, the Council of Ministries decided that it was important to enter into an experimental ministry of temporary housing. Parenthetically, it should be noted that people had been living in the church for years. People

suspected that such might be the case, but could never sub-
stantiate it for sure. After some diligent sleuthing on the part
of the custodian, evidence was uncovered that confirmed
the suspicion. In October of 1980, the Administrative Board
of the church voted to launch a residential program. I was
not present at the meeting, because I thought it was important for the board to make this decision in my absence. The
board authorized the program and gave permission to use
three rooms on the third floor of the educational building.
The program was called The Upper Room.

The program was launched and now has been in operation for six years. Hundreds of lives have been touched
within that short time. The ministry is administered by a
board of lay people who are responsible for policies, continuing education, finance, public relations, nutritional education, jobs, and helping the residents set their goals for
re-entry into the mainstream of life. In addition to the board,
lay people lead in the worship on Wednesday evening; a
dentist in the congregation provides services for dental needs;
and various people from the community provide supervision each evening.

With regard to the matter of supervision, an unusual
event happened to me in an airplane (as I was returning to
South Bend from a trip to Puerto Rico). I was taking the
six o'clock flight from O'Hare to South Bend. The plane at
that hour was filled to capacity. The seat next to me was
vacant and a man sat down beside me. After we reached our
flying height, I asked him if he lived in South Bend and inquired further as to his work. He said that he traveled for
Bendix. He asked me the same. When I shared with him
that I was the pastor of First Church, he asked was that
the church that housed The Upper Room. What a question
from a total stranger!

When I told him that it was, he said that he and his
family had just moved from Detroit. They were Roman

Catholics and were looking for a place where they could be involved in ministry. They had called various places and someone had suggested they call the Upper Room. He told me they had been working in the program for a month. They were the lay supervisors on Friday nights. Needless to say, the thrill that I experienced in that moment was indescribable. God was truly at work in this ministry; and I was meeting one of his instruments for the first time, and the meeting took place seven thousand feet above Lake Michigan at that!

The key to such a ministry as the Upper Room is in the matter of leadership. Initially, we had live-in supervisors, people who tried diligently, but for various reasons were inadequate as leaders. However, when people desperately need a place to live, you do with what you have.

In the area of leadership, the manner in which God works renews one's certainty in the living presence of the Holy Spirit. One weekend a couple from Holland, Michigan was attending a convention in South Bend. They visited the church and shared with us in morning worship. The couple noticed the various ministries which were listed in the worship bulletin, and after the service they wanted to stay and discuss the church ministries with me. They returned to worship several times after that, and even supported the ministries financially.

But they did more than just financially support the programs. Henry Cort's niece, Cecelia Drenth, had just returned as a missionary for the Christian Reformed church in Argentina, where she had spent ten years. "CC" was a graduate of Fuller Seminary and desired a place for service. After several discussions, "CC" decided to serve the Upper Room for a month, but stayed for nearly two years. At first she lived with the people full time, but she discovered that such an arrangement did not afford her enough personal space, so she worked with the people during the day and lived in a private apartment the rest of the time. "CC" related that the cultural shock she experienced as a result of living with the people was more widespread than when she had gone from the United States to Argentina. While she was on the staff of the Upper Room, she truly was a minister of the presence of God. By the way, she is the only person I have ever known who studied Hebrew diligently while she was doing the daily washing for residents.

As a result of a providential chain of events, Larry Elliot became the counselor-director of the Upper Room. Larry has two degrees from Purdue University in finance and he is a certified alcoholism counselor. Before that, Larry had worked for fourteen years in New York City for major corporations. He had lived in a condominium on the Hudson River and ran a fast track straight into alcoholism. After years in this condition, having experienced a divorce and not seeing his only son for several years, he had entered a treatment center.

After getting out of the center, he spent the next year studying the Bible and reading such spiritual classics as Oswald Chamber's, *My Utmost For His Highest*, and Thomas Merton's, *Seven Story Mountain*. During that year Larry made a commitment of his life to Christ. God has given Larry a compassionate heart, incisive wisdom with regard to administration, and an empathetic ability to identify and listen with people. That dedication is shown in the fact that he worked for $7,200 a year, ($5,000 of which comes from the North Indiana Annual Conference). Two years ago I had the privilege of uniting Larry and his wife, Michelle, in marriage. They have become members of First Church, and Larry is now an alcoholism counselor for the Memorial Hospital treatment program. One of the wonderful aspects of Larry's life is that this summer he is beginning to re-establish a relationship with his son.

In addition to Larry and "CC," Peter Stitsinger, a seminary student from the Elkhart Mennonite Biblical Seminary, came to do his field work at First Church. An alcoholic himself, Peter wanted to work with chemically-dependent people, but he wanted to do it in a pastoral context. A mutual friend said, "I know exactly where you can do that." Peter spent a rewarding and wonderful summer with us, and we hope it is the beginning of several such summers with students from the seminary. Again, First Church has the opportunity not only to model ministry for other churches, but also to impact the lives of the church's future leaders.

The ministry as a result of the presence of the above mentioned people is an ecumenical effort. "CC" is from the Christian Reformed denomination. Larry is from the People's Church, and Peter is from the United Church of Christ. Larry was succeeded by Bill Wachs who brought tremendous organizational strengths to the program. Bill is a Roman Catholic. Bill was succeeded by Betty Olena who was a member of the Nazarene Church, but eventually became a member of First Church.

The Upper Room has one room for men and one room for women and their children. There are twenty beds for both rooms, and it is the only co-ed community living in the city. The purpose of the program is to guide people in making their own decisions about returning to the mainstream of life and living in a responsible manner. In order for this mainstream realization to take place, there are guidelines built into the program.

One of the greatest personal needs of the residents, in preparing for life within the normal structures of society, is to learn how to deal with authority and responsibility. The responsibility facet begins with their entrance into the program. A contract is signed which is tantamount to their agreeing to work at setting the directions they would like to see their lives take. The intent of the contract is to encourage them to take positive steps with regard to their own personal life goals. The emphasis on the positive is important because most of them function from a negative lifestyle and mind set. It is also wise to encourage residents to set achievable short-term goals so that they can have a sense of accomplishment. Many of the residents have never had many, if any, accomplishments, or they have descended from immense achievements and feel that they cannot summon up the energy to achieve again. What would seem minuscule to the average person is a major realization to some of these people.

The guidelines of the contract are not inflexible rules. The person is more important than anything else, so the contract is interpreted for each personal situation. To those who observe from the outside, it might appear that the only consistent factor is the inconsistency with which the contract is administered. But when persons are your primary concern, grace always reaches beyond the law, and often law becomes a vehicle of grace. In fact, through this ministry, we have learned that genuine love begins at the very point where some Christians want to stop loving, and that applying the rules, which at times seem cruel and are not consistent with the supervisor's sensitive nature, is the graceful thing that must be done. It goes without saying that there are times when you simply want to quit, but it is at those very moments when the cross of Jesus looms highest and there is strength for the next step. In truth, it is impossible for the Christian to know what it means "to take up the cross," until one comes to that moment when natural love has been exhausted.

I do not want to leave the impression that the only residents of the Upper Room are alcoholics or drug-oriented people. Others who have made the Upper Room their home are abused wives and children, families, youth who are troubled or have troubles with their parents, people just out of jail or prison, people whom the police find on the streets, people in other forms of transition, people who miss their bus, and hosts of others. On one occasion, we had a young woman and her children there because, in the past, she had sold one of her babies on the black market so that she would have enough drug money, and she did not want that to happen again. Could such a thing happen in South Bend, Indiana? Yes. And it can happen in your city, town, hamlet, or rural area also. It does happen. Every day babies are sold for booze and a quick fix.

It would be wonderful, indeed, if it could be said that most of the experiences with the residents were positive, but the rending heartaches are part of the daily ministry of the Upper Room. You never get over the suicides. You never get over those who return to prison. You never get over those who have received unconditional love, yet who send another person to jail, simply out of revenge for a small wrong they did to the informing person. You never get over the college girl who was doing so well, but returned home to her parents for the weekend, drank secretly, and drowned in the family swimming pool. Sometimes the world is too much for you. There are those who do not find a rest upon the way. These are the ones of whom you do not read in the church growth success stories. Our prayer is that the success stories will occur more often. The Upper Room is there, a mistake leading to a far-reaching ministry, which through compassionate care has been "a rest upon the way" for hundreds who were hungry for hospitality. In the Upper Room they have experienced hospitality at its highest.

The following letter emphasizes how important it is to have such a ministry.

> When I came to the Upper Room, not only was my heart broken, but my spirit, mind, and every part of me was crushed by all the things life had continually thrown upon me. After being in the Upper Room for a couple of days, and letting God take away some of the hurt and bitterness, things started to change.

Never before have I seen so much love flow among peo-
ple. I was able to see so much of God's work until some-
times it filled my heart and tears would come to my eyes.
Thanks to all the residents and the people at First Church.
I love "CC" who is such a beautiful example of a Christian.
I thank you all from the depth of my heart. May God con-
tinue to pour His abundant blessings upon each of you.

This wonderful expression of gratitude came from a woman in her mid-thirties who came with her high school daughter to live in the Upper Room. The church, through a special designated gift for such situations, provided funds for her, so that she did not have to go to prison on a fraudulent check charge. Sylvia now has a full-time job and is working diligently at becoming a contributing member of the community.

If all the ramifications of such an episode were to be positive, it would be wonderful, indeed. However, a word needs to be said about how some others in the church felt about this woman and the help which she received. There was a small group in the church, long-time United Methodists, who thought that it was wrong to help this woman. In fact these people were opposed to all of the programs of assistance for the poor and wounded.

When mission to the unwanted is taken seriously, there will be a continual conflict. Surely no one enjoys such constant engagement, but it will be present as long as such ministries are present. The present obsession of being positive at all costs is eventually far too great a cost for the unwanted and their antagonists. There does come a time when the positive does not automatically win over those who are incessantly opposed. In fact, in reality, church conflict over social ministry issues as presented in this book does not turn out as neatly as some of the stories one hears in sermons or sees in movies dealing with pressing social issues, where the protagonists and antagonists "kiss and make up to live happily

ever after." Now it is certainly true that there are such situations of reconciliation, but there are as many more where
love is nailed to a cross by well-meaning religious people;
and more often than not, such impalings take place when
ministries to the unwanted of the world are at stake.

There does come a moment when the penchant for the
positive must give way to the prophetic penetrating Word
which confronts people with their systemic misunderstand-
ings of the Christian faith. No matter how gracefully and
lovingly such confrontations take place, there will be certain misguided and sometimes calloused people in the congregation who will assess your approach as less than the
positive which has come to be synonymous with Christian
faith. But, it is time for Christians to realize that sometimes
the prating of the positive is a coverup for an unwillingness
to take the risk and be involved in the program and plan
of Jesus — the program which he set forth in his inaugural
sermon at the synagogue in Nazareth. (Luke 4:14-30)

One of the underlying reasons for such conflict is due
to the presence of what Paul refers to as "principalities and
powers." (Ephesians 6:12) These are the bases behind the
antagonisms, and such powers do not respond to Gospel reality, even when the Gospel is presented from a very positive perspective. When such powers are present, no matter
how positive the message is set forth, it will be construed
as negative by the opposition group.

Such a group, for the most part, is composed of nice,
well-meaning people, many of whom are considered to be
leaders in the community. And are. There are others making up the opposition who are simply entrenched neurot-
ics who need a target on which to vent their feelings of anger
and helplessness. Some of the latter are those who have, for
some reason or the other, been denied power in the secular
structures, and see the church as the context where they
can exercise their otherwise frustrated power needs.

Whoever the opposition happen to be, it must be understood that the directions of Jesus for his church are clear, and the opposing group's exercise of power, even if it has the backing and support of powerful, well-respected leaders, does not alter the intent of Christ's concern.

There is a deceptive power in the world whose sole purpose is to detract the people of God from the mission and methodology of Jesus. The temptations Jesus experienced at the beginning of his own public ministry conclude with the words: "and the devil departed for a season" (Luke 4:13), or as the RSV has it "Until a more opportune time." We know from our study of the gospel record that the Deceiver reappeared on the scene at crucial points in order to divert Jesus from his purpose. The Tempter usually made his assaults on Jesus through well-meaning, religious people. And he still does! For this reason alone, religious people should take great care, and scrutinize, intently, who it is that is working through them.

The Deceiver continues to "appear as an angel of light" (2 Corinthians 11:14) as he motivates sincere religious people in an intense attempt to divert the church from the missional mandates of Jesus. The deceptive method is more than subtle. It is religiously acceptable in that the Tempter employs such fine Christian categories as the over-concern for a plastic unity through the maintenance of positive, non-disruptive personal relationships.

The unity of the church is definitely a primary Christian concern. It is a repetitive theme of the New Testament. But a counter harmony of the Bible is that Jesus also brings division. When faithfulness to the mission of Christ issues in division, the missional motive of the church must not be sacrificed to a spurious unity which is more the dominant motif of fraternal orders than it is the theme of the community of Christ. Such an obsession with unity is more a ploy for doing away with Christ's concerns than it is priority for New Testament concepts of the church's unity.

The penchant for the positive at all costs, when it is demythologized, has as its foundation (especially among pastors), the primacy of fulfilling their "like me scripts," or is a component of pastoral cowardice. Positivity and unity may fare them better for future appointments, but when such is the motivation, it has a stench of hell about it.

· There does come a time in ministries of outreach when the demons must be named and exorcised so that the antagonists (pastors and lay people) can be liberated from a malignant bondage if they so choose. The "hard word" must be spoken in loving manner so that the cause of Christ is not reduced to pursuing the Tempter's purposes.

Those in the church who do not understand the concerns of Christ must be continually encouraged to do so, but at no time can the leadership of the local church capitulate to their gospel which in Paul's terms is no Gospel at all. (Galatians 1:6-17)

Jesus Christ sets the agenda for the church. The church is a theocracy, and is not, in the purest sense, a participatory democracy. Those who are at systemic odds with the Gospel must be hindered from setting the agenda of the church. If you think such a group is truly democratic, it would do you well to notice how fascistic they become when the so-called democratic processes mitigate against them.

It is part of the pastoral calling to enter into compassionate dialogue with antagonists. At times when this is done, the pastor's "like me scripts" will be obliterated; and the pastor will experience an intense loneliness, but such is the risk the pastor takes, especially when the pastor knows that the unwanted others are experiencing the grace of God as a result of the minister's being faithful to the missional agenda of Jesus. That they are recipients of his love is far more important than the fact that the pastor may be experiencing acute discomfort from those of "another gospel." (Galatians 1:6-17) The pastor must, along with the hosts of supporters which are present in all such situations, remain steadfast in faithfulness due to the fact that the very Gospel itself is at stake. It is much more important to have a Gospel without total personal acceptance and unity than it is to have total personal acceptance and unity without a Gospel.

The following letter makes the confrontations diminish into the background where they really belong. It is this which should gain our attention, for it is the following letter that compels us to continue. We cannot let the opposition so ensnare us that we have nothing left for our calling. We are not to be so naive as to believe the opposition does not exist. They exist. We confront and name them. The Holy Spirit disarms them, leaving them without power that they were certain they possessed, and full of resentment. The attention is focused on those whose lives are being made different, because the majority of faithful church people, and there are many, dare to be different in their positive commitment to the unwanted.

> *Dear Upper Room — I wanted to thank you for allowing me to stay at the church for a few weeks. I was in pretty desperate straits and I do appreciate the fact there is a place like the Upper Room in South Bend. Will you thank the pastors? I am sorry but I never learned either of your last names. That is the reason I had to send this through Bobby.*
>
> *Your friend in Christ.*

The person did not know the pastors' names but, for some reason, that does not seem important. As I read the letter, what is more important is that this person found acceptance and had an experience with the one who is the Way and gives rest to those who labor and are heavy-laden.

As I close this chapter on the Upper Room, I want to share with you the nicest thing that has ever happened to me. I was asked to give the message at the Wednesday evening Upper Room service a few days before I left the First Church appointment. Following the service a man sixty-five-years old asked me to stand and he presented me with a beautiful plaque, which had been signed by sixteen "strangers who had become dear friends." In that high and solemn moment, as we embraced and said our farewells, the constant conflicts seemed so insignificant, and the warmth and smiles of their faces made me want to do it all over again at another place in history.

Chapter Nine

Witness from Weakness

My grace is sufficient for you. My strength is made per-
fect in weakness. (2 Corinthians 12:9)

As I wrote to you about two years ago that I had then
suspicions of the first germs of leprosy being in my sys-
tem — the natural consequence of a long stay with these
lepers — be not surprised or too much pained to know
that one of your spiritual children is decorated not only
with the Royal Cross of King Kalakaua, but also with the
cross more heavy, and considered less honorable, of
leprosy with which our Divine Savior has permitted me
to be stigmatized.[7]

The reader will recognize the above words as Father Damien's moving witness as regards his identification with the
lepers of Molaki. The witness is contained in a letter he sent
to his superior in 1886. At one time in my life it would have
been impossible to understand these words except as the personal profession of an heroic disciple of the cross. When
I first read them years ago, they would not have resonated
with my personal experience in any way. However, their
distance in experience is not distant any longer. Although
I know nothing of Damien's stigma, I do know something
of the scars of a modern leprous disease. The leper stigma
for me was a personal journey through, and recovery from,
alcoholism. For a Christian clergy person, there is a certain
leprous untouchableness about alcoholism.

A pastor never thinks this malicious malady will be a
problem for him or her. From time to time, the pastor may
experience obesity, ulcers probably, marital disruption, com-
pulsive sexual fixations, incessant professional gossip, the
use of the pastoral role for personal power, financial
problems, and other personal tragedies from which immu-
nity is impossible; but the likelihood of alcoholism is

something against which the pastor thinks himself impenetrable. Surely the historical abstinent stand of United Methodists and many other denominations would seem to guarantee that this would never be a problem for them, but such guarantees are not guarantees at all when alcohol has been a part of your life since childhood.

It was certainly not difficult to rationalize drinking as a pastor. I vividly remember how the rationalistic ritual took place. Luther had a beer stein with the ten commandments on it, and, when you got down to the tenth commandment, it meant that you needed more beer in your stein. Marney quaffed a few with his friends after a long night at the Interpreter's House. The Bonhoeffers spent wonderful times together at the Berlin beer gardens. Wesley was not a stranger to ale, despite what his American interpreters say about him. During a Chicago theological discussion, Barth could work a bottle for over an hour. Minister friends of mine could make a beer last through a whole evening. They could drink and be normal. My experience was that I did not do it normally, no matter how normal I was when I drank, at least normal at the beginning of the drinking years.

The alcoholic threat on my life started when I was nine months old. My grandmother told me of the incident when I was older. My grandfather, who was the son of a United Brethren Bishop, was so proud of me, since he had no sons of his own, that he took me to a bar with him to show me off to his friends and to celebrate a boy coming into his family. He had no idea how many celebrations this was going to preface in my life. Alcoholics will find a reason to celebrate, even a strike-out if you did it swinging. Being an alcoholic himself, he did not know for sure what he was doing, but in the course of the evening he gave me my first drink. Grandmother said, "You acted strangely when you came home." She said, "You acted like a drunk baby," and then, when I vomited on her, she knew what had happened.

You say that it is crazy for a person to give a baby alcohol. You are absolutely correct. But alcoholics do many crazy things.

There was never a time in my life, from that time on, when alcohol was not, directly or indirectly, an important part of my life. Later on it was my life. I did not know as a child what was going on. I did not know what was happening when, at two-years old, I would go to the bar with Grandpa and be served a Strohs in a Kraft cheese glass. I did not know what was happening when, as a child, I loved to drink vanilla extract. I did not know why I liked Hadocol so much, or why such products as Vicks 44 served as a refresher to me instead of a medicine. I just liked those things. I did not know what was happening when I would clean out the glasses after parties in our home or in any home. I did not know what was happening when a friend of mine and I drank all of my grandfather's whiskey one evening when I was ten years old. I did not know what was happening when I drank more than my high school friends.

Later in my life, I did not think I had any problems when I would drink six to eight beers an evening. After all, if you could hold that much every evening and still work, how could you possibly have a problem? The subtlety is that what you once did not know, you later do not want to know. You do not want to know why you will not go to a restaurant which does not serve alcohol. You do not want to know why, when a parishioner gives you a bottle of Harvey's Bristol Cream, you drink it before you leave the office. You do not want to know why, when you are involved in a preaching mission and staying in a motel with an abstinent song leader, not able to drink beer, you drink his mouth wash. You do not want to know why you would drink ten beers while driving home with your son in the car. You do not want to know why you miss a very important meeting because you have blacked out in a Fort Wayne motel room. You do not want to know why you would take bottles from residents of the Upper Room and drink them yourself. You do not want to know what is happening when beer isn't enough and you start with drinks that you do not even like, but need. You do not want to know, and earlier you did not know, but, in the beginning of the end, it is happening anyway. As William James says, "You may not think it counts, but it is being counted deep down in every tissue of your being."[8]

I started to think that I might have something seriously wrong with me when I would throw coffee off the church wall as a result of a delayed alcoholic response. I started to have very short blackouts when dictating, and I would forget what I had said or what I wanted to say. This seemed very strange to me because I have always had a very good memory. Yet, in all this, my alcoholic mind would not allow me to admit that the cause was alcohol. I told myself that my problems must have been psychological, or perhaps a result of working too hard. But then things began to happen that could not be related to my lame excuses. The blackouts were not temporary and always occurred when I had been drinking too much.

I would come home at night and go to bed, but the bed was often the car. I could not make it to the parsonage. When I would go through my pockets the next morning, I would find credit card tabs from places I did not even remember visiting the night before. Worse, I did not even remember how I had returned home. Then the most bizarre of all things happened. I started talking with people who did not exist. Now I had seen others do this while they were in an alcoholic stupor, and I knew it was due to their continued and excessive drinking. When it started happening to me, I knew that all the problems I was having could be traced to the one problem I did not want to admit or face.

After making a call one evening, I went to a local pizza place to watch the World Series on their big screen. It was also convenient that they served beer and wine. I went there at eight o'clock, and, at one o'clock, the manager asked me to leave because I was talking to persons who were not there. They were there to me. One of them was kneeling at my table. He had a Bible in his hand and he wanted to pray for me. We had a lengthy conversation on the nature of spiritual matters. If, as the manager said, he was not present, I had a very deep problem on my hands. The manager must have been correct because, to my knowledge, it is not a common occurrence in public pizza places for people to be kneeling at your table, wanting to pray with you. At least I had never seen that happen before and have not seen it happen since.

I decided the next day I had better go to Alcoholics Anonymous. My intention was good. I lasted for a month and then I went out, drank, and celebrated my month's victory. My condition got worse, although during this time First Church was making some momentous decisions. It was at this time that I also finished my doctorate. There was a celebration in connection with that graduation, but as you will soon see, there was a more significant graduation to come.

During this time, I enjoyed going on special speaking engagements. My prime motivation for going was not so I could be alone in a motel room, unharassed, to drink. It just·so happened that I was alone and I did drink. When I would leave the local airport, I would promise myself I would not imbibe, and then the stewardess would come down the aisle. When I deplaned, I promised myself I would not drink the rest of the week. Such promises were fleeting as soon as I caught glimpses of the local area beers that I had heard of but never tried. I would sample one plus one plus one, ad infinitum. I was the exact opposite of Robert

Frost at that point in my life. I had promises I could not keep and miles to go before I slept, if I could sleep at all. As I type this now, those days seem like they never happened, or at least happened to a different person. But they did happen. At least that was what I was told by people who watched and experienced it. Much of it I do not personally remember. Other people remember it well, and some of them will take years to recover from the episodes.

Home life was made up of people whose lives centered around my habit. Verbal abuse was commonplace; and nights of sleep were disrupted, when I would go into seemingly unbelievable alcoholic tirades. My wife informed me that, on one particular evening, I walked the floor most of the night like a caged tiger. Such is not normal behavior. If you think it is, try walking back and forth in a room for fifteen minutes, let alone most of the night.

I began to come to myself on February 29, 1980. I had just spoken at a Lenten breakfast and started drinking shortly after that. By late afternoon, I had downed ten beers, two bottles of wine, and a fifth of Cutty Sark scotch. That evening I harangued my sons for four intense hours. In a drunken stupor I decided to leave home. I messily packed my clothes and started down the middle of Jefferson Street, one of the busiest thoroughfares in the city. Cars were swerving on the icy pavement so as not to hit me, for my suitcase had fallen open and I was trying to pick up my clothes. I remember thinking (why I do not know, and the fact that I could think at all was remarkable), "I must be insane." Those were the most honest thoughts I had entertained in years. I was insane. At that point, for some reason, I went home.

Sitting in the home that I had literally made into an emotional shamble, I was a totally and thoroughly broken person. Surprisingly, my wife and sons were still there with me, and I said to Marilyn, "I am sick and I need help." It was at this point that my son, Rod, said, "Dad does not have any energy or love left, but I have enough love for this whole family." He was sixteen years old at the time.

The next morning I was admitted to Memorial Hospital. My doctor thought it best that I not be admitted to the alcohol ward, so I was put in a private room. On the medical chart it was recorded that I was suffering with heart pain and fatigue. Both descriptions were correct, but not in the literal medical nomenclature.

I was put on Librium for a time and then they took the drug away. For the first time in years I had no chemical on which to depend, and that evening I made a shamble of the hospital room. The nurse came in and said, "There is more wrong with you than chest pain and fatigue." Hostilely, I replied to her, "As far as you are concerned that is what is wrong with me."

When she left, I started to think about how I could get something to drink. It was after midnight. Nothing was open that would deliver, and they would not deliver to a hospital anyway. What was I going to do? I called one of my street "wino" friends and asked him to bring me something. For one who used to be very selective as to his drinking, I had now come to the point where I was not particular at all. Anything and anyone would do. A little later my friends were standing at the door of my room. They were in miserable shape. They smelled like a brewery and were empty-handed. Oh, it was not that they had not made a purchase. On the way to the hospital they had also proceeded to drink it.

My wino friends arrived about one o'clock in the morning, but they did not stay very long. How they entered the hospital and came to my room will forever remain a mystery to me, but such things are not obstacles to people who spend their lives getting what they want. I do know how they left, however. The nurse literally sensed their presence.

They were escorted from the premises and I spent a miserable night with nothing, absolutely nothing, to anesthetize my condition.

The next morning the doctor came to the room. He asked, "Do you really think you have a problem?" After the night before, no answer was needed. He suggested that I go to Brighton Hospital in Michigan. Two weeks later I was on my way to the Brighton Hospital for alcoholics.

During the two weeks of waiting for a bed at Brighton, I experienced the love of people as I had never experienced it before. When I admitted my sickness, I did not know what the future would hold as far as my ministry was concerned, but that concern was not paramount on my agenda. I only wanted to get well.

Lay people from First Church, those few who knew, came to visit me. Doctors from the church stopped regularly. The lay leader prayed for me at my bedside. One day as I was standing, looking out the window at the church only two blocks away, my district superintendent, Dr. Robert Jackson, came to see me. He put his arm around me and said, "I know that is the city you love." I replied to him, "Oh, Bob, what am I going to do?" In his inimitable, compassionate manner he said, "You are going to get well." There was no condemnation. There was not any sharing of pseudo-psychological jargon, nor theological inquiry as to what the deep secret causes of my state were. (By the way, there is constant debate going on as to whether alcoholism can be cured just by conversion, reconversion, and whether Alcoholics Anonymous is needed if a person opens the self up to God. Those are concerns usually discussed by people who do not have the disease. They are usually more concerned that their theological and psychological presuppositions stay intact than they are about the help which the alcoholic person needs. The suffering and recovering alcoholic knows these erudite excursions for what they are —

irrelevant inanities. The sick person only wants to get well and stay well; and the person will use whatever makes that possible and is not terribly interested in the discussions of such detached disputants.) No questions from Bob at all. He simply exuded pure sensitive love. I was going to get well. Could it be?

At Brighton I discovered that I had destroyed more brain cells than I would like to think about, and I was diagnosed as the worst type of alcoholic there is. That was a shock! I had always thought the worst alcoholics were on skid row. Only about three percent of Americans who are alcoholics are on skid row. Most of them are like me. Numbers of them are clergy persons who are not receiving the help they desperately need, because they are fearful of admitting their disease. They are held in secret bondage because they think that they have morally transgressed the historic abstinent stand of the church. I am writing this chapter of the book for the sole purpose of encouraging these people to face their sickness, and to know that the church will stand beside them. If the church does not, it is not worth belonging to in the first place. But the church will stand with you. Get well!

Time will not permit me to write about the excellent care which I received at Brighton Hospital. That would take another book. I can only say that the hospital saved my life. While at Brighton, Scott Shoaff, the associate pastor, sent me a quote from Watchman Nee, the Chinese Christian, which directed my times of meditation during those secluded days. Nee said, "Sometimes God shuts you up in prison so He can talk to you." When I read those words, words from Stanley Jones came to me. "When you give the mess and the messer to the great Unmesser, he unmesses the mess and makes an asset out of the messer."

For several months after leaving the hospital, I stuggled with how I could be an asset if people did not know about my personal descent into hell. After much personal discussion, searching, and prayer, I decided to be open about my disease. Six years have authenticated that God does not fail to make an asset out of the messer. I prayed many times that God would take the disease away. In one of those times of prayer and meditation, the words of 2 Corinthians came to me with an impact that I had not previously experienced: "My grace is sufficient for you, my strength is made perfect in weakness." What a word for me! God wants me to trust him and not some experience I wanted God to give me. Had he taken the disease away, knowing myself as I do, I would have trusted the experience more than the one who gave me the experience.

His strength has been made perfect in my weakness, and not just for me but for others. It has been six years since my hospitalization. In that time I have seen many faces in the congregation for which I cannot find a name. During the fellowship time I have asked them, "Where do I know you from?" They would immediately reply, "Alcoholics Anonymous."

God does work through our weakness. Let me tell you about Ryder. I met him at the area hall A. A. meeting one day. He is in his seventies and had not been in a church for years. After the meeting he asked me where I worked. I told him I was pastor of First United Methodist Church. He said, "I used to belong there. I will see you Sunday." He has been there regularly for six years now; and he and his wife, Billie, joined the church and are dedicated supporters of the ministries described in this book. Part of getting the story straight is to share with people how God works and witnesses through our weakness.

One morning before worship a member told me that his wife had begun to attend Alcoholics Anonymous. I affirmed him in what he had shared with me and said, "I belong to that group." He said, "Would you tell her that? It will give her so much encouragement." Following the service I saw his fine wife and I said to her, "I am proud of you and your decision. I belong to that fellowship. Would you like to go to a meeting together?" Her eyes and face shined. She said, "I am glad you told me. It means so much to me right now." Later, Molly told me, "There are some Sundays, when I just do not want to come to worship, because I think no one would understand what I am going through. When I come, I look around and see so many I know who are just like me. Then I look in the pulpit and I know there is another who really understands." "My strength is made perfect in weakness."

At another meeting, when I walked into the room, I saw a woman who had transferred her letter from First Church because of personal difficulties she had experienced. After the meeting she said, "I was surprised to see you here. I did not know about you. I still have difficulties with First Church. I will tell you about them some day." I asked, "Why don't you tell me now, and then you will not have to carry your heavy load any longer?" She then shared with me about the burden she had carried for a number of years. Although she was dealing well with her alcoholism, this matter was literally eating her up on the inside. In an attempted spirit of acceptance and love I said to her, "God forgives you for those things. What else is new?" The tears rolled down her cheeks. Her face totally relaxed and an instantaneous shine came into her eyes. The load disappeared before my eyes. She left the meeting a new person. "My strength is made perfect in weakness."

There are many gifts which God bestows upon us, but one of the tremendous gifts God gives to us is the miraculous manner in which his strength is made perfect in our weakness. It has happened again and again during the past six years. I cannot begin to tell you about the numbers of people who have come to see me as a result of a referral from the District Superintendents and the Board of Ministry. There have been leading United Methodist lay people who have sat in my study as we discussed their struggles with this most deceptive of diseases. I cannot tell you of the number of Upper Room people who have experienced the life changing grace of Jesus, because they knew that I had walked the same valleys which they had experienced.

All I can say is that alcoholism is one of the greatest gifts God has given me. The people come. They are getting well. They are experiencing Jesus. It really is a strange gift. God, to this day, has not taken the disease away; but what is more important is that countless others are finding new life and hope because God's strength is made perfect in my weakness. In a sense, I guess I too can say that I have been stigmatized with a very honorable cross. Thanks be to God.

In the chapters that follow I want to share some of the stories which are a result of that witness through weakness. The names have been changed to honor their privacy.

Chapter Ten

Prone to Wander

Prone to wander Lord I feel it. Prone to leave the Lord
I love. ("Come Thou Fount of Every Blessing")

It took a week to drive the eight hundred miles to
Lynchburg, Virginia, 1,300 miles from where Frank lived.
Every so often, Frank would drive as far as fifty miles off
the direct route looking for something to drink. Frank re-
counted for me the trip that had led to the culminating change
of direction for his life.

His family had lived in a small town, and used to go fishing in the local river. "My father would sink a tub in the
river to keep his beer cold," related Frank. "I was always
curious about what was in those bottles. One day, when
I was ten years old, my brother and I tasted a sample; we
became violently ill, but I loved what I tasted. After that
I would sample the beer whenever I could. I found it mostly
in the refrigerators of relatives and neighbors."

By the time Frank was sixteen years old, he had missed
enough school that he was only in the seventh grade, so he
quit. As I talked to him one day, he continued his story.
"Late one November I was poaching ducks in a snow storm
on the river. I slipped on some ice in the bottom of the boat,
the gun went off, and shattered my right arm. The doctor
took the arm off just below the shoulder." Frank does not
remember that the accident made any great change in his
life. Nonetheless, soon after the accident, he began his thirty-
odd years of wandering. A loner, he traversed the United
States many times. He said, "I worked at odd jobs for just
enough money to buy the alcohol my body craved."
Throughout his wandering years, Frank was followed by
the prayers of his mother and brother.

He said, "My brother watched Jerry Falwell on television." One night Dr. Falwell described the Heal 'Em Home for alcoholics at Lynchburg. Dr. Falwell's father died an alcoholic, and the home is one of the ministries of the Thomas Road Baptist Church. Frank had stopped to visit his brother who told him about the home. His brother urged Frank to go; and, subsequently, it was the trip that turned out to be a week-long binge. But he arrived sober, because he knew they would not admit him in an inebriated condition. On July 16, 1983, a day etched in his memory, he arrived at the home; and an equally important date took place three weeks later, when he accepted Jesus as the Lord of his life.

Following a two-month stay at the home, Frank purchased a bus ticket to South Bend. He said, "I do not know why I chose South Bend. Perhaps it was the guidance of God. I was afraid to return to Michigan. The gang I used to associate with was still drinking, and I knew I could not cope with that situation."

When he arrived in South Bend, Frank was directed to the Upper Room by the Salvation Army. Both the Upper Room director and Frank thought he would be comfortable with the program, so Frank unpacked his bag and settled in for an eleven-month sojourn. The first Sunday he joined a Bible class and went to the worship service. He said, "I knew the Lord wanted me to do that, but I did not feel comfortable around the people. After the service, I was the first person out the door and I was like that for quite awhile. Now it is different. I know many of the people and I like the place. I could stay all afternoon."

Feeling uncomfortable around the people was only one of the problems Frank faced. He could not find a job. There just were not even enough jobs for persons with two good arms. He did not think he stood a chance with only one arm, so he finally applied for disability and SSI payments.

When asked why he had not applied for these before, he grinned and said, "I was too proud to ask for help when I was drinking." While Frank waited for the payments to come, he earned money by selling his blood serum at the blood plasma center. A person can earn sixteen dollars a week for two blood donations. Frank ceased that practice when he got the opportunity to earn twenty-five dollars a week doing the Friday set-ups for the food co-op. When his disability payments started coming, he gave his co-op earnings to the Upper Room program.

Frank said that living in a confined area with anywhere from six to sixteen other people was especially difficult for a loner, and almost intolerable for an alcoholic. The residents were assigned housekeeping chores in the living area and custodial tasks in the building. Frank, a workaholic, did as much as he could do. Some of the other residents very often did as little as they could do. As a result of this situation, resentment built up in Frank. He said, "I prayed for patience and understanding." There were many compensations for his industrious attitude. The staff, church members, and regulars in the church building valued his willingness, skill, and dependability. In fact, he was so dependable that, when the building engineer went on a two-week vacation, Frank was entrusted with the heating plant and other responsibilities. He said, "I look upon what I do around the building as the Lord's work."

There are other ways in which the Upper Room affected Frank's life. Plans for his future gradually came into focus, and we discussed his emerging desire to go into some kind of Christian service. I suggested that he go to school and made an appointment for him to see the admissions people at Bethel College. Frank signed up for a summer course in Bible Introduction. This fifty-year-old man who had not made it to the eighth grade completed the course with a hard earned C. He was encouraged by his success and journeyed promptly to Lynchburg for a visit. Two weeks later he was back with exciting news. He had enrolled in a two-year course at Liberty Baptist College that would train him to go into church ministries or the mission field.

Frank made the trip back to Lynchburg a few days later, but he did not go back to Michigan first, for he knew that the lurking danger was still present there. He made a responsible decision and started out on the trip right. As Frank had been followed throughout the years with his mother's prayers, on this trip he would be supported by the prayers of his friends at First Church.

It does appear that his proneness to wander is over — or that his wandering *now* will be to those places where God leads him, as he tells the story of how Thomas Road and the Upper Room, hundreds of miles apart in more ways than one, enabled him to meet the One who is the Way followed by both groups of Christians for the sake of people like Frank and for the glory of God. In fact, when the Franks and Christ become central in the lives of both churches, perhaps some of the deep differences between the two churches will pale into insignificance.

A happy addition to this story is that, on the day we moved from South Bend to Lafayette, Frank came by to help us move. With great delight he showed me his grade card for the year. He had taken six courses in which he had received grades of A or B. It reminded me of what E. Stanley Jones once said in his book, *Conversion*, "When God converts the soul, he also enlivens the mind"[9] — even the mind of one who had not made it to the eighth grade. Keep wandering Frank. But wander now for the Christ.

Chapter Eleven

Leftovers from the Army

But when he came to himself . . . (Luke 15:17)

Not all of the people who find their ways to the Upper Room come from out of the city. Over the years, several of the people that have found the way back to life have come from the congregation. Such a one is Ward. One day he said, "I knew about alcoholism those days; but I did not know the seriousness of it and I did not know I was an alco-holic." Ward was describing how it was in his suburban high school in the late sixties. He said, "There were not a lot of drugs then, not even probably a lot of alcohol during school hours." He went on to say that there were not a lot of bad influences at that time. Many of the students were thoroughly active in their churches and held leadership po-sitions. Ward stated that he had started drinking on weekends. He was a very good musician and had played in several bands, traveling as far as Chicago. He said there is an unwritten agreement that the band members can drink as much as they want. They played at weddings and other places where there was alcohol and everybody drank, but Ward took his work seriously. He said, "Anytime I would play in school performances or band contests I would not drink. I wanted to be as good as I could be."

At Indiana University, Ward got into a dance band right away and "I was drinking before classes as well as at night. I was beginning not to take my music and a lot of other things seriously. My draft number was about to come up. I didn't know what to do. I really didn't care. I didn't even try to get a deferment. I wanted to be a pilot. An officer. I wanted to fly 'copters. I enlisted.

"I didn't fly 'copters or anything else," he said. "I had

no depth perception. I ended up being a door gunner. You hung out the door, shot your gun and got shot at.''

Along with a few others in his unit, Ward was sent to Vietnam. He said, "I was totally surprised. It was about as unreal to a kid from the midwest as you can imagine. Personnel there were listed in two bunches. You were either into drugs or you were a juicer. I was a juicer. We stayed in that realm ninety percent of the time. I didn't know anyone not involved. You might get killed at any moment, so what's the difference. I didn't get killed, but I was hospitalized for a bleeding ulcer and some minor injuries.''

After eight months, Ward was sent to West Germany, another alcohol environment. It wasn't so blatant, but it was so much in the open. It was just as bad. Such drinking was perfectly acceptable in Germany with the right people, and he was one of the right people.

What did he do in Germany? He was put on border patrol. He said it was the most hypertensive unit in the whole country. There were alerts all the time. The Russians might be coming across the Czechoslovakian border. You never knew. He told his C.O. that he couldn't take it.

Ward said he knew a commander on the other side of Germany, so the C.O. got him out of the combat area and into an engineering unit as a supply sergeant. He knew nothing about it. He was tense, he was homesick, and he drank every night. He said, "I got myself so loaded I could go to sleep. I did it for three years." At the end of his tour of duty, Ward received an honorable discharge.

He got out of the army and thought, "Once I get out of this situation, I can stop drinking. I don't need this. I can stop. I can stop. I can stop." Well, he tried.

In 1974 the situation for a soldier getting out of service was really bad. It was the Vietnam syndrome. The stigma was still there. Ward felt like an alien. "I couldn't get along with people. The only thing I could get along with was the bottle, or so I thought.''

In spite of a sense of alienation and drinking, Ward held a job at a local store for three years. He went in every morning with a hangover. No one really knew it, and if they did they never said anything. He finally got fired. "No one said I was fired because I was drinking. I didn't drink at work, but I drank a lot when I got home."

Ward got another job . . .

Got fired.

Ward went into printing. He said, "At first I didn't drink on the job, but then I started to. Then I knew in here [rubbing his chest] I had a problem, but not up here [pointing to his head]." That job lasted three years.

Then another firing.

About that job, Ward says he drank all the time.

"Then my bleeding ulcer sent me back to the hospital; how my gut hurt." He said, "Was there no end to my misery? Sandy was there. She knew my problem but did she care?

"When I got out of the hospital, I got another job. I wasn't fired. I got laid off. My boss laid me off so I could collect unemployment. Then again that was not a kind thing to do. It let me not work. It let me drink all day long. Sandy had taken me in; Sandy kicked me out. I had no place to go. In my desperation a fellow traveler found me. I recognized my pastor; he cared. His caring was real. He told me I could live in the Upper Room.

"There was a no drinking rule for the men living in the Upper Room, but I had a room to myself. I wasn't ready for that. The monkey was still on my back.

"One day I can remember, I went down to the favorite place of the alcoholics. I bought as much liquor as I could carry. I was going to go to that room and die. Instead of dying, I got sick, sicker than I had ever been in my life. That was my bottom right there. That was my bottom. In desperation I called my sister. She cared. She came to find me. I remember crawling on my hands and knees to the chapel. I had to crawl because I was starting to have D.T.s. I just sat there and prayed. 'I need help. If you can help me, I can help me.'

"I heard someone in a room across the hall. I dragged myself over. I pounded on the door. The associate pastor was there. My sister came. I collapsed. They couldn't get me to the VA hospital until the next morning. The pastor held onto me, the lifeline that kept me from disappearing into the abyss. Will morning ever come?

"At the hospital I asked for help for the first time and, for the first time, I admitted that I was an alcoholic." Ward's two counselors, fellow alcoholics, asked him, "How do you want to do this?" He said, he didn't know. How do you do it? They said, "We can bring you down hard, or we can bring you down easy. If we bring you down hard, you are going to remember it. We are not going to let you die, but you are going to want to die."

Ward said it was just a nightmare. "It took me seventy-two hours to do it, about three days. I got D.T.s. My arms were sore from my wrists to my elbows. I wanted to die or go to sleep. I couldn't do either. I was resigned to die because it hurt so badly."

Ward said, as the counselors said, "I didn't die. After several months of rehabilitation, I was ready to go back to South Bend. I needed a place to go where there was no pressure. It is almost a fearful thing being released, knowing that you have access to alcohol again. You need a place where you are not pressured. You need an interim place before you go back into society and that is what the Upper Room is. They took me in again. I thought of the hand that helped me through the night and I knew the answer was 'yes.'

"Again without a job, what do I live on. I had a small veteran's pension, was still collecting the unemployment insurance that let me almost kill myself, and I applied for food stamps." Ward said, "This was an important step for me, going to the welfare office. You begin to know yourself. Pride is not important.

"I was still on very shaky ground," he said. "I still felt the ground shaking before the state music contests, I could still see the Russian guns sighted on me, the animal eyes of my Vietnam buddies, and my whole body shaking with D.T.s. But if you do everything they tell you to do, you can make it. They tell you not to get involved in any relationships and get back into society gradually. I didn't do what they told me. I moved back in with Sandy; I started drinking again. We quarreled, and she threw a telephone which hit me squarely on the side of my head. In two weeks I was having seizures. I went to a South Bend hospital. They sent me back to the veteran's hospital in Indianapolis.

"The seizures continued daily. They didn't have enough staff at Veteran's Hospital to watch me. They had to send me to a hospital where I could get twenty-four hour surveillance, and it turned out to be a mental hospital." Ward goes on to say, "It was probably a good thing for me. It added something to keep me off of alcohol. I saw people who were definitely affected by alcohol, most of them young men twenty-five to thirty-five. Many were Vietnam veterans, leftovers from the Army. In another year my liver and heart would have been where there was no hope for them.

"After several months the seizures went away and I was discharged. For the third time I went up to the Upper Room. This time I had a roommate, the supervisor. I become his assistant and gradually assumed some responsibilities. I began to socialize with people at the church. I followed A. A. this time with the right attitude. I followed the program to the letter. I was going to get it right this time.

"Things were getting better for me. I found a job; and I went back to college, but I went back with the idea that I would do well. One of the classes I took was physics. I was horrible at those kinds of things. I said to myself, 'If I can get an A in physics, I'm on my way.' And I did. That slammed everybody out, including me. I never got anything under a B after that." (Ward will graduate this year from Indiana University.)

"My newest job did not turn out so well. I got fired. I got fired, not because I was drinking, but because the boss thought I was. I was honest and told him I was an alcoholic, but I didn't let it get me down like it did before. I just went out and got another job.

"I have been working there for two and one-half years. I have learned not to tell them I am alcoholic. I learned to protect myself.

"Sandy and I are married. I don't know if it will survive. I care for her, but like a woman I heard at an A. A. meeting. I will do anything to stay sober," and stay sober he has. Ward is active in the church. He has served as a lay reader, and he has become a light of home for those who, like him, think maybe they won't make it.

Chapter Twelve

A Coal Miner's Son

". . . one thing I know, that though I was blind, now I see." (John 9:25)

Question: Johnny, when did you start drinking?

Answer: I started when I was six, or thereabouts. We lived in West Virginia. My daddy was a coal miner. He made home brew and hid it around the place. We had an outhouse then. That was a good hiding place. For a long time he did not know I'd find his bottles. I'd drink the stuff and fill the bottles with water. He always thought it was mom who found them. Later on, when I would be with him, we would get a bottle some place and drink it on the way home. Mom never smelled it on us. She had cancer. When it got worse the doctor said it would not hurt her to have a drink now and then. That made it easier for my dad and me to get away with it.

Question: Johnny, how far did you go in school?

Answer: I went about half-way through the tenth grade. When I was sixteen, I joined the Marines.

Question: How long were you in the Marines?

Answer: I was drinking so hard, they wanted to put me in the hospital but I told them I would quit. Later on I was locked up in New Hampshire. I was locked up for two years due to my drinking. I drank in lockup too. You can always get booze. I learned to make suits. The guards would see to it that I got extra material. I would make them suits so they could sell them, and they would bring me alcohol. I was discharged in 1964. They took me to Boston and gave me a train ticket to West Virginia.

By then drink started getting to me. All I wanted to do was lay around drunk. My sister and her husband had come up to Lapaz, Indiana in 1965. I worked for a company there for three years. One day the boss smelled liquor on me and gave me a warning, so I quit. I got another job right away. I would finish my work by noon and drink the rest of the day.

My boss picked me up every day. I always put rum and coke in my thermos. One day he asked me for a drink thinking it was coffee. I forgot what I had in it and said, "Sure." He gave me thirty days probation. He said my drinking didn't interfere with my work. I was a welder and they couldn't find anyone to replace me. After three years I was to get bumped. There was this guy they felt sorry for. They finally gave him my job.

Question: Were you ever married?

Answer: Two times. I got married first in 1968. I worked at a trailer factory. We lived in Lakeville, Indiana. We had a boy. He is sixteen now. By 1974, I knew I was a winehead. That is what I called myself. I left them and came to South Bend to live on the street. That is what I wanted to do.

Question: Why did you give up the street life?

Answer: I met Beth. We were married in 1980. I was 39 and she wasn't 18 yet. We lived with her family for awhile and then went down to West Virginia. Penny, our little baby, was born in West Virginia. There weren't any jobs. I just helped my brother-in-law put on a new roof, things like that. My brother was a coal miner; but I wasn't going to work in the mines, so I said to Beth, "have your mother send us the bus money and we will go back to South Bend."

This is how it is with Beth's mother. Beth and I and the baby got over $100 in food stamps a month; her mother got food stamps. A younger brother made out he was retarded on some tests and got a check. Her sister had several kids who got a check. Several brothers got government checks. Why there was over $1,000 in food stamps a month coming into that house. Beth and I ate only one meal a day. The rest of them sat around and ate all they wanted when they wanted. They said we were to turn over food stamps to them. I said, "I have a baby and wife to consider." It was Beth's sister who talked her mother into throwing us out.

Question: Where did you go?

Answer: We went to the Morningside Hotel. I was going to Madison Center for my alcoholism. They had me work at Goodwill. It wasn't much money but they were trying to help. I'd come here to the church to get some food for Penny from the food pantry.

Question: How did you know about this church?

Answer: That fellow Jerry told me about it when I was living on the street, and Dr. Forbes said I could bring Beth and the baby here to live.

Question: Does that mean that you had given up drinking?

Answer: Let me tell you about that. I wouldn't drink anything around the church. I'd go downtown and buy vodka and think I could keep everyone from smelling it on me. I have this to say now that I have quit drinking, living on the third floor had a lot to do with it, and being with the people here had a lot to do with my wanting to quit drinking.

Question: How did you get your job at the funeral home?

Answer: I felt I owed the church a lot. The only way I knew how to pay it back was to work around the building. There was always a lot to do and I felt good doing it. I guess they liked the way I did the work. The funeral home needed a janitor. The church staff told the owner they thought I could do a good job. I have been working there for three years.

Question: Did you ever drink after moving out of the church?

Answer: Yes. We moved out of the church in April. We found a house near the funeral home. I started drinking on weekends. One of the bosses told me that if I drank anymore, I'd lose my job. Another thought comes to mind. I lost my first wife to booze. I knew that. I believe I was on the verge of losing Beth and the kids. It was about time I did something.

Question: You're one of the winos that cared more for your family than your bottle then?

Answer: It took a lot for me to see the light but I finally saw it.

Question: How long has it been since you quit drinking?

Answer: Two years. It came about like this. We moved down on Scott Street. Some people from the Pentecostal church picked up Beth and the kids. She was saved there. One Sunday they came into the house and begged me to go. I was sitting there with a fifth of vodka. I said, "Look, I am sitting here drinking. People, when you go to church, don't want to smell the booze on you." They said, "That is no way to look at it," but they took my wife and kids and went on. She didn't say much when she got home. I didn't know she was going back that night. When the people came in, I had just finished that fifth. I wasn't so drunk that I staggered, but you could smell the booze on me. They talked me into going with them, so I went and the next thing you know, I was saved.

Questioner: Praise the Lord!

Answer: I went back home, took my clothes off, and put on overalls. It was like a swimming pool. I call it the drunken spell taken off me. I hate to call it "saved." People may think I am a full-fledged Christian. I don't want to deceive anyone. I have lots of faults.

The couple asked, "Would you like to take Bible study?" I said, "Yes, I'll take the Bible study." It was on Tuesday nights. I was walking down William Street going home from work, and I said, "I think I will walk over close to Main Street. This way I can stop by the liquor store, have a beer and no one will smell it when I get home." When I got close to the bar, it struck me, "You've got Bible study tonight. People don't drink. They'll smell it." I went straight on home and got cleaned up for the Bible study. That is the last time the urge for a drink hit me.

Question: Why do you come back to First United Methodist now?

Answer: Even though I went to church with Beth and the kids, my mind would be back at this church. That is no good that way. I stopped going and stayed home a few Sundays. Then one Sunday while I was shaving and getting cleaned up, my little girl said, "Daddy, are you going to church with us?" I said, "No honey, Dad is going to church. He is not going to your church, but he is going to church."

People say to me, Johnny you were saved in the Pentecostal church. Why do you go to First United Methodist? I tell them there are some things you don't know about. I wouldn't have a family if it weren't for First United Methodist Church. First Church could have put me out a few times when I was drinking beer. But by the grace of God, you didn't.

Questioner: That is right, Johnny. By the grace of God that is one mistake we didn't make.

Chapter Thirteen

A Wanted Man

". . . for this my son was dead, and is alive again; he was lost and is found . . ." (Luke 15:24)

When the bishop appointed me to an historical down-town church, only God knew that the parish would extend to a large metropolitan court room hundreds of miles away from South Bend. But when we become seriously involved in local ministry, the world does become our parish. The well-known Wesleyan phrase becomes more than just a well-worn piece of Christian folk lore. It in fact becomes an extension of daily ministry as a result of one's local appointment.

Dan made the phrase a reality in my own ministry. Dan came to the Upper Room via the route of the Salvation Army in South Bend, Chicago, and another large midwestern city. Dan was a kind, affectionate, unassuming, simple person.

From the beginning he was the kind of person we could entrust with responsibility. He became the live-in director of the Upper Room program. He cared for the security of the building. Up until that time we had not had a person that carried out his responsibilities with the dedication and thoroughness which Dan displayed.

Dan was the kind of person you simply liked. The last thing that would have occurred to you was that he was a "wanted man." Quite the opposite would have been your continual impression. Dan was accepted and liked by the people of the church, and he felt at home in the church's fellowship. One Sunday, during the singing of the invitational hymn, Dan became a member of that fellowship. He was wanted and felt accepted. Events, soon to emerge, were going to rapidly disrupt that serenity.

One day soon after his wonderful Sunday, the associate pastor asked me to come to his study. As I walked into
the study, there were Dan and two detectives whom I recognized. I asked, "What is happening?" Before the detectives
could answer, Dan in his customarily simple and humble
fashion said, "Gary, I want to tell you why they are here.
What I am going to tell you is true. They are only doing
their job. I am wanted on suspicion of murder in another
city. It is time for me to go and face this thing. But I want
you to know I did not do it."

Stunned, confused, shocked, I still could not help but
believe what Dan had just told me. But I thought to myself, "Not Dan. Not simple and loving Dan." Either way
I remembered that the God of the Gospel in whom we believe is no stranger to murderers. Once he called a person
his friend who was a murderer. (The story of David and
Bathsheba is a sad piece of sex and murder any way you cut
it.) And there was Paul. All of us standing in the study that
day owed to that Pharisaic executioner the concept of grace
which changed his life and ours. That was what Dan needed
in that moment. "Grace, grace, God's grace, grace that is
greater than all of our sin." In a moment I learned that grace
is not an academic doctrine to be studied and discussed in
the hallowed halls of academia. Grace is the actual concrete
unconditional movement of God toward Dan during that
most tense time in his life.

During what followed, I was afforded the opportunity
to be a conveyer of that grace. Finally, such is the only ministry we have — to be dispensers of God's love in situations
that seem to hold nothing but haunting uncertainties.

Dan knew that a possible lengthy prison sentence might
await him, and possibly the death penalty. I said, "We will
be with you through this entire thing." Dan responded,
"Would you do that for me? You have only known me for
a few months." I said, "How long I have known you does

not matter. I know that Jesus loves you and I love you. Loving Jesus means we walk through the deep waters with those who belong to him. We will see you soon."

Dan gave me his parents' phone number, parents he had not seen in years. When the murder had taken place, he had simply left the city without notifying anyone.

As the detectives and Dan left the study, Dan was handcuffed. I remember that he looked like a trapped child in those handcuffs. The only handcuffs I had ever seen were on television, or were the toy variety my sons used in their play when they were young boys. But, believe me, when you see the real thing, you know they are the first step of belonging to a system from which you are not going to escape unless you are released. Handcuffs are shackles, and when I saw Dan with them on, I felt that someone had shackled my heart. I said to the detectives, "Do you have to put those on? He will not hurt anyone or try to escape." But Dan said, "Gary it is all right. They are doing their job."

The three started down the hall. One of the detectives came back and said, "This man is no murderer." The detective did not like what he had to do. As a result of that episode my attitude toward policemen underwent a radical change. To put all policemen in a stereotypical category as insensitive people is as fallacious as putting any humans in categories. This detective was different. He truly cared about Dan, and he displayed that care keeping me in touch with the progress of events surrounding Dan, as he sat in the county jail waiting to be transferred to the city where he would be tried.

Later that day I called Dan's parents and informed them of the situation. A few months passed before they called back and told me of the trial date. At the trial I met his lovely mother. She was like any mother who had lovingly done all the right things in raising Dan, but she was heart broken by the intense anxiety which surrounded the uncertainty of the day that was before her.

In the court room the story unfolded step by step. The events that had led to the entire situation simply underscored the character of the Dan we had all come to know. He had had an apartment in the city where the trial was being held. He had befriended an older man who desperately needed a place to live, and so Dan had let him live with him in the apartment. Later he became friends with another person who needed shelter. He said, "I do not think my older friend would mind if you shared the apartment with us." That was Dan through and through. The new friend came and Dan shared his home, food, and belongings.

One day while Dan was in another room in the apartment, the other two men became involved in a violent argument because the older man would not give the other the little money which he possessed. The younger man beat the older to death with a shoe. When Dan came back into the room, the murderer said, "You are an accessory to murder." Dan helped stuff the old man's body into the closet. They both ran their separate ways. Dan never saw the murderer again until he saw him that day in the court room.

At the trial the lawyers talked with Mrs. Lovejoy and me. We gave our impressions of Dan and the lawyer said, "That is the Dan I know. He is no murderer. He is a simple, caring person who was taken advantage of by a known criminal." Dan was declared "not guilty," and our support and statements, along with the evidence, helped to make him a free man. When Dan was released, tears flowed down all of our cheeks. As we embraced I told him, "This is one of the most wonderful moments of my life." He immediately replied, "I knew you would be here. Can I come back to my church in a couple of weeks?" "My church." What beautiful words.

We drove to Dan's home, a home he had not seen for years. There his father met him and said, "Welcome home, son." Does not that bring another similar episode to your remembrance? A time when another father welcomed his son home. A story told by the one through whose death and resurrection it is possible for all his sons and daughters to come home.

Dan, in fact, did come back to the church and to his former job, which he once again performed very well. No one had known where he had been. They thought he had been on an extended vacation to see his parents.

As the months passed, the day came when Dan informed me he was going to leave the church and go to the Salvation Army. I strongly retorted, "You can't do that. Where was the Salvation Army when you needed them?" I was incensed to think that a person we had helped liberate could even think of joining another church. The director of the program helped me to see that, when you aid in the liberation of persons, that does not mean that those persons are at your beck and call the rest of their lives. People must be freed to pursue their own destinies and purposes. Grace means that God truly frees people to serve him and not the ones who were blessed enough to have a small part in the liberation process. One cannot keep them around indefinitely, so as to continually inflate one's own ego. I became aware that liberators can use the liberated to support their already dangerous messianic consciousness. People are free to live as persons in their own right. "Thank you, God, for Dan's ministry of liberation to me."

Months later I heard from Dan. I have not been in contact with him since that day. He did write to me, saying he was living with his parents; and they are getting to know one another again. He said, "Home never felt so good." He had reestablished contact with his child, and he and his girl friend were planning to be married. He wanted to know how the Upper Room was doing. Now the "wanted man" was truly wanted. He was free and, in the process, this pastor, (more often than he wants to admit), was liberated from the need to control the lives of others. Perhaps I find myself in that trap because I do not see that I am wanted, am important, and do not have to prove my worth by being important as I exercise my paltry power. Indeed, both Dan and I learned that we are both wanted simply because God wants us just like we are.

Chapter Fourteen

Happily Ever After?

*"O Jerusalem, Jerusalem . . . How often would I have
gathered your children together . . . and you would not!"*
(Luke 13:34)

"When this session is over, may I see you for a few
moments?" One of the pastors of the annual conference had
asked me that question. At the close of the plenary session,
I met my colleague in the hall outside the auditorium.

His conversation started in a hesitant manner. It was
obvious that he was going to have a difficult time opening
the subject. He started by saying, "I don't know how to
ask you this." He stopped, paused, grasped for words that
would not come. Realizing the obvious dilemma, I tried to
lessen his discomfort. "Tom," I said, "You know I am an
alcoholic. Do you have someone you want to discuss with
me?"

Tears came to his eyes. "Yes, it is a close friend of mine.
She is addicted to drugs and alcohol. She lives in your city.
She has no place to stay. Could she stay at the church?"

The following week Tom brought his friend to First
Church. That began a year-long venture which appeared as
if it were going to issue in a new life. Instead, it ended in
a tragic death.

As I waited for Tom to bring his friend for the initial
appointment, I surmised that Tom held some rigid views
about alcoholic persons; but isn't it amazing how quickly
and drastically our views about issues and people are altered,
when the people are no longer impersonal categories and
statistics, but members of our own families, or close friends.
Our impregnable theologies and rigid ethical systems change
in the twinkling of an eye, and our inflexible moral universals undergo almost instant rearranging, because the people

with the problems are much more valuable to us than is keeping our mind sets intact. During my first meeting with Marcia the thought came to me — what could begin to happen to people, people we know or do not know, whose life styles are radically different than ours, and who very often are people whom we put in the categories of "detestation," if we were to relate to them not as categories or depersonalized universals, but as individuals very much like those closest to us? What would happen to these people who have problems which often ostracize them from the fellowship of the church, if we were to treat them as if they were one of our children?

When Tom and his friend arrived, she was in a stupor. In order to relate with her I could not be concerned about whether I would offend Tom's sensitivities. I asked her about what was going on in her life. Had she been drinking? Had she had a fix lately? To all of my questions she responded with a definite "No."

Then the confrontation began. I said, "You are not telling the truth." At twenty-seven she had deceived herself through several treatment programs, dropped out of a major university, brought continual personal pain to her family, and still, in the presence of offered help, was in a state of continued denial.

She responded, "That is no way for a Christian minister to talk to me. I do not even think you should be a minister." I said, "That may be what you think, but what you think about me does not change the fact that you are not telling the truth. In fact, you are living a lie."

After a long discussion, for some reason of grace, she decided to live in the Upper Room, a stay which would haunt me to this very writing and beyond. Marcia responded wonderfully to the surroundings and to the strokes she received for the positive progress she was making. But she fell prey to the often accepted position that a good environment would permit her to pursue her addiction in what she thought would be a controlled manner. She thought it had been a pressurized environment that had caused her problem. Less pressure would permit her to im- bibe in a moderate manner. So she thought. Marcia was truly the product of contemporary enlightenment thinking which does not take seriously the nature of one's disease. Instead it leaves one with an easy conscience which says that the problems are the result of everyone else's failure, and the malady does not in any way reside in our nature and choices.

She started to practice her life style again, surreptit- iously, she thought. She attempted to delude everybody con- nected with her by attending worship, talking religious lan- guage, bringing her mother to see us, and stating she was on the way to a new existence. It was a masterpiece of manipulation and deception. But, as is often the case, no one was being fooled or deluded, but Marcia. Paul offers a truth which became incarnated in Marcia, "Be not deceived. God is not mocked. Whatsoever a person sows that will the per- son also reap." (Galatians 6:7) Life does do back to us what we do to life.

Her control outlook resulted in her being with people of a destructive life style, people she did not know or remem- ber after she became aware the next day. In those times of blackout, she would sell expensive items to pay for a short fix or a bottle. She would fall and badly bruise or cut her- self. Many nights I would find her in dangerous sections of the city where she had collapsed or fallen asleep. In her sane moments, Marcia was a person of high moral standards and personal expectations, but under the influence, she lived a life which was the exact opposite; and she was totally un- aware in those states of what had taken place.

When Marcia learned what she did during those times, she decided to spend some time in a private home, hoping that a new environment would bring the change she was progressively coming to know that she needed. But, again, environmental changes do not, for the addictive personality, bring personal structural changes. Within a few days her alcohol blood level was at a lethal point.

I took her to the emergency room of the local hospital; and after days of observation, the doctor, in consultation with several other people, decided someone had to commit her to a long-term treatment center. With the support of her parents, she was committed to an alcohol program in a state hospital.

While waiting for the transfer to the state facility, without anyone knowing, she left the local hospital; and a few days later she was in jail, having been arrested for public intoxication. When we appeared before the judge, she said, "You do not give a damn about me." These were hard words for one who is possessed by a dominant "like me" script. But, in the ministry, when one is truly concerned about people, you learn how to disregard some of your script needs, and you do what needs to be done for others, no matter how much it will pain you as a person. During her stay in the hospital I visited her on various occasions and the "don't care" litanies composed the substance of our conversations. It is not an easy task to continue your pastoral ministry when one continually hooks you at such painfully vulnerable spots.

She, against her court committal, left the hospital again. The incessant cravings of her habit were too much for her. I did not hear from her for months, but just because one loses contact does not mean that one in turn loses concern. Months later, the phone rang. "This is Marcia," she said. "I have been with my mother. I have thought things through and I have decided to admit myself to the hospital." That was a first for her.

While she was at the hospital, I received many letters from this beautiful woman, a woman with nothing but tremendous gifts and potential. The letters did imply an honesty and sincerity, not before present in our previous contacts. The church staff and others were encouraged and pleased with what they read. She said she was serious about her future and her relationship with God. In fact, there was more in the letters about her new-found relationship with God than any other subject. It really did appear as if Marcia might become one of the few "happily ever afters." It looked like she was going to make it for sure.

In July I was preaching a mission near Fort Wayne, Indiana. As usual, I called home in the evening. My wife told me that Marcia had taken a weekend pass to be with her mother. While her mother went shopping, Marcia drowned in the family swimming pool. Two months after her death I happened to meet her lawyer in a store. He asked, "Have you heard from Marcia?" I said, "What do you mean?" He said, "She walked out of the state hospital." It was not difficult to piece together why she had gone home. The old pattern of deception was exerting itself again. I told her lawyer that Marcia was dead. Those words that day carried a terrible finality. Marcia is dead!

Marcia is dead! Once again Marcia tried to control her addiction, but it controlled her; and this time it killed her. Sometimes in the ministry you just want to quit. In the real world, with real people, ministry does not always turn out "happily ever after." However, love does continue, and all that remains is the fact that Jesus Christ understands Marcia, even when she could not understand herself. Oh, that she could have understood and experienced Christ's loving presence that releases us from the bondages which destroy us. What a difference Christ could have made in her life.

As I bring her story to a close, the painful questions are still present. I pray they never go away. Their presence is a constant reminder that we, as representatives of Christ, are daily dealing with life and death issues. Those matters which occupy much of our time in the ministry are just not important. Marcias are important.

I must, as you must, realize that we are responsible to Marcia, but we are not responsible for what Marcia finally does with her life. No person can carry the latter load and be effective with other people. However, even realizing that fact, there are lives that end far too soon, and we are in daily contact with them. Their presence should put us under constraint to be about the mission of persons, and to make that the priority — more important than anything else we find ourselves doing.

Marcia is still inextricably embedded in my memory and heart. She is there to keep me very sensitive to the myriad of Marcias I will meet in the future, ever challenging me with the fact that this matter we call ministry carries with it issues which are final in more than one sense. All ministry does not lead to "happily ever after."

Chapter Fifteen

Silent Night — Lonely Night

. . . That he who made all nations is not willing one soul
should perish lost in shades of night. ("O Zion Haste")

The second Christmas Eve service had just concluded,
and I went upstairs to the Upper Room to share in the residents' celebration. I especially wanted to extend holiday
greetings to Craig, the director, who in the previous few
months had made tremendous progress in his own personal
growth; and had also become a close friend.

Craig, at forty-five years, was an architectural drafts-
man by trade, with grown children whom he had not seen
for some years. His wife would have taken him back, but
he would not return to her, because he knew his priority
was his addiction and he did not want to put her through
more misery. (Alcoholics are not totally insensitive people.)
On one occasion his children were going to visit him, and
to have done so, they would have had to travel over five
hundred miles. Craig did not want to see them, as he was
not in the condition he wanted to be at the time when such
a reunion might take place.

The First Church people had made possible the residents'
party. They did not want the people to be deprived of the
Christmas celebration. For some of the residents, Christmas was a reminder of better days and became a symbol of
hope for what might be possible in their futures. But to
others the familiar sounds of "Silent Night" lead to unend-
ing lonely nights. The loneliness brings on deep depression,
since their minds remember the meaningful days which were
obliterated by their addictive life styles. Remembrances such
as Christmas are just too much for them, and they resort
to that which anesthetizes their hurt and guilt, at least for
a time.

Lonely nights lead to long, lonely, and unremembered days. When I returned home from a short Christmas visit to my parents, the associate pastor said that they had not been able to get Craig to open his door for three days. It certainly did not require any imagination to know what had been going on inside that room.

I knocked on the door and said, "Craig, it is Gary." The door opened. Why would he open the door so quickly for me and not for the others? It is simple; and underlying the simplicity is a truth that we in the church have forgotten, and such a lapse of truth has contributed to our ineffective-ness as witnesses for Christ. People respond to those who have experienced what they have experienced more readily than they respond to those who have never shared what is specifically the "dark side" of their lives. It is true that most Christians will admit to the fact of being a sinner, or only human, or not being perfect, but these are usually very safe words to keep them from revealing what their own per-sonal pains and existences really are. Such safe stances separate and insulate us from rapport with people whose existential pain only reminds us of our own dishonesty; and acceptable words as "sinner" subconsciously make us feel that we have already dealt with the shadows, when in truth they are still dealing us.

Now is the time for Christians, if indeed they want to be in touch with themselves and others, to express what is the specific pain and shadow which keeps them from being genuinely human and personal. What is it with which they still struggle? What is their secret that seethes below the safe symbol of "sinner?" These safe, acceptable symbols af-ford us a pseudo-respectability (at its most devious among the clergy) and enables people to still think well of us, while our humanity pulsates within us and defeats those in our presence who do not know of the divided souls that inces-santly harass us in the depths of our being. Life-changing

witness and redemptive rapport come in the opposite manner from which we think. It is only as I name, admit, and
share these demons which lurk in my life that I become a
contact with others through which the power of the living
Christ can work. General moral or immoral categorization
only retards our personal and spiritual growth; and such
dishonesty distances us from those who are more honest
about their existential pain, but are still entrapped. And our
image of having it together under the usage of acceptable theological nomenclature does not help them in the least.

The door to Craig's room opened; and it opened up to
a scene I had never experienced in my life before, and hope
I never experience again. The stench was indescribable.
Standing before me was a personal friend I literally did not
recognize. His facial features were the features of a total
stranger. The voice was not his. (I am not saying that the
person before me was a male Regan in the sense of the little
girl in the famed *Exorcist*, but this was not the Craig I had
known, nor was he, in appearance, like any staggering drunk
I had ever encountered.) His hair was matted and most of
his body was coarsely encrusted by human feces.

As I entered the room, Craig lay down on a sheet and
pillow which were totally stained by urine and excrement.
The soiled surroundings of this usually meticulous person
were not even part of his awareness. Then I saw them,
empty bottles of vodka and two empty containers of rub-
bing alcohol which he had procured from the Day-Care
Center. Why he was not dead no one knew. There he lay,
this usually neat person, in lower-than-animal conditions.

After some of us had gagged ourselves out, the associate pastor went into the shower with Craig, soaped and
scraped him down with a table knife. It took the knife to
get him clean. Four showers later, repeating the same routine, Craig was somewhat clean, at least externally. The experience of the showers is not something you learn about

in your seminary education. At least it was not a part of my core curriculum.

Later, Craig was committed to the security room at the hospital where he was observed carefully due to his poison-saturated system. During these days he came to himself, and that is to employ a loose description to express the horrors he experienced during those days. When able, he discovered what depths of hell he had experienced and he began the steep ascent back to becoming a human being again.

Part of the sojourn for Craig was a forthright facing of his failures which were an inescapable part of his personal past. Months later, looking like himself again, he came to my study and said, "I am going home."

The honesty continued. I put him on a bus; and he set out to face the hardest facet of coming home to one's self, and that is going back to the home where the hurts were still present and having to face those whom he had destroyed as much as he had destroyed himself.

Craig entered a long-term treatment center in his home state. His counselor kept in touch with me. Craig sent me a letter, saying in other programs he had tried, he had done most of what they suggested but he had never taken Christ seriously, and now he knew this was indeed the presence he wanted in his life. In the letter he asked, "Gary, you have told me many times before how to find Christ but I have forgotten what you said. This time I really want to know. Will you tell me again?" Dear reader, this moment would never have happened if I would have insisted on not revealing who I was, or hiding my life journey under some safe, innocuous theological term such as "sinner," or some psychological incantation such as "I'm OK; you're OK." It does not work that way. Life changes at the human systemic level take place when you share your real sordid honest journey with another person. It is then that hope comes for others because they realize you were once exactly where they are, but that now you are different; and that says that perhaps they can be different, too.

"Will you tell me now?" What an awesome question. I felt that the letter I was about to pen was a life and death matter for him. Does your witness with people ever take on that kind of urgency? On a plane, flying to a mission in Michigan, I wrote one of the most urgent and important letters of my life. As I was writing, I became aware of the fact that more people than we know live their desperate lives on what we write and say. Who is up to such awesome demands? I am certain that most of us would say none of us are equal to the task, but it is the task given to us by the very name we carry: Christian.

A year or so later, while I was away on a preaching mission, Craig came to South Bend. The other pastor said that he looked very well. His wife was with him. He was dressed neatly. From a very lonely night a new life was being fashioned. To reverse the title of one of Eugene O'Neill's plays, Craig was making a long night's journey into day.

There are many stories I could have shared with you in this book. These only begin to enable us to see that there is a world which is "white unto harvest." (John 4:35) There are literally thousands who need a "rest upon the way." Can your church, as First Church, be the place where they can rest their heads long enough to find that what the apostle said can be true for them: "If any man be in Christ he is a new creation; the old has passed away, behold, the new has come." (2 Corinthians 5:17) They want to be made new. Oh, how they want newness of life. Can we be honest and open enough about our own lives so that they can experience the Christ through us? Our openness can open the way so their nights are no longer long and lonely.

Epilogue

The Fragility of a Mighty Fortress

"I know your works. Behold I have set before you an open door which no one is able to shut; I know that you have little power, and yet you have kept my word and have not denied my name." (Revelation 3:8)

There are numbers of downtown churches throughout America just like First Church in South Bend, who were once the powerful bastions and representatives of Christianity. As they led the Christian revival in the opening years of this century they can do so again. In fact, it is these congregations which can remind and call the faith to the awareness of what were the motifs of their founders — people who went to the unwanted masses when many established churches were totally insensitive to the fact that there were unwanted masses.

The "Old First Church" is fragile at its best. If the church insists on pursuing yesterday, it will in fact be just that — a memory of a bygone age. Old First Church might exist on the National Historic Register as an architectural wonder, or it might be purchased at a ridiculously low price by a sect group, or it might just stand, hauntingly empty, as passers-by might remember what it at one time meant to the city of which it was a part.

But it does not have to be that way. Old First Church is fragile, but it is not finished. When the people of that fortress listen to the mandate of the Master, they will discover themselves growing into faithful fruition, and they will be to the future what their ancestors were to the past. Fragile? Definitely. But finished? Never! The choice before such a church is whether the church will rest on the laurels of the past (and there are certainly those in the membership who will want to do just that), or whether the church will be a rest upon the way for those who are so very tired, but have not forgotten that the church represents the one who said, "Come unto me all you who labor and are heavy laden and I will give you rest." (Matthew 11:28)

Notes

[1] Daniel T. Niles, *The Message and Its Messengers*, (Nashville, Abingdon Press, 1966), p. 69.

[2] Will Campbell, *Christian Century*, June 1984.

[3] Emil Brunner, unknown work.

[4] John Carey, *Carlyle Marney — A Pilgrim's Progress*, (Macon, Mercer Press, 1980), p. 47.

[5] Henry Nouwen, *Reaching Out*, (Garden City, Doubleday, 1975), p. 46.

[6] Ibid, p. 47.

[7] Hanley, *Ten Christians*, (Notre Dame, Ava Maria Press, 1979), p. 61.

[8] Charles Allen, *When the Heart Is Hungry*, (New York, Revell), p. 81.

[9] E. Stanley Jones, *Conversion*, (Nashville, Abingdon Press).